PRETTY DEAD GIRLS

Also by Monica Murphy

Daring the Bad Boy
Saving It

PRETTY DEAD GIRLS

MONICA MURPHY

YA

Entangled Publishing, LLC
2614 South Timberline Road
Suite 109
Fort Collins, CO 80525

Entangled Teen is an imprint of Entangled Publishing, LLC.

Visit our website at www.entangledpublishing.com.

Edited by Stacy Abrams and Alexa May
Cover design by Erin Dameron-Hill
Interior design by Toni Kerr

ISBN 978-1-63375-891-9
Ebook ISBN 978-1-63375-892-6

Manufactured in the United States of America

First Edition January 2018

10 9 8 7 6 5 4 3 2 1

entangled teen
an imprint of Entangled Publishing LLC

To all those creepy urban legend books I started reading when I was twelve—thanks for the inspiration.

"Is all that we see or seem but a dream within a dream?"

—Edgar Allan Poe

CHAPTER ONE

I finally get her where I want her, folks, and wouldn't you know, she starts giving me attitude within seconds.

"And why am I here again?" Gretchen snags the lit joint from my fingers and brings it to her mouth, taking a long drag. She holds the smoke in, her bright green eyes narrowed, her expression almost pained, before she blows it all out.

Straight into my face.

God, she's such a bitch sometimes. Though I envy her fearlessness. She's rude and mean and she just doesn't give a damn.

I realize she's waiting for me to speak and I clear my throat.

"Look, I know you're never going to believe me, since we haven't talked much in the past. But we've gone to school together for a long time and I just wanted us to...g-get to know each other better." I stumble over the words, and I am thoroughly pissed at myself.

I practiced this little speech over and over again the last

few days, preparing for this moment. In the mirror, reciting the words back to my reflection. Late at night, while I lay in bed and stared up at the ceiling, mesmerized by the slow spinning ceiling fan above my head.

Yet I mess it up, falter because I'm actually in front of her, just the two of us. Gretchen Nelson, one of the most beautiful, most popular girls in school. She has *everything*.

I have nothing.

All I want is a little taste. Just a tiny sample of what she is. What she has. What I could possibly be.

"So what? You tricked me to go out with you?"

"It's nothing like that," I reassure her.

"What do you mean by getting to know me better, then? What exactly are you talking about?" She takes another drag off the joint, this one short and fast, and she coughs out the smoke, hacking a little. The glamorous, perfect Gretchen Nelson mask falls for the briefest moment, and it's like I've just been treated to a sneak peek of the real Gretchen. She's just a girl who likes to get high, who's aggressive, and who treats other people like shit. I mean, I already knew she was like this, but... "Please don't tell me this is your idea of a *date*."

The contempt in her voice is obvious.

"No, not at all!" I sound too defensive and I clamp my lips shut. "That wasn't my intention. Can't we just be... friends?"

She shoots me a sardonic look, her lips curled, her delicate eyebrows raised. She's still wearing her shorts and T-shirt from volleyball practice and she has to be cold, since both car windows are rolled down, and once the sun disappears, the temperature around here drops rapidly.

My gaze falls to her legs. They're sturdy, her thighs are thick, and I can't help but stare at them. They're thicker than the other cheerleaders', which made her a great base. Gretchen was known for tossing the flyers into the air higher than anyone else. I remember watching her. Watching all of them…

Not that Gretchen's a cheerleader any longer. She quit at the end of her sophomore year, wanting to focus on volleyball instead. She's a strong player. Fearless. Downright mean on the court. Yet she's also beautiful and poised and smart.

"*You* really want to be *friends* with *me*?" She makes it sound like an impossible feat.

I nod.

"We have nothing in common."

"We have a lot of things in common."

"Name ten."

I frown. "You really want me to name *ten*?"

She nods slowly, places the joint between her lips. It dangles from her mouth, giving her this tough, rebellious air, and I can't help but admire her all over again. At school, she's absolute perfection. Right now, in the passenger seat of my car with a joint hanging from her lips, her dark-red hair a wild tangle about her head, eyeliner smudged, and her cheeks still ruddy from the chilly nighttime air, she's not quite as perfect.

But she's a lot more real.

"That's stupid," I tell her, and she sits up straight, yanking the joint out of her mouth so she can gape at me.

"Did you just call me stupid?"

The venom in her voice makes me recoil away from her. "N-no. I mean, I just took a hit off that joint. My head is spinning. How do you expect me to come up with ten things we have in common, just like that?" I snap my fingers for emphasis.

"*God.* You're just like everyone else. Always thinking you can buy me off with sex or booze or weed." She tosses the joint at my head and I dodge left, so it sails out the driver's side window and lands on the ground outside. "Bringing me to a church parking lot, too. Real classy."

With those last words, Gretchen climbs out of my car and slams the door behind her, so hard she makes the vehicle rock.

Panicked, I bolt out and follow after her. Her long legs take her far across the parking lot as she heads straight toward Our Lady of Mount Carmel Church. But I can run fast when I need to, and I catch up to her quickly. I grab hold of her arm and she snags it out of my grip, whirling on me with wild eyes.

"Get away from me!" I grab her again and she shakes me off, her expression full of disgust. "God, you're so freaking *weird*! Just leave me alone!"

It's the *weird* comment that gets me. It always gets me. They all single me out. They all point their fingers and laugh. With every step forward I make, something like this happens, and I'm pushed four steps back.

She turns away, breathing heavily, but she's not going anywhere. Odd. She's usually dying to get away from me.

That's when I realize she has her phone in her hand. And she's tapping away on the screen, like maybe she's texting someone.

Hell.

"Gretchen, come on." I keep my voice even, like this is no big deal. Like I'm not hunting her down in the church parking lot on a Tuesday night. The wind whips through the giant pine trees that surround the lot, I can hear the branches swing and sway, the hoot of a lonely owl in the near distance. It's dark up here. Quiet. No one drives by.

The street is abandoned and the nearest house is a quarter mile away.

Feels like it's just the two of us out here.

All alone.

"Fuck you, you fucking weirdo!" She turns to face me and starts to laugh. No doubt when she catches sight of the stricken look on my face. "I can't wait to tell everyone about this. Wait until I spread this story around—I will *ruin* you."

A roar leaves me, unlike any sound I've ever made before in my life, and it makes my lungs ache. I run up on her and shove her hard, so she tumbles to the ground. She's distracted, in shock that I shoved her, and I take my chance and sock her in the face. I meant to hit her mouth, but my knuckles only glance off her jaw and my entire hand throbs from the impact.

I can't believe I hit her.

"What the hell?" She touches her face gingerly, working her jaw to the side, and she winces. "You punched me!"

"You deserved it." My voice is eerily calm as I stand over her, both of my hands clutched into fists.

She tilts her head back, all that glorious red hair spilling past her shoulders. Even after I hit her, she still challenges me. I don't know whether she's brave or just stupid. "What are you going to do to me now? Beat me up?"

I say nothing.

I don't need to.

Instead, I smile. Laugh.

Actions speak louder than words, after all.

CHAPTER TWO

"So yeah. They found a...*body* this morning. Rumors are flying it was a teenage girl."

"Are you serious? How do you know?" Wednesday morning before third period and the halls are packed, everyone trying to get to class. I'm desperate to dump a few books off in my locker so I don't have to carry them around. Bad enough I have to wear the school uniform what feels like every day of my life. Don't need my backpack to stretch out my navy blue cardigan sweater and make it look even worse.

"I just...know. I have sources." My best friend, Danielle Sanchez, is practically whispering as she stands by my side; I can hardly hear her. Not that it really matters, considering whatever she's telling me is most likely pure rumor and speculation. Maybe she's hallucinating. I mean really—a dead body found before eight in the morning in our privileged little community?

No freaking way.

"Who are your sources? And please, speak up. I can't

hear you. No one's listening to us anyway." My voice drips with skepticism and I resist the urge to roll my eyes. I'm the realistic one while Dani's the idealist. She's all in, all the time, believing every little thing she hears, from the stupid lies some jock tells her in Spanish class to the rumors buzzing around the quad at lunch.

Me? I trust no one. I've been burned far too many times.

"Cops were on campus first thing this morning. Didn't you see their cars in the parking lot?" Dani frowns when I shake my head. "They showed up at the main office just before first period. A whole bunch of them, too, with serious expressions and looking badass in their uniforms." Only Dani thinks cops are hot. She loves a guy in uniform. "They looked like they were going to a funeral or whatever." Her eyes go wide the moment the words leave her lips. I can read her mind. She's thinking of funerals and murder and dead teenage girls.

"I was at the Larks meeting before first period." And what a worthless meeting that had been, not that I'm telling Dani. Half the girls in our community-service group weren't even there—every one of them seniors. The juniors all show up because they're trying to secure their Larks spot for next year, but they're clueless most of the time.

This is why meetings before school are pointless. No one wants to get out of bed a minute earlier than they have to, not even for their fellow Larks or for the good of the community. "You didn't show up," I remind her.

Dani shrugs. "I figured you'd fill me in, considering you're President Penelope." Ugh, I so hate it when she calls me that, but I say nothing. Just give her a little grin.

She smiles serenely in return. "But back to the cops. Supposedly they wanted to see recent attendance records for all seniors."

"Please. They might've been looking for a truant senior, and I can think of two right off the top of my head. I seriously can't remember the last time I saw James Fuller or Craig Howe in class." Grabbing my physics book, I slam the metal locker door so hard it rattles before I take off down the crowded hall toward my third period class.

Dani falls into step beside me, the heels of our loafers clicking in time on the concrete floor. "Valid point." She's always saying *valid point*. Usually because I'm explaining that whatever lies someone fed her were just that—total lies. "But I think you're way off. I heard they only wanted to look at the girls' attendance records. No guys."

"So?" I can't even focus on what she's saying right now. I have that test in physics to study for—Mrs. Emmert said we could use both sides of an index card to write notes to help us, and I want to get a head start. I do well in school. Okay, fine, I do great in school, but this year, physics is tripping me up, and I don't like it. I can't put my future at risk, which means I need to do everything I can to ace this test. My college applications must look impressive. I've got everything mostly covered.

Advanced classes, check.

Volunteers within the community, check.

Social and athletically involved, check and check.

Problem? I'm going to look *less* impressive because I suck so badly in that stupid freaking class. I'm barely keeping my head above water with a C that could slip into D territory if I don't watch it.

And I can't have that. Within my group of friends, we're all a bunch of overachievers. And the Larks isn't just about community service—it's the ultimate overachievers group. The outgoing seniors nominate the best of the best before the end of their sophomore year. The Larks is a small group of ten girls who are the smartest, the most respected, the most athletic, the most popular in our school. We all try to make the top grades so we can get into the best colleges and make our school and our families proud.

Sometimes, it feels like we don't really have a choice, either.

"So put two and two together. It was a girl's body that was found this morning? And they're checking out seniors' attendance records?" Danielle's the one who rolls her eyes when I say nothing. "Duh, Penelope! The dead body is someone from school! Someone from *our class*." The last two words are said in a ragged whisper.

"No way," I tell her, but she's nodding frantically, her enthusiasm level shooting up about fifty notches. "You always think the worst when something happens."

"That's because bad stuff happens to good people!"

"I'm afraid you're watching too much Discovery ID channel again." It's true. My best friend loves to jump to conclusions. There was the time during sophomore year Danielle thought Melissa Hankins got caught up in a sex-slave ring but it turned out Missy had mono. Or when she thought Brent Villanueva was a drug dealer who got tossed into prison when really Brent spent the night in juvie because he was caught with a little baggie of weed in the front pocket of his jeans.

The cops didn't even want to take him to juvenile hall. They were ready to cite and release, but his parents wanted to *prove* a *point*. They wanted him to *suffer* the *consequences*. He stayed the night, picked up some excellent leads on who to score even better weed from, and was released the next morning. He proceeded to go to his best friend's house, where they smoked a bowl together before they came to school.

Typical.

"Maybe I am, but come on. It's just too weird of a coincidence." A little shiver moves through her and she frowns. "I just hope it's not someone we know."

"Ah, Dani." I wrap my arm around her shoulders and give her a side hug. We've been friends for so long, and I love her dearly, even though she's a little nutty sometimes. "I think you're getting ahead of yourself."

"Something is definitely up." Dani smirks, looking rather pleased with herself. "Courtney answers phones during second period in the main office. She said the cops called in twice. *Twice.*"

"It's probably nothing." Maybe. Maybe not. How often do the police call the high school? I know we have rent-a-cops who put on a big show when they strut around campus, supposedly scaring us straight or whatever.

"Or it could mean everything." Danielle glances over her shoulder, her eyes narrowing. "Touch me and die, Pearson!"

I blow out an exasperated breath when I hear Brogan Pearson and all his football buddies laugh at Danielle's useless threat. She's the one dying for Brogan to touch her. She's just playing hard to get.

"I'm sure we'll find out what's going on eventually," I tell her once we reach the wing where my class is. "See you at lunch?"

Dani nods and waves before we go our separate ways, Brogan chasing after her with his friends. He's a goofball, always playing pranks on people, and for some reason everyone loves him, especially Dani. I tolerate him because she's had a crush on him for so long, but I don't get the appeal.

Pushing thoughts of Brogan Pearson out of my head, I hurry to class, slipping into my seat and pulling a few index cards and my pen out of the front pocket of my backpack before I scan the room.

Everyone's talking in low whispers, their wide-eyed gazes lingering on empty desks. Unease trickles down my spine and I jump a little when the guy who sits next to me brushes past and settles into his seat, sending me a curious glance when he catches me gawking.

I look down, not wanting to engage. Weird boys who keep to themselves and rarely talk really aren't my thing. Plus, his background story is weird and sort of sad and warped. Something about a dead father and a mom in prison for murdering him? I don't know if it's true—the information did come from Dani, after all.

But I do know he lives with his grandma up on Hot Springs Road, which is like, the most elite neighborhood in town. We're talking multimillion-dollar estates with views of the Pacific that stretch as far as the eye can see. He's also really smart and prefers to keep to himself, which ups his weird factor around here. No one wants to keep to himself on purpose.

Meaning no one can figure him out.

Within minutes, Mrs. Emmert strides into the classroom and dumps a stack of books and a can of Dr Pepper on top of her desk before she surveys everyone sitting at their desks, her hands resting on her hips. "Ready to get this review started?" she asks, her overly cheery voice making everyone groan in agony. Including me.

She does a quick roll call, not missing a beat when a couple of female students come up absent and the whispers start all over again. Mrs. Emmert shushes us before she launches into the chapter review, talking so fast I can hardly keep up. I finally prop up my physics textbook in front of me and switch my phone to record mode, so I can catch every word she says and not have to worry about writing it all down. I prop my elbow on my desk and rest my chin on my hand, the sound of the teacher's droning voice making me sleepy. Not a good sign. I usually don't feel like this until after lunch.

Why did I take this class again? To look good to future colleges? Or to torture myself?

A crackling sound suddenly comes over the school intercom and Mrs. Emmert clamps her lips shut, all of us swiveling our heads in the direction of the speaker that's on the wall, just to the right of the American flag. We hear a throat clear.

It's our principal, Mr. Rose.

"Attention everyone—we're asking that all Cape Bonita Prep students please leave their classrooms in an orderly fashion and go to the main gymnasium for an emergency assembly." There's a pause, the static from the speaker loud in the quiet classroom. "Again, all students and faculty. Please come to the gymnasium for an important announcement. Thank you."

Mrs. Emmert blinks repeatedly, her expression one of surprise, her lips tight with seeming concern. "Well, you heard the man. Gather up your things and let's go to the gym."

Shutting off the record button, I shove my phone into the front pocket of my backpack. "What about the test tomorrow?" I ask as we all seem to stand at the same time, earning a few irritated groans for my efforts. I need to know everything that's going to be on tomorrow's test. I refuse to fail.

More like I *can't* fail.

"We'll postpone it." Mrs. Emmert actually looks disappointed. Me, on the other hand? I'm thrilled for the extra day of reprieve. And so is the rest of the class as they all start to cheer. "All right, all right, settle down." She hesitates for a moment before she continues. "Just to let you know, in all my years at this school, I've never seen *anyone* call a surprise assembly."

"You don't know what it's about, Mrs. E.?" someone yells from the back of the room.

"No, I do not." Mrs. Emmert's smile is strained, her gaze worried. "Trust me, I'm just as curious as the rest of you."

"This ought to be interesting," the guy who sits next to me mutters under his breath as he shoves his textbook into his black backpack. He pulls the hood of his navy blue regulation school sweatshirt over his head, slings his backpack onto his shoulder, and heads out of class.

"Cass is so weird."

I turn to see my friend Courtney Jenkins sneering in the direction the boy just left. "He's not so bad," I say, wondering why I'm defending him. Seriously, I do think he's a little weird. I've never really talked to him.

In other words, I know nothing about him.

"Please. His mom murdered his dad—she actually cut his throat open because she's a vengeful bitch, and now she's in prison forever. So freaking creepy. Makes you wonder if that sort of thing is hereditary." Courtney mock shudders. "So. Do you think the assembly is about the body that was found up at the church?"

Wait a minute. A body was found at the church? Maybe Dani was right. She did mention that Courtney told her about the police calling in. What if they're going to talk to us about it because the body they found is of someone we know? "I have no idea."

"I think it's someone who goes to this school." Courtney looks around, her perfectly curled, perfectly blond hair barely moving. "The question is, who's not here today?"

A shiver runs down my spine at Courtney's foreboding tone. "I don't know."

"Girls!" Mrs. Emmert's shrill voice makes me wince and I turn to find her glaring at us. "Let's go!"

I exit the classroom without a word, Courtney following behind me and chirping away, though I'm not really listening to her. All I can think about is someone's dead. Someone we might know.

And I have no idea who it is.

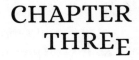

CHAPTER THREE

The small gymnasium is packed, freshmen and sophomores sitting on one side of the gym, juniors and seniors on the other. I settle in between my usual group of friends, Dani on one side, Courtney on the other. Brogan sits directly behind Dani, talking endlessly as we wait for Mr. Rose to make his appearance. Courtney taps away on her phone, no doubt spreading gossip about the possible dead student announcement.

Me? I wait anxiously, scanning the room, my gaze snagging on our principal as he marches to the center of the gymnasium with a microphone clutched in his right hand. His expression is grim, like he's about to blow our minds with some serious bad news and I sit up straight, bracing myself for the verbal blow.

"Oh God, there he is," Dani whispers, ducking her head close to mine. "Mr. Rose looks *so* upset."

She's right, but I say nothing. Nerves are eating at my insides, making me tense, and I suck in a sharp breath, exhaling slowly.

"What's he so upset about?" Brogan yells, making Danielle wince.

I turn and send Brogan a withering glance. "Don't eavesdrop on private conversations, *Brogan*."

"Give me a break, *Penny*. You can't have a *private* conversation in the middle of the gym surrounded by everyone," Brogan says, his voice dripping with sarcasm before he sends a little smile in Dani's direction.

Ugh. I hate it when anyone calls me Penny, especially someone I can't stand, like Brogan Pearson. Though the jerkoff has a point—private conversations are impossible in situations like this.

"Students." The speakers screech with reverberation and Mr. Rose winces, holding the microphone far out in front of him before he attempts to speak again. "Everyone. Please. Settle down."

His calm voice isn't very effective. Mr. Rose is a short and stocky man, probably in his mid to late fifties. Everyone loves him because he's such a pushover. The one to watch out for is our vice principal, Mrs. Adney. She's the one who'll kick our asses seventeen ways to Sunday if we get too out of line.

And hey, I didn't make up that quote. Supposedly Mrs. Adney did.

She marches out to the center of the gym right at this very moment, swipes the microphone from Mr. Rose's hand, and sticks two fingers in her mouth before she whistles so loudly, I automatically cover my ears with my hands.

"Listen up!" Mrs. Adney yells, her voice booming throughout the gym. The crowd immediately goes silent and she hands the microphone back to Mr. Rose, a satisfied smile on her face as she returns to the benches and sits.

"We've been notified of a…tragedy this morning." Mr. Rose clears his throat. Dani reaches out, grabbing hold of my hand and clutching it tight. I think deep down she might be enjoying this moment, not that I'd ever say that to her face. "Involving one of our own."

The murmurs start back up again and the terse look Mr. Rose sends all of us doesn't stop the rumors' momentum. "Gretchen Nelson is…no longer with us." He drops his head for a moment in prayer. "They found her body this morning," he murmurs into the microphone, his head still bent.

A collective gasp rips through the gym, and I gasp along with everyone else. *No.* Gretchen? I've known her forever. She is—*was*—a Lark. We cheered together our freshman and sophomore years before she quit and became captain of the volleyball team. She was a fierce competitor. She was also a friend—and sometimes an enemy, if I'm being completely honest.

And now…she's dead.

I can't believe it.

"The police haven't released any details and not much is known, so please, respect the Nelson family during this difficult time and keep the rumors to yourselves." Too late for that. I can already hear the whispers all around me. "We've brought grief counselors onto campus, so if anyone needs to speak with them, they're available." A sob sounds at this offer and I look around, though I don't know who cried out.

All I see are chalky, pale faces, shock etched into their features, eyes wide and full of fear. Of sadness. I wonder if I look the same. I can't believe she's gone—I just saw Gretchen yesterday. She'd seemed perfectly normal, like she had no problems, and at the time, I guess she didn't.

One of our own has been taken. Not just someone from Cape Bonita Prep, one of *my* own. Granted, Gretchen and I hadn't been that close lately—

"We need to call an emergency Larks meeting," Courtney whispers close to my ear, interrupting my thoughts.

I say nothing. It's like I can't. Words are stuck in my throat, which never happens. I'm all about voicing my opinion, but I swear I feel almost...emotionless.

Void.

I think I'm in shock.

"Hey, I'm serious," Court continues to whisper fiercely. Her expression is fierce, too. Her eyes are narrowed and she's watching me carefully. As if she fully expects me to say no. "We all need to talk about this."

"About what?" Dani asks as she leans over me, practically thrusting her face in Courtney's.

Court rolls her eyes, a sneer curling her upper lip. "About what happened to Gretchen. This is serious. Someone is *dead*. Someone we know and was a part of our group, a part of the Larks. She was our friend."

"Yeah. But what do *we* have to do with that?" Dani sounds genuinely perplexed.

"Who could've done this to her, Dani? That's what we need to talk about. You know how sometimes Gretchen hung out with...unsavory people." Courtney wrinkles her nose.

Unsavory? Where did she get that word from? And Gretchen hung out with all the same people we did.

"She did not," Dani says indignantly.

"Penelope." Courtney jabs me in the side with a pointy elbow, making me wince. "Say something."

Glancing around, I make sure no one is paying us any attention before I duck my head and murmur, "If you really want to talk about this, let's meet right after school. Should I bring in one of those grief counselors?" Maybe we need one.

"Absolutely not. What we want to discuss is private," Courtney says.

"Are we meeting in the library?" Dani asks. When I glance up, her brown eyes are so wide I feel like I could trip and fall right into them.

I nod. "Room three." Our library is huge. Hardly anyone uses it. There are large conference rooms in the back of the building, and that's where we always meet.

"Girls!"

We all three lift our heads to find Mrs. Adney staring at us, her gaze razor sharp, her mouth tight. My cheeks go hot at being caught chatting during what is most definitely a somber time.

"Sorry," Dani squeaks, and Mrs. Adney nods once, turning her attention back to Mr. Rose, who is still droning on about grief counseling and how what we might know in regard to Gretchen's death could be important. How any information, *any* at *all,* he stresses, could be a major help to the case.

I wish I knew what was going on. How did it happen? Was it an accident? Or do they suspect Gretchen was... murdered by someone she knew? Could the killer be someone *we* know? The thought is terrifying. It's much easier to put this on a complete stranger who wandered into town and killed her without thought. Cape Bonita is a small, wealthy town along the northern California coast. We don't *do* murder.

I can literally hear one of Mom's friends saying that, I swear.

But seriously. The danger you *don't* know is far more understandable than the danger you *do* know—at least in this case.

I scan the room, noting the unfamiliar men standing near the exit. They're wearing cheap, rumpled suits, their hawk-like gazes sweeping the room, no doubt sizing up every one of us. Cops. They're so obvious it's almost pitiful.

But maybe they want to be obvious. Maybe they're trying to send us a message.

Looking away, my gaze snags on a boy sitting directly across the gym on the bottom riser. In the freshman section, though he's not a freshman. He's leaning his elbows against the back of the riser just behind him, his legs spread wide, his expression bored. He lifts his dark head, his gaze snagging on mine, and I can't look away.

It's the boy from my physics class. The one Courtney called weird. Cass something—such an unusual first name—he's the one with the murdering mom. And he's staring right at me.

He smirks, this tiny, lopsided smile that's...I don't know how to describe it. Irritating? Smug? Intriguing? Cute.

No. *Not* cute. There's nothing really *cute* about him. I don't like how he's watching me so carefully. I glance over my shoulder, making sure he's not staring at someone behind me, and when I look back at him, he's inclining his head toward me. His expression clearly saying, *Yes, you.*

"Is he looking at you?" Dani whispers close to my ear.

"Who?" I pretend I don't know what she's talking about.

"Him," Dani stresses, tilting her head in his direction. "Cass Vincenti." She pauses. "He's *totally* staring at you."

"No, he's not."

"He so is. Ooh, do you have a crush on him, or what?" Dani starts to giggle but quits when I glare at her. For some reason, I don't want Courtney to know about this. She gave me a weird vibe earlier about Cass.

"Absolutely not," I say vehemently.

"Uh-huh." Dani smirks. "I thought you didn't like high school boys."

"You're right. I don't. I'm waiting until college to find a real boyfriend." The last boyfriend I had—Robby Matthews,

star football player, gorgeous, and a cheating bastard—
graduated last year, and I haven't been interested in any
boys at school since.

"That's so boring," Dani mumbles.

"But safe," I remind her.

Besides, Cass Vincenti isn't boyfriend material.

Not even close.

CHAPTER FOUR

The call comes during sixth period when I'm in American Government. We're all quietly reading a chapter while our teacher tries to take a nap, which is typical. Mr. Gonzales answers the phone sitting on his desk, listens for a moment, and then slams the receiver down, glaring at all of us like we interrupted his siesta.

"Penelope Malone," he barks. "Go to the main office."

I frown. "Why?"

"I don't know," he snaps. "Just go. They're waiting for you."

Shoving my stuff into my backpack, I stand and glare at Mr. Gonzales as I exit the classroom to catcalls and those low *oooh*s boys like to make when they think someone's in trouble.

There's no way I'm in trouble. And who could be waiting for me? It's such a strange thing for Mr. Gonzales to say.

When I enter the main office a few minutes later, the secretary Mrs. Boyer takes one look at me from behind her desk and says, "Hi Penelope. You're wanted in Mrs. Adney's office."

Dread fills me. I've never been called to the vice principal's office before. Ever. Not in all my many years of attending school. What could this be about? What did I do? More like, what is someone *saying* I did?

I may never get in trouble, but I definitely have enemies. We all do.

The office door is partially open, and when I peek in, the dread leaves me. It's not anything I've done. It's all about Gretchen.

Those cops I saw in the gym earlier are standing in Mrs. Adney's cramped office, and she's sitting behind her desk, chatting with them in low murmurs. I'm guessing they want to talk to me. One is staring at his phone—the younger one—and the older one has a small notepad, his pen scratching across the paper so hard I can actually hear it from where I'm standing.

I clear my throat to warn of my existence and then knock on the door, flashing Mrs. Adney a bright smile when her gaze meets mine. "You wanted to see me?" My tone is pleasant. Like it's any other day.

Mrs. Adney scowls because it is most certainly not like any other day. "Detectives Spalding and Hughes would like to speak with you, Penelope—" she starts to say, but the older detective interrupts her, which makes her scowl deepen.

"We won't take up too much of your time." His voice is gentle and he steps forward, indicating the empty chair in front of me with a casual wave of his hand. "If you don't mind having a seat, Miss Malone?"

I sit, smoothing my blue-and-white plaid skirt down around my thighs, making sure I'm covered. My hands are shaky and I hope they don't notice. "I'm not sure if I can help," I say with a small smile.

The older detective sits next to me, but the younger one remains standing. "I'm Detective Spalding," the older one offers. "And that's Detective Hughes. We're here to ask you a few questions about your friend Gretchen Nelson."

"Okay," I say slowly, resting my hands in my lap.

"When was the last time you saw Miss Nelson?"

"Um, yesterday afternoon while I was at cheer practice."

Hughes frowns. "She's not a cheerleader any longer. Why was she at cheer practice?"

"She wasn't. But I saw her here on campus when I was at cheer. Gretchen plays volleyball and they practice in the gym," I explain. Then correct myself. I blink hard at the sudden wave of emotion that washes out of me and I choke out, "Played, I suppose I should say."

The room is silent for too long and I drop my head, staring at my clutched hands. I still can't believe she's gone. That Gretchen is...dead. It doesn't feel real, like this is some sort of awful nightmare I'm going to wake up from at any moment.

But I don't wake up. I'm still sitting in Mrs. Adney's office, and when I lift my head, I swear it looks like she's going to cry. If she starts, I'm going to start, too.

"So you saw Gretchen here yesterday after school," Spalding reiterates. "Do you remember the approximate time?"

"I don't know." I shrug and frown, trying to think. "Around four thirty, I guess? Practice was almost over but I think hers already ended."

"Good, good." Spalding scribbles on his notepad while Hughes taps away on his phone. "Did you talk to her?"

I think of Gretchen yesterday. Wearing blue Nike shorts and a Bonita Academy T-shirt, the late afternoon sunlight catching on her vibrant auburn-colored hair and making it shine extra bright. I waved at her, and she looked irritated when she first saw me.

"Briefly," I tell them with a slight frown.

"What about?" This came from Detective Hughes.

"Our Larks meeting this morning. I called her over and reminded her about it, and she whined because it was going to be held before school started, and none of the girls like an early morning meeting. But I'm just too busy and can't really schedule it any other time, you know?"

"What exactly is a Larks meeting?" Hughes asks.

I lean forward, my gaze locking with Detective Hughes's. "The Larks is a student-led organization that provides various charitable services within the community." I sound like I'm reading from a brochure, but I can't help it. "It was formed to help build character and create leaders among the girls at Cape Bonita."

"And what exactly do the Larks do?" Hughes asks.

"Oh, we put together all sorts of fund-raisers, we volunteer at the local children's hospital and many of the retirement homes in the area as well." If there's one thing I love to talk about, it's the Larks. Some people probably make fun of me behind my back for my enthusiasm, but I don't really care. I'm proud to be a Lark. It's a family tradition.

"Penelope is the Larks' president," Mrs. Adney chimes in.

"You are?" Detective Hughes's eyebrow lifts.

I nod. "Just following in my sister's footsteps." More like I worked hard and earned that position. No one handed it to me because of Peyton, that's for damn sure. "Not that I didn't earn the position fair and square."

Okay, now I sound like a rambling, nervous idiot. I need to shut up.

"Her older sister, Peyton, was president of the Larks when she was a senior here as well," Mrs. Adney says.

Hughes looks like he wants to laugh as he turns his focus on me. "So your sister's name is Peyton? And you're Penelope?"

I smile demurely, though deep down I'm irritated. This guy is kind of rude. "I guess my parents like the letter *P*."

"Their brother's name is Peter." This again comes from Mrs. Adney. I sort of wish she would stop talking.

I can tell it takes everything within Detective Hughes not to do a massive eye roll. "Cute."

"Is this all you wanted to question me about?" My voice is pleasant, but I am thoroughly confused. Why are we talking about my family and their love of the letter *P* when we should be discussing what happened to Gretchen? A girl I know is gone, yet we're talking about miscellaneous stuff. It makes no sense.

"So after you talked to Gretchen, where did she go?" Spalding asks.

Okay, maybe that was just a minor blip, their getting sidetracked. "I'm not sure. I still had to finish practice, so I didn't notice her again. I assume she went to the girls' locker room, grabbed her stuff, and left," I say.

"How many members are in your Larks group?" Detective Hughes suddenly asks.

I glance up at him. "Ten. It's always ten. Well." I hesitate, my chest getting tight. "Now we're only nine." I look to Mrs. Adney, who offers me a sympathetic smile. My chin wobbles and I'm terrified I'll start crying. That's the last thing I want to do. Showing emotion is a sign of weakness. "Can I go now?"

She nods. "Will that be all, gentlemen?"

Hughes looks put out, but the older detective just smiles.

"Thank you for your time, Penelope." Detective Spalding stands and I do the same. "We might have some more questions for you, though, over the next few days. Just to warn you."

"That's not a problem." I flash them a polite smile and then hurriedly make my escape.

I pass through the main office when I see him sitting there—the boy from my physics class. The boy who stared at me at the end of the assembly.

Cass Vincenti.

He's slouching in one of the four hard chairs that line the wall. Usually that's the spot where students wait to see the principal.

I'm frowning as I study him and he's frowning in return. Is he in trouble? Or is he going to talk to the detectives, too?

"What are you doing here?" I ask, my curiosity getting the best of me.

He arches a brow. "Wow. The queen actually speaks." He rests his hand against his chest, like he's shocked.

I roll my eyes. "We've talked before."

"Not really." He drops his hand.

His answer makes me hesitate. "Sure we have."

"Name five times."

"Uhh…"

Cass smiles, and it transforms his entire face. His dark brown eyes crinkle at the corners and his smile is…nice. He's actually really good looking. Not that I thought he was a hideous troll, but still. He's not someone I've paid much attention to before. More like he always blends into the background. I think he prefers it that way.

"I'm just giving you a hard time," he murmurs, his smile dimming. "Did you talk to the cops about Gretchen?"

"Are *you* talking to the cops about Gretchen?"

"I asked you first."

"What are we, twelve?"

"Maybe." He flicks his chin at me. "So. Did you?"

"Um, yes. I did. We were friends." And I don't think they were. I glance around, thankful Mrs. Boyer isn't at her desk. "Why do they want to talk to you?"

"I don't know. They called me down here a few minutes ago." He shrugs, drawing my attention to his broad shoulders.

They're very nice, capable-looking shoulders.

Ugh. Stop thinking like that. Your friend just died. And they're possibly questioning this guy about her murder. What if they believe he—

"I didn't kill Gretchen, if that's what you're thinking," he says, interrupting my thoughts.

I frown. What is he, a mind reader? "I never said that.'"

"But you were thinking it."

"You're putting words in my mouth." If he were any other boy I've dealt with at this school, he would've jumped on that opportunity. He would've said, "I'd like to put *something* in your mouth," before laughing his ass off with all his crude friends.

But Cass is alone. There are no friends around for him to impress. And I guess Cass doesn't have that type of sense of humor. Though there's something about him—like this underlying anger, that's just bubbling beneath the surface.

Despite the smile and the joking attitude, he seems mad.

He slouches in the chair, kicking out his long legs. He's wearing the uniform khakis and they're kind of wrinkled. Like they sat in the dryer for a few days before he finally pulled them out. Beat-up, faded black Converse cover his feet, and he crosses them at the ankles. I have to take a step back to get out of his way. "I can practically read your mind," he says, his gaze locked on his feet. "You're all the same."

"Who are all the same?"

"All of your group. Your girls. Your *squad*." He says the

last word with contempt as he looks at me, his mouth tipped up on one side. "There's not a single thing that's different about any of you. You're all cut from the same cloth."

I glare at him, insulted by his assumption. "You don't know me."

"Ah, but I do." His smile fades. "You just don't realize it yet."

My heart racing, I hurry out of the office before Cass Vincenti can say anything else to upset me.

CHAPTER FIVE

I enter conference room three in the library promptly at three thirty to find eight panicked girls sitting around the table, all of them deathly serious. Deathly pale.

Deathly quiet.

We are normally not a quiet bunch. Not by a long shot. So I know they're all affected by Gretchen's death, not that I can blame them. Only a few days ago, she sat at this very table with us, laughing and trying to take command of the entire meeting, as was her usual way. I always found that so irritating.

Now I know I'm going to miss it. Miss her.

"Ladies." I smile at them and take the seat at the head of the table. Dani sits to my right, Courtney to my left. The rest of the girls watch me, their eyes wide and unblinking, some even shining with unshed tears. I decide a gentle approach is best. I don't want to make any of them sadder than they already are, so I need to remain strong and hold it together. "I know this is a difficult day, and I appreciate you coming to the meeting."

"What are we going to do to honor Gretchen?" asks Alyssa. She's one of the new members of the Larks, and I've learned fast she has a soft heart. As in, she's blatantly crying at this very moment, tears streaking down her cheeks.

"They're having a candlelight vigil for her tonight at seven," adds Maggie, another one of our new Larks. "Coach Smith is giving a speech and everything."

The volleyball coach adored Gretchen. To the point that we all found it sort of weird, how seemingly…obsessed she was with Gretchen.

"We should make a donation in her honor," Dani suggests. "What was her favorite charity?"

"Good idea. She loved the animal shelter." Gretchen much preferred animals to people. "Let's also send flowers to the vigil." I open my notes section and write myself a reminder. "Is someone providing a photo of her?"

"I don't know," Courtney starts, and I turn to look at her.

"Find out," I say gently, and she immediately starts texting someone. God knows who.

Courtney is well connected. Not only is her family a huge donor to Cape Bonita Prep, but she also assists in the office, she's in student council, she's a cheerleader, she's dated the quarterback of the football team—a few other members of the football team, too, but let's not talk about that at this time—and she knows freaking everyone.

Everyone.

She's my source. When I can't figure something out, Courtney always can.

"Did anyone else talk to the cops?" This comes from Alexis, a fellow senior, a fellow cheerleader, my nemesis. But I heed the words, "Keep your friends close and your enemies closer," because Alexis Nguyen is my absolute worst enemy.

And she feels the same exact way about me. We've been

in competition for the same positions since elementary school. Leads in the school plays, positions on teams, a few times that we've fought over a boy…she's always my direct competition.

We get along because we have to. We share the same inner circle. We're "friends." Everyone believes it, except for us. We know the truth. We barely tolerate each other most of the time.

"What do you mean, talk to the cops?" Maggie asks. She's a junior. Very enthusiastic. Almost too enthusiastic, if you know what I mean. She usually steps up and volunteers for everything.

"I was briefly questioned," I say quietly, wanting them to know I'm just like them. "Were you, Lex?"

Alexis nods, rolls her eyes. "The young one was cute, but rude."

"I was questioned, too," Courtney says, sounding bored. "I think it's standard procedure. Nothing to get our panties in a twist over."

"They talked to me," Dani says, her eyes wide. I really hope she doesn't lose it and start crying again. I don't mind as much if the juniors do, but they're young. They haven't heard the "stay strong, we're Larks" speech enough times yet.

Because that's what Larks do. We stay strong. We are the ones others can lean on. We're leaders who are committed to helping others. We support our school, our community, those who are in need. Those who are troubled and lost.

And now we've lost one of our own. This is not the time for us to fall apart.

Even though I'm pretty sure we all want to—at least secretly.

"They questioned us because we were Gretchen's friends," I remind Dani, patting her arm. "They're probably going to question everyone who was close to Gretchen."

"I hated her." This comes from Courtney. The juniors gasp, even Dani. Alexis doesn't look surprised by her statement, and I'm really not, either, but I wouldn't make that sort of declaration out loud, for the love of God.

The girl's been gone not even twenty-four hours yet. Show some respect.

"God, why would you *say* that?" Alyssa asks, sounding horrified. She shakes her head, her long, curly black hair swaying around her shoulders. "You should never speak ill of the dead!"

Courtney shrugs. "We never really got along. She's a man stealer."

I raise a brow. "She stole your *man*?" What boy is Courtney even talking about?

Now Court just looks irritated. "There was someone I was…*interested* in, and she snatched him up before we were through."

"Through with what? Hooking up?" Lex smirks.

Courtney glares. "Shut the hell up, whore."

Lex's eyebrows shoot up, but she doesn't look offended. "Funny, you talk about random hookups and call me a whore, all in one breath."

"Please, stop arguing. Gretchen's gone. We shouldn't talk bad about her," I say, sounding weary because I so am. I've heard this sort of argument between them before. And sometimes Gretchen was involved, too.

Let's be real—these girls *are* all the same. As in, they're all banging the same guy at one point or another. High quality males who are potential boyfriend material at this school and in the nearby vicinity are hard to come by. So they end up…sharing. Not on purpose. Never on purpose, because *ew*.

So yeah. They steal each other's "man" all the time. And if one calls the other a whore, then they're all whores together. You know what I mean?

But I'm not one to slut shame so…

"Coach Smith is already having a poster made out of Gretchen's senior portrait," Courtney announces, smoothly changing the subject. "She just texted to let me know."

"Awesome. Dani, will you order the flowers for tonight?" I ask.

Dani nods and whips out her phone. "No problem. Anything else?"

"I assume Sally is providing the candles and cups for the vigil?" I look at Courtney, who sends off another text to the volleyball coach to ask her. "I think that's everything we need to talk about today. I hope to see you all there tonight. We should be a solid unit, showing our support and love for Gretchen."

The words feel like obvious lies as they fall from my lips. I am just like Courtney. I would never wish anyone dead. Once upon a time, Gretchen and I were friends. But the last couple of years, our bad moments far outnumbered the good. I don't know where it went wrong, but we weren't close. Not at all.

Maggie raises her hand, her freckled face wary. She looks downright scared to ask a question, and I do my best to smile pleasantly at her. "You okay, Maggie?"

She nods, dropping her hand to her lap. "Maybe we should make signs? They could say, 'We love you, Gretchen.' Or, 'Heaven gained an angel today.' Something like that?"

"If you want to head up sign making for Gretchen's vigil, I say go for it. That's a great idea," I tell her, and she looks pleased.

At least I can pass the project on to a bunch of juniors.

There are only four of us seniors now, what with Gretchen gone. And the last thing I want to think about is a replacement. Though tradition states we need an equal number of seniors to juniors.

For once, I think we're going to have to buck tradition. At least temporarily.

Maggie puts together a sign-making group—basically all the juniors. They'll head to her house as soon as the meeting is finished, and I go ahead and declare it over, because what else can we hash out? It doesn't feel right to talk about serious Lark business when Gretchen is dead.

I leave the library with Courtney and Dani, all of us walking together to the mostly empty parking lot.

"Court is giving me a ride," Dani tells me just as we're about to part. "See you tonight, right?"

"Absolutely," I say with a nod, hugging Dani close when she embraces me. If Courtney weren't here, I'd let Dani cry in my arms, but I pull away from her instead, offering a reassuring smile. "You'll be there early?"

"For sure," Courtney chimes in, answering for Dani. "Dani and I will come together. Want us to pick you up? I don't mind."

"I'm okay with driving."

"You don't mind going alone?" Dani asks, concern lacing her voice, filling her eyes.

"I'll be fine. See ya." I smile at them and wave before I turn and head toward my car. The sun is shining but I can see the clouds in the near distance, hovering over the ocean. The breeze is crisp and cool, slightly salty. Feels like a storm is coming.

Fitting, what with the somber mood today.

As I approach my car, I see someone standing beside it. Two someones.

The police detectives—Spalding and Hughes.

I stop short, staring at both of them before plastering on a polite smile. Detective Hughes is leaning against my BMW like he freaking owns it, the jerk. But what am I supposed to do, tell him to step away from my car?

He's a cop. And I'm a…possible suspect?

I do my best to keep my smile pasted on, but it's shaky at best. "Hello," I greet them.

"Miss Malone." Detective Spalding nods and takes a step forward, his smile kind, though his expression is bland. The complete opposite of Hughes right now—he's glaring at me like he wants to throw me to the ground and cuff me. "Glad we caught you before you left campus."

"What's going on?" I stop near the back end of my car, keeping my distance just in case Detective Hughes decides he really does want to cuff me.

I'd give anything to have Mrs. Adney or Mr. Rose here with me. I'm not comfortable talking to the cops alone.

"We were speaking with Barbara Nelson earlier— Gretchen's mother. She mentioned a tiny detail we found rather interesting, and we were wondering if you knew anything about it."

"Isn't this illegal? Your questioning me?" I frown, unease slithering down my spine. Why are they questioning me here in the parking lot? When they both remain quiet, I decide I might as well ask another question. "What did she say?"

"She told us Gretchen texted her while she was at volleyball practice, letting her know she was going to a surprise Larks meeting," Detective Hughes explains, stepping forward so he's standing next to Spalding. "Did you call a surprise meeting yesterday afternoon?"

I shake my head. "No."

"Who's the person who normally organizes Larks meetings?"

"Me," I admit shakily.

"But you didn't organize this one?"

"No," I repeat. "I didn't. I don't know who would do that."

"Neither do we," Spalding says easily, slipping his hands into the front pockets of his pants.

"Maybe Gretchen was lying to her mother," I suggest. I wouldn't put it past her. She'd done it before. So have I. Haven't we all?

"Did she do that often?"

"I don't know. Probably?"

"Do you lie to your parents very often, Miss Malone?"

"No." Funny how one word can sound guilty.

Spalding decides to change tactics. "Did you and Gretchen spend a lot of time together?"

"We weren't that close." Not anymore.

Hughes looks surprised. "Really? I thought all the Larks were close."

"We work together. Some of us are friends. Some of us aren't." I don't like the way he's looking at me, like he suspects me of…what? Gretchen's *murder*?

As if. Maybe they should take a look at that creepy Cass Vincenti. Though really, maybe that's unfair. What does Cass have to do with this? What do any of us have to do with Gretchen's murder? Beyond providing information on her whereabouts, no one at school is responsible.

At least, I don't *think* anyone at school is responsible.

"We might need to call you down to the station to question you further, Miss Malone. Do you have a problem with that?" Detective Spalding asks, his voice kind yet his expression serious.

"You'll have to talk to my dad," I tell them, lifting my chin, hoping I look stronger than I feel. "He's a lawyer."

"Ah." Spalding nods like that explains everything. "Well,

we'll be in contact with him soon, then."

Dread washes over me, but I pretend I'm fine, hitting the button on my keyless remote so my car doors unlock. "If you'll excuse me, gentlemen, I have a candlelight vigil to get ready for." Oh, I sound megaconfident. Where did that come from?

"Talk to you soon, Penelope," Hughes says as I climb into the car. I shut the door before he can say anything else.

I wait until they walk away before I reach out to start the car. But it's hard.

My hands won't stop shaking.

CHAPTER SIX

This candlelight vigil is complete bullshit.

Pretty sure everyone from school is here. Like, every single person—the popular people, the band geeks, the burnouts, the brainiacs, the losers. And they're all clustered together in smaller groups, hugging one another and sobbing into one another's shoulders and chests—though the chest sobbing is more like guys trying to press their faces into girls' boobs.

But yeah, they are all literally sobbing like they can't contain themselves. Like they're so overcome by the queen bitch's murder.

It is the most vulgar display of fake emotion I've ever seen in my life.

Volleyball coach Sally Smith is standing next to a giant poster of Gretchen Nelson that's propped on a stand. There are two obscene floral arrangements of blood red roses flanking either side of the photo of the grinning, forever-gone Gretchen.

Coach Smith is still in her volleyball gear. She's wearing

a Cape Bonita Prep T-shirt and dark blue Nike shorts that show off her thick legs. There's even a whistle around her neck, for Christ's sake. She's droning on and on about what a great player Gretchen was—ha, that could be taken in so many ways. What a great person Gretchen was, which we all know deep down is a complete and utter lie.

She was not a great person. She was a snob and a bitch who loved putting people down. Who loved stealing guys right out from under her friends' noses. I've seen her do it once or twice.

"We will all miss Gretchen so, so much," Coach says just before she breaks down in tears. She hangs her head, bends forward a little, and her whistle swings to and fro. It's downright mesmerizing.

With a big sniff and a little cough, Coach Smith turns to stare at the photo like she wants to make out with it, and speaks, as if she's actually talking to Gretchen. "I hope heaven knows how lucky they are to have a pretty angel like you."

People start waving the corny signs they made in honor of Gretchen. I'm surprised the band isn't set up, ready to play at a moment's notice. If you squint and forget the recent tragedy, you would almost imagine this is your typical high school pep rally.

My gaze goes to the giant Gretchen poster. She's leaning against a tree and her arms are crossed in front of her. The smile on her face is smug, her red hair is bright and shiny, and her eyes…let's just say, she looks mighty pleased with herself.

The complete opposite of what she looked like last night, begging for her life in the church parking lot.

Bitch got exactly what she deserved.

CHAPTER SEVEN

I don't even know what to make of this vigil we're having for Gretchen. It feels so over the top, and the volleyball coach is not making it any easier. She's literally sobbing into the microphone and I'm half tempted to cover my ears and scream, "Make it stop!"

But I don't. Of course I don't. That would be the worst thing I could ever do. Larks don't make a scene. No one in Cape Bonita makes a scene. Not really. We're so polite it's almost comical.

Besides, I really am torn up over Gretchen's death. Yes, we had our ups and downs. Yes, we were in a down when she died, but that doesn't mean I won't miss her. No one really *deserves* to die, and while I haven't heard any confirmed details yet—and trust that the rumors are flying around school, let me tell you—I do know she was for sure murdered in the parking lot of the Our Lady of Mount Carmel Catholic Church.

It makes no sense. Gretchen's family went to that progressive Christian church on the other side of town, and they attended infrequently. The typical holiday appearances and whatnot. So what brought her to Our Lady of Mount Carmel?

Supposedly it was me, since I called the surprise Larks meeting—at least, according to the detectives.

I spy the detectives now, standing off to the side but not too far from where Coach Smith is still sobbing into the mic. They're just behind the giant portrait of Gretchen, their faces unreadable, their eyes shifting and moving as they scan the crowd, their hands resting on their hips. Looking for suspects, no doubt.

I'm pretty sure the entire school is here, and they are all collectively in mourning for Gretchen. I've never seen so many people cry in one spot in all my life. I've swiped at my eyes more than a few times myself, though I'm not big on crying in public. My father instilled that in us since we were little kids. Tears make us weak.

And we need to stay strong.

"This is so incredibly sad," Dani says to me. I can tell just by the sound of her voice that she's been crying, too.

Wrapping my arm around her slender shoulders, I pull her in close and give her a one-sided hug. "I know. It's hard to believe she's gone."

"Is it wrong to admit I'm kind of glad she is?" Courtney asks snidely.

My mouth falls open. So does Dani's.

"Too soon? Yeah, I thought so," Court says with a slight nod.

I don't quite understand the animosity between Courtney and Gretchen, but it was bad. And it looks bad, too, what with how Courtney can't stop talking about it. So why aren't the detectives questioning her more thoroughly? She's the one who's acting suspicious, not me. They make it seem like I'm the one who lured Gretchen to her death. While Courtney's going around telling anyone who'll listen she's glad Gretchen is dead.

Or maybe I'm just paranoid. When I told my parents everything that happened at school today, Daddy told me he's calling in a few favors from work associates, so I know I'm covered. But still. It's scary, having the cops snooping around and looking into our lives.

But maybe someone else is looking into our lives, too. Someone we don't know.

"What exactly was your problem with her anyway?" I ask, curious. When Courtney whirls on me, her eyes narrowed, I plead my case. "Come on, Court, we're all friends here. I had no idea you two were fighting so badly."

"We weren't fighting. It was more like an unspoken disagreement," Courtney explains.

I frown. "About what?"

"A boy," Dani adds, sending me a *duh* look. "Remember what she said earlier this afternoon at the library? Supposedly Gretchen stole her man."

"She *did* steal my man," Court adds.

"Who did she steal from you?" I turn to look at Courtney.

She sighs, resting a hand on her hip. "The last one isn't even worth mentioning," Courtney says, her voice low as Mr. Rose starts to speak. All three of us are standing close together, our own little island among the many mourners who are sniffling and crying openly. "It's the fact that she stole yet *another* guy from me that pisses me off. I confronted her about it, too, but she just laughed." Courtney scowls. "I'm so over it. I'm over *her.*"

Huh. If Court says he's not worth mentioning, then he is most definitely worth mentioning. She's just trying to keep him her little secret.

"Then why are you here if you're still so mad at her?" Dani asks innocently, her brown eyes wide.

"Where else am I supposed to go? If I didn't show up tonight, I'd look like a bitch," Courtney says. "So instead I'm here pretending I'm sad she's gone."

"You really shouldn't talk about Gretchen like that, Court," Dani says timidly. "What if someone else heard you?"

"Please, she had so many enemies. I could hand over a long-ass list of people the police should talk to, trust me. Besides, I already spoke to the detectives. I was upfront with them. They know we didn't get along very well, and they acted like it was no big deal." Courtney shrugs, scanning the crowd until her gaze alights on someone. "I'll be right back, girls."

She walks away before we can say anything, getting swallowed up in the crowd.

"Who is she going to talk to?" I stand on my tiptoes, trying to find her, but it's near impossible in the sea of black-wearing, crying students.

"Who cares?" Dani tugs on my arm, forcing me to look at her. "I don't like how she's talking, Penelope. She seems suspicious."

"They've always sort of hated each other." I know where Dani is going with this, but Courtney would never actually hurt someone. Come on, we're Larks. We're not murderers.

"Yeah, but we've all sort of hated each other at one point or another. It's like Court doesn't give a crap who hears her say she despised Gretchen." Dani lowers her voice. "She's giving herself motive."

More like major motive, not that I want to think Courtney would ever do something like that. "Come on, D. You don't think she murdered Gretchen, do you?"

"No. But I don't like being seen with someone who

everyone else is going to think murdered Gretchen," Dani explains.

Huh. She has a valid point.

I scan the crowd, looking for Court's familiar blond head, but I don't spot her. It feels like everyone's looking at one another, suspicion in their gazes, their arms wrapped around themselves like they're trying to ward off bad spirits. The mood is somber, unlike anything I've ever seen at school before, but I guess that's expected considering the circumstances.

My chest feels tight and I rest my hand over my heart. It still hits me every few minutes that Gretchen is never coming back.

Ever.

"Thank you, everyone, for taking the time to gather together tonight, and to help remember the bright shining light that was once Gretchen Nelson."

We all go silent when Mr. Rose starts to speak. His voice is strong and firm, totally unlike how he spoke to us earlier this morning in the gym, when he'd still been rattled and shocked.

"It is always devastating when a young life is snuffed out too soon. But the way we lost Gretchen is particularly painful for all of us." Mr. Rose pauses, like he's letting that bit of information sink in. "I hope that if there's anyone out there who has even a tiny bit of information, or who might've seen something yesterday—or perhaps you heard something—I hope you will do the right thing and talk to the detectives in charge of the case." He waves a hand at Detectives Spalding and Hughes, who both give this weird sort of wave at the crowd, like they're embarrassed that Mr. Rose pointed them out.

Maybe they didn't want to be acknowledged at all?

"Cape Bonita Prep is proud of its students. We are strong, we are smart, and we are capable. And right now, we need to band together and take care of one another in our time of need," Mr. Rose says, his voice rising. "Some of us will remain strong. Others will do their best to not fall apart, and that's okay. You're allowed to feel pain. We all deal with loss differently, and this will be a difficult time for all of us to endure, especially those who were so close to Gretchen." He pauses, letting his words sink in yet again. "Please don't forget we will have grief counselors on campus for the remainder of the week. And if necessary, they will be here next week as well."

Mr. Rose goes silent and scans the crowd, his gaze alighting on…me.

"Penelope. I know you and Gretchen were close. Would you like to say something?" He tips the microphone in my direction.

Oh. My. God. He totally called me out. I know I should stand strong before the student body and say something thoughtful about Gretchen, but…I'm scared. Nervous, too. And I usually never get nervous when speaking in front of a crowd.

A shuddery exhale leaves me, and I part my lips, ready to answer, when Courtney appears out of nowhere, standing next to Mr. Rose and swiping the mic right out of his hand.

I can't help but admire her outfit as she takes the stage. A plain black dress that's not plain at all if you look for the right details. Like the delicate lace collar that circles her neck, and the intricate pleats in the bodice's wispy, thin black material. The dress fits her to perfection and is extremely expensive.

Very funeral chic. If that's even a thing.

"I have something to say about our dear, sweet Gretchen,"

Court starts, a giant smile curving her lips as she studies the students. She has no fear of crowds. Not only is she a cheerleader, Courtney has also performed in lead roles for the drama department since we started high school. This is definitely her element.

She turns to look at Mr. Rose. "Do you mind, Bob?"

We all call Mr. Rose *Bob* behind his back, since that's his first name. But we never say it to his face.

"Go right ahead, Courtney," he says with a weak smile. He looks nervous.

Knowing Courtney and what she just revealed to us, he should be.

She faces the crowd once more, beaming. Her blond hair shines, her blue eyes sparkle, and she is elegance personified in that gorgeous black dress. But it's all a facade, hiding her ugly, angry heart.

Courtney can turn on the sweetness like no one else, but she also knows how to infuse every word she says with venom, too. Over the years, I've learned it's better to keep her on your good side versus your bad. And lately she's acted even more out of character. Angrier. More outbursts, more irrational behavior.

"I've known Gretchen since kindergarten. Isn't that sweet?" Everyone makes an *aww* noise, and her eyes dim. Is it just me or is she starting to look weird? Like she's suddenly exhausted. Maybe she is. I know I am. "We were the very best of friends. We did everything together, up until about fifth grade, when we drifted apart. It happens, you know? We make new friends. We find new interests. It hurts, but it's normal."

What's not normal is Courtney's behavior. Her words seem to slur together and her eyelids are droopy, like she might fall asleep at any moment.

Dani leans over and whispers, "Do you think she's drunk?"

Shaking my head, I shrug. I have no clue.

"But then in high school, we came back together," Courtney continues. "We bonded. We became best friends again. We were in cheer together. We were both appointed to student council positions. Our junior year, we became Larks, and we made a promise to each other at the beginning of that school year. We were going to *change* the *world* and make it a *better place*. We were going to *do* things that *mattered*. The Larks are leaders of the school, bright and shiny representatives of the future."

I brace myself, waiting for the verbal blow, because it's coming. Courtney is a master at delivering them. Dani clutches my arm, so tight I'm scared she's going to cut off the circulation, but I don't try to shake her off. I'm clutching at her, too.

"So how was I to know that when she said she wanted to *do* things that mattered, she meant she would *do* all the guys who mattered to *me*? Why did I always have to take her sloppy seconds? Yeah, not cool, Gretchen." Courtney glares at the giant portrait. "Not cool at all."

There is no more sobbing. In its place is absolute silence.

Oh, and Bob Rose frantically trying to grab the mic out of Courtney's waving hand.

"Hold on, Mr. Rose. I'm not finished." She dodges him and laughs into the microphone. "Let's be real, people. No one liked Gretchen Nelson. She was mean. She was calculating. And she didn't care about any of you. Not even you, Coach Smith." The volleyball coach makes an unintelligible sound and presses her hand against her mouth. "Think whatever you want, say whatever you want, but Gretchen didn't give a flying fuck about any of you!"

The sound of multiple cameras snapping makes me glance around to see everyone's got their phones out, and the local news stations are filming away.

The vigil is definitely going to make the evening news. And the people of Cape Bonita are going to flip. We're the quintessential beach town. Wealthy, with giant mansions on cliffs and glamorous cars and overachieving children, our little enclave doesn't like it when bad stuff happens.

And the murder of Gretchen Nelson is the epitome of bad stuff.

Mr. Rose rips the mic out of Courtney's hand just as the detectives approach. She laughs hysterically, trying to jerk away from their grasping hands, but they each grab Courtney by her upper arms and take her away.

We are still silent.

We are shocked by what Courtney just said.

Well. Some of us are.

And some of us aren't.

At all.

CHAPTER EIGHT

Saturday is Gretchen's funeral. Dani and I drove over to the cemetery together for the graveside ceremony, the both of us all cried out after the long service in an overly crowded and extremely hot church. It is an unusually warm fall day, pushing almost ninety degrees by the midafternoon, and there isn't a cloud in the sky. All the colors are so intense, like a saturated lens. With the blue, blue sky and the green, green grass, along with the trees and their changing leaves of burnished gold and orange and red.

It's too beautiful a day to bury someone so young.

Standing by Gretchen's gravesite, staring at the beautifully polished wood casket that's covered with dozens and dozens of white roses while the minister drones on and on about the loss of such a beloved young soul, it almost feels like some weird form of punishment. Having to stand out here and suffer on such a gorgeous day.

But at least I'm not Gretchen, gone too soon. There's still so much life to live, so much more she could've done. It's still hard for me to believe she's gone.

The minister is reading from a piece of paper, rattling off Gretchen's attributes one by one, adding in all sorts of comforting words that I suppose should make her family feel better that she's gone. I bet he barely knew Gretchen. I'd guess all the stuff he said about her was standard, words he'd repeated a hundred times before about other nameless, faceless dead people.

God, my thoughts are deranged and sad, but I can't help it. When you go seventeen years without thinking about death, and then it's suddenly thrust into your face? It's weird.

Dani sniffs a lot and dabs at her face with the giant handkerchief that once belonged to her grandfather, who died when we were thirteen. He's buried in this cemetery, too, and Dani told me on the drive over that coming here would dredge up old memories.

I didn't know what to say. I've never really dealt with death before. I have my mom and dad, my older brother and sister. My grandparents on both sides are still alive, and all my aunts and uncles and cousins are, too. This is my first brush with tragedy, and it's kind of overwhelming.

More like really overwhelming—and awkward. I never know the right words to say or how to act. I'm trying to be respectful and do the right thing, but it's difficult. Sometimes I think it's easier—and smarter—to just be quiet.

The minister finally finishes talking, and there's nothing but silence as the family murmurs among themselves. I have no idea what's coming next, but it can't be good. Gretchen's mom stands, and she's clutching a handful of pale pink roses. A sob falls from her lips and she nearly collapses. Gretchen's dad grabs hold of her arm and guides her back down into the chair behind her. Dani gasps next to me, new tears streaming down her face, and I send her a sympathetic look as I reach out and squeeze her hand.

"You're a good friend," Dani whispers to me as we stand behind the row of chairs that were set out for Gretchen's immediate family members. "Thank you for being so supportive and not making fun of me."

I send her a look. "Who would make fun of you for crying at a funeral?"

She shrugs and looks around before she says out of the corner of her mouth, "Courtney."

Who did not make an appearance at the church service, and she isn't here now, either. She hasn't been back to school since her outburst. Turns out she was high as a kite on anti-anxiety pills the night of the candlelight vigil, and they made her ruder than normal. At least, that's what Courtney's mother told us when Dani and I went over to the Jenkins's house on Friday night to check on Court. Her mom wouldn't let us come inside to see her.

Rumors are now spreading that Courtney's been sent to rehab.

"Well, she's not here," I remind Dani, hooking my arm through hers. "And you're allowed to cry at a funeral."

"It's just, I feel like I'm crying more for my grandpa right now than Gretchen." She meets my gaze, blinking at me. "That's awful, isn't it?"

"No, you're not awful. You're just being honest." I give her a brief hug, clutching her close. "When is this going to be over?" I whisper in her ear.

"Probably in a few minutes." Dani withdraws and turns to watch as Gretchen's mother stands once more and approaches the casket.

"Pink was your favorite color," Gretchen's mother says to the shiny wood box as she sets the roses among the mountain of white ones. "I will miss your sunny face more than you'll ever, ever know."

And then she promptly collapses to the ground.

A chorus of cries and gasps rises into the air as Mr. Nelson rushes toward his wife. The minister stands over them, praying for them both, and I can actually hear Gretchen's dad crying.

His loud sobs are making me incredibly sad and I'm on the verge of crying. I sniff loudly and wrap my arms around my middle, trying to ward off the sudden chill that washes over me. It's like Gretchen's entire family is falling apart in the most public way and we're all just watching it go down.

Dani and I exchange glances, and then we both hightail it out of there without a word. Not that anyone noticed, which is fine by us.

"That was awful," I say once we've walked far enough away that no one can hear us.

"I know. I feel so bad for her family. I can't imagine what that must be like for them," Dani says, her voice hushed. "It's such a pretty day, too. It doesn't seem fair."

"I was thinking the same thing earlier." I glance over at Dani. "Are you holding up okay?" My best friend is probably the most sensitive out of all of us. She doesn't want to hurt anything, won't even step on a spider or slap a mosquito. I know Gretchen's murder has to be tormenting her.

"Sort of. I cry a lot." She tries to smile, but her lips tremble and I'm afraid she's going to start sobbing again. "It's hard for me to believe that someone would do that to Gretchen."

There's nothing I can say to that, so I keep quiet.

We walk across the smooth grass of the cemetery, my gaze drawn to the headstones. So many of them dot the landscape, some tall and grand, others small and plain. The cemetery is high up on a hill that overlooks the town and the ocean just beyond, and I can see the whitecaps that dot the seascape, the occasional fishing boat far out on the water.

Such a beautiful view. So many tourists come through our tiny town, but no one knows the best view of the ocean is at the cemetery. Kind of weird, but true.

It's breezy up here, too, the wind catching my long dark hair and whipping it into my face, and I bat it away. A squeal leaves me when the wind catches the hem of my black skirt and flips it up, causing Dani to giggle, which is a relief to hear. I catch it before my butt's exposed.

"Almost saw your underwear."

The unfamiliar male voice makes both of us stop, then turn.

It's Cass.

"What are you doing here?" I ask, my tone snide. I can't help it, after our last encounter left me so unsettled.

"I came to pay my respects to Gretchen." He slips his hands into the front pockets of his black pants. He's wearing a black button down shirt, too, and those faded, beat-up Converse. "We were…friends."

"Funny, she never mentioned your name to us before," I tell him.

"Penny," Dani says, her voice low.

I send her a look. She knows how much I hate the Penny nickname, though she's one of the rare few who can actually get away with it.

"We weren't the kind of friends you brag about." He smiles and slowly approaches us. "More like we met in secret."

Dani's mouth drops open. "What are you saying? You two were hooking up?"

He throws back his head and laughs, like Danielle just told the most hilarious joke ever. "Not quite."

"Then what's your deal with Gretchen?" Ugh, I sound like a complete snob, but I can't help it. It's like this guy brings out the worst in me and I don't even know why.

"Did you ever think that maybe it's none of your business?" He lifts a brow, smirks, and then brushes past us, bumping into me as he goes. "Have a nice afternoon, ladies."

We turn and watch him go, Dani sending me a strange look when he finally disappears out of our view. "What the hell was that about?"

"I don't know." I'm fuming. I start walking toward the small parking lot nearby where my car sits. Dani practically has to run to keep up with me.

"You were totally hostile toward him," she says, puffing like she's out of breath.

"I don't like him. Court's right. He's weird."

"I think Court was hooking up with him."

My mouth drops open, and I come to a stop. "Say what?"

She skids to a stop, too. "I'm serious. She was always talking shit about him, but I saw a bunch of texts between them once. She was sending him tit pics."

Great. So he was hooking up with Courtney? And possibly Gretchen, too? What a man whore.

"Please don't tell me he sent her dick pics in return," I say, both curious and a little disgusted. I've had my fair share of dick pics via text. More like they were sent via Snapchat, since those can disappear in less than ten seconds.

"Not that I saw. I'm totally speculating, by the way. She was sending tit pics to someone, but maybe it wasn't Cass, you know? Maybe she just used his name as a ruse." Dani shrugs, and we start walking again. "Courtney sends topless photos on Snapchat to everyone. You know this."

She's right. I do.

We approach my car and once we're inside I turn to look at her. "What exactly do you know about Cass?"

"Not much. His mom murdered his dad and now she's in

prison. He lives with his grandma up here, on Hot Springs Road."

"In that brick house at the top of the hill, right?" It's on the most coveted piece of property in the entire area, with a view of Cape Bonita and the ocean that most would pay huge money for.

But the house is small—an old, brick structure with ivy covering the entire front of the building, even draping over the front porch, giving it a spooky vibe.

Figures.

"Yeah. Have you ever been there?"

"Why would I have reason to go to Cass Vincenti's house?" I start my car and drive slowly along the road that meanders through the cemetery, suddenly desperate to get out of here. I've had enough with funerals and graveside services and strange boys who make ominous statements, thank you very much.

"I don't know," Dani says. "Weirder things have happened. I remember there was that one time in the eighth grade when he had a Halloween party."

"I don't remember that."

"Of course you don't. Because you didn't go."

"Did anyone go?"

"Oh yeah, pretty much everyone, though I couldn't. I went to a party with my parents instead, and it sucked." Dani shakes her head at the memory. "I guess Cass's party was super creepy and a lot of girls got freaked out, including Gretchen and Courtney."

I frown, thinking back to eighth grade. Why didn't I go to that party? Did he not invite me? I can't imagine he would exclude me…

But then I remember. I was in cheer that fall, for a local youth football league, and our last playoff game landed on the Saturday before Halloween—most likely when Cass's party was held. And none of my friends cheered with me except for Alexis.

"Why was his party so creepy?"

"It was like, literally scary. He scared the hell out of everyone who went, boys and girls. Some of the guys threatened to kick his ass at school on Monday, but he just laughed. Practically dared them to do it," Dani explains.

"Isn't that the point of a Halloween party, though? Like, we get older and we want to be scared," I point out.

"There's being scared and laughing, and then there's being scared and shitting your pants." Dani's tone is dead serious. "Cass's party was the last one."

"Oh." Yikes. Glad I didn't go.

"But there's always been something kind of…attractive about his creepiness," Dani continues as she stares out the passenger-side window. "That sounds weird, I know. But he *is* weird. And he's cute. If you like them quiet and sort of goth."

"I don't," I immediately say as I pull out of the cemetery and turn right, so fast I make the tires squeal.

"Neither do I. Not normally." Dani watches me carefully. I can feel her gaze on me, but I refuse to look at her. "I never said you did, either."

"Good, because I don't. He's definitely not my type." I don't know why I'm arguing. Or who I'm trying to convince.

Her or me.

CHAPTER NINE

Last week at school was a study in tragedy. Grief counselors on daily standby, open weeping in the halls, teachers breaking down midlecture. All tests and any fun activities were temporarily postponed. The football team didn't play their home game Friday night as a show of respect toward Gretchen, which meant they forfeited the game. No big deal, since they suck anyway...

It's like Cape Bonita Prep came to a complete halt, the entire school nearly falling apart after losing one of its own. The local news stations talked about Gretchen on a nightly basis, but with no new leads and no suspects mentioned, the story has gone quiet.

Typical. Cape Bonita would rather sweep Gretchen's death under the proverbial rug. Pretend it never existed. Same with our school.

This week, it's business as usual. The physics test just about killed me on Tuesday. I worked on an English paper long into the night on Wednesday and emailed it to my teacher at 11:59 p.m. — it was due by midnight. Now it's

Thursday afternoon, and I've called a Larks meeting after school in conference room three in the library.

Everyone's there, even Courtney, who wasn't put in rehab after all. Her parents kept her home for a few days after her mini-outburst, and when Court showed up at school first thing Monday morning, fresh-faced and seemingly eager to be back, she explained that she had a hard time coping with Gretchen's death, but she was feeling much better now.

It was really tough for me to keep a straight face when she said that, because I know she's lying. I think Courtney's pissed Gretchen showed her up yet again — even when she dies. And I know it's wrong to think like that, to believe Courtney would act that way, but I can't help it. I've known her a long time. I know how she operates, and how she always wants to be the center of attention.

I am glad she's back, though, and that she can help with the Larks. We need to keep things going, not let it fall apart because we lost a member.

Once I get the meeting started, we discuss the little stuff first, then I move on to serious business.

"I need two new volunteers for the children's hospital this month," I start, my gaze briefly landing on every girl sitting at the table. Since the Larks organization's main requirement is that we give back to the community, we've chosen specific charities to work with — most of them dealing with disadvantaged and sick children. We volunteer at the hospital, we help out in the special-needs classrooms at the local elementary schools, and a few of us are even a part of the Big Brother/Big Sister program.

Sometimes I think I'd like to be a teacher, but my parents always try to convince me to do something bigger and better — direct quote. They've controlled my life since I was born, so I usually just nod in agreement and keep my thoughts to myself. But being a teacher is a noble profession, right?

"I'd like to do it," Alyssa says with a shy smile. I like her. She has great potential. She speaks up when necessary and knows when to hold her tongue. She's always volunteering and helping out, and no one ever has to ask her twice. Plus, she's a cheerleader, which is practically a prerequisite for the future Larks president.

Why, I'm not exactly sure. That's just always the way it is.

"Great. Thank you, Alyssa. You're always so helpful." I scan the table once more, curious when no one looks me in the eye. Dani just came off the volunteer round, so I'm not going to ask her to do it again. Courtney is currently too unstable, so I'll wait until next month. Lex lifts her head, her gaze almost defiant when it meets mine, and I wonder what her deal is.

I decide to challenge her. "You up for volunteering this month, Alexis? We could really use your help," I say, my voice sickeningly sweet.

Her bold red lips twist into a semi-smile. "Not particularly. I need to finish writing my senior essay. College applications and all that."

"Um, I'm fairly certain we all have to finish writing our senior essays." I glare at the remaining quiet juniors, and anger makes my blood hot. I have no time for this. "Time for you to step up, junior Larks. Someone needs to pipe up before I choose one of you to take the job. And I really hate doing that." I pause. No response. "It's a requirement, girls. You *must* volunteer. That's the whole point of being a Lark. Remember?"

Maggie sighs and tilts her head to the side, her lank brown hair falling across her shoulder. I'm surprised she's not volunteering, because she's usually one of the first to speak up.

The put-out expression on her face is annoying. How did she get into the Larks again? Oh, that's right. She's a legacy member. Her sister was a Lark four years ago, when I was still in the eighth grade, so I never got a chance to work with her, though my sister did. I heard nothing but good things about Lysette Fawkes from Peyton.

Not so sure about her little sister, though.

"Fine, I'll volunteer," Maggie finally says with a slight frown. "Though don't forget, I was the one who organized the sign making for Gretchen's vigil last week."

"Oh, that's right." I snap my fingers. "So…what are you saying? Would you like a medal?"

Maggie's surprised expression is straight out of a cartoon. She's all bug-eyed, gawping shock. "I just wanted to mention it—"

"When we feel it's necessary to list our accomplishments, we do so. Otherwise, it just looks like you're bragging. A bit of advice? It's best if you keep your mouth shut and let us judge you by your actions." I smile serenely, trying my damnedest to look presidential. I swear Courtney looks like she's about to burst out laughing. "I do appreciate you taking the initiative and helping out with the signs, though. And thank you for volunteering at the hospital this month. The children will be ever so grateful."

Maggie's face is tomato red. "You're welcome," she mumbles.

She probably thinks I humiliated her on purpose, but I have to keep the juniors in line. I hate being so tough on them, but I'm the Larks president. I need to be extra tough.

"Anyone else have something they wish to discuss?" I ask pleasantly.

"I do," Lex says, sitting up straight. "I think we need to seriously consider who to choose as Gretchen's replacement."

"Already?" I ask. "She's barely been gone a week, Lex. I don't know…"

"I think it's a good idea," Courtney adds. "The bylaws say we must maintain ten members at all times—five seniors and five juniors."

I turn on her. "You *read* the bylaws?" No one reads the freaking bylaws. They're boring. They date all the way back to the seventies, when people had to actually write them on a typewriter.

So primitive.

"Yeah, I did." Court shrugs. "After Gretchen died, I figured we'd need to do something. So I checked up on the rules."

"If we don't find a replacement for Gretchen, we might have to disband," Lex tells me.

How in the world does she know? Did Lex read the bylaws, too? What, are they ganging up on me? "Says who?"

"Says our rulebook," Lex stresses. "I read the bylaws with Court. Come on, Penelope. Don't be difficult. We need to nominate a potential new member."

"Shouldn't we declare special circumstances?" I can't even begin to fathom who we might nominate. The choices among the senior girls are so slim.

"Maybe," Dani says, finally piping up. "I mean, we've never dealt with a…murdered member before. I would definitely count this situation as special circumstances."

"Then let's look into it."

When Lex starts to speak, I cut her off. "I'm serious. Finding another member is the last thing I want to do. There are so many other tasks we need to focus on."

"Like what?" Court asks.

I glare at her. I shouldn't have to explain myself to Courtney—or any of them. And I don't appreciate how she's calling me out in front of everyone. I thought she had my back.

"Let's discuss potential new members at the next meeting," Dani suggests, ever the peacemaker. "And if we can't make a decision, then we should look at the next step."

"What? Disband?" Lex says with a smirk.

"No!" Maggie practically shouts. She pounds her fist on the table so hard, it makes everyone jump in their seats. "We can't disband! The Larks are too important to this school, to the entire community! We can't quit just because Gretchen was *murdered*!"

I watch her, surprised by her outburst. She looks furious at the thought of the Larks breaking apart.

Alyssa reaches out and pats Maggie's arm. "Calm down. Everything's going to be fine," she murmurs, but Maggie only glares at her before she slumps in her seat. Like that mini tantrum just took everything out of her.

"Thank you, Alyssa." I smile at her and she smiles in return. I probably look like I'm playing favorites, but I can't help it. She's my pick for next year's Larks president. "And that would never happen," I reassure Maggie. More like I'm reassuring everyone. I make sure and look them all in the eye. "Just because one of our members is gone doesn't mean we're all going to quit. Gretchen wouldn't have wanted us to do that."

I don't know if that's true, but it sounds good.

"Speaking of murder. Have the police released any other details about what exactly happened to Gretchen?" Courtney asks.

The room goes silent at her question. Someone clears her throat. Dani fidgets in her chair.

I mean seriously—does Courtney want all the dirty details? How gross is that? The local paper ran an article right after the body was discovered and identified, but they didn't mention how she was killed.

It's like they're keeping it a secret.

"I haven't heard anything." I glance around the table to find them all watching me with hallowed expressions. "Has anyone else been questioned by the detectives?"

Mostly shaking heads, except for—of course—Courtney.

"They came by my house on Sunday to talk to me again," she says quietly, her gaze dropping to the table.

"Really?" Lex's voice perks up. She'd probably secretly love to see Courtney go down for Gretchen's murder. "All that smack talk about Gretchen finally bit you in the butt, huh?"

"More like the public scene she made at the vigil," mumbles Jessica, one of the quieter junior members. The rest of the juniors giggle nervously until I send them a stern look that immediately shuts them up.

"None of that was the reason." Courtney lifts her head and glares directly at Lex. "They found texts on Gretchen's phone about me and…someone else. Ugly stuff, like she wanted to kick my ass or something stupid like that."

"*Really?*" Dani breathes, her brown eyes wide with surprise.

"Yes, *really*," Courtney mocks. "They wanted to know if Gretchen had threatened me in any way over the last few weeks."

"Had she?" I ask. What does she mean, texts about her and someone else? Who's the *someone else*? Why won't she just say the name?

Courtney levels her gaze on me. "No."

Huh. I don't know if I believe her.

"Then they asked to look at my phone," she continues.

"Did you let them?" Lex sounds like she wants to start laughing.

"No." Courtney's gaze sweeps around the table, alighting on each of us. "Be careful. Because they'll probably ask to look at all of your phones."

Dani gasps. Lex laughs. The juniors remain quiet. But I'm still watching Courtney.

What exactly does she have to hide?

CHAPTER TEN

Later that night, I'm sitting on my bed with my laptop, trying to work on my American Government project, when I get a text from a number I don't recognize.

Unknown: Don't trust her.

Frowning, I stare at the three words, then at the number. Even the area code is unrecognizable.

I have no idea who it is. I have no idea who I'm not supposed to trust, either. I know a lot of *her*s.

So I decide to call their bluff.

Me: Don't trust who?

I set my phone down and try to concentrate on the article I'm reading for research, but it's boring. And I'm suddenly anxious. Who's sending me random texts late on a Thursday night? Who am I supposed to not trust?

My phone dings with a reply.

Unknown: All of them. They're liars.

Me: Who is this?

Unknown: Consider me a friend.

I open my text thread with Dani and shoot off a message to her.

Me: Plz tell me you're getting weird rando texts from strangers.

She replies quickly.

Dani: I'm not...r u?!?!?

I stare at the screen, wondering how much I should tell her. My phone chimes with another message and I check it. It's from my random stranger.

Unknown: Courtney isn't being honest with you. She knows more than she's saying.

My heart twists. It's like this person is in my head and knows about my earlier suspicions. And it's freaking me out. Who the hell is this?

Me: What does she know more about?

Unknown: Gretchen.

Me: What do you mean?

Unknown: They've been fighting for a long time. G&C.

Yawn. That's old news.

Unknown: And it got serious the week before Gretchen died.

Me: How do you know?

Unknown: Trust me. I know.

Me: So I'm not supposed to trust my friends I've

known for years. But I should trust you, a random creepy stranger?

Unknown: I'm not a random creepy stranger. You know me.

I stare at the last words this person texted me. *You know me.*

Unease slips down my spine.

Me: How well?

Unknown: Well enough.

Me: Maybe you should tell me who you are.

Unknown: Maybe you should do a little more investigating and see just how much Courtney really hated Gretchen.

Me: Why don't you tell the police yourself? Let them investigate.

Unknown: I don't trust cops. They're idiots.

Okay, this conversation is stupid. Though this person isn't too far off the mark. I didn't like the detectives, either.

Me: You have trust issues.

Unknown: You're right. I do. But I think I can trust you.

Why in the world would he or she trust me?

I get another text from Dani, so I check it.

Dani: Why aren't u responding to meeee? What's going on?? Whooz texting uuuuu??? Tell me!

God, sometimes I really hate her bad text grammar.

Me: Turns out it wasn't meant for me.

My finger hovers over the button. Should I lie to her? Keep this from her? According to my new anonymous text friend, I'm not supposed to trust anyone. But Dani is my closest friend. She's my *best* friend. I pretty much tell her everything, and I know everything about her. I don't like keeping secrets from her, even if she does blab them to other people sometimes and I end up getting mad.

Yes, if you haven't guessed, this has totally happened before.

Giving in, I tap the screen and send the message. And get a fast reply.

Dani: Dang! I was hoping it was some mysterious guy who's hot for you.

She's always hoping I'll hook up with some guy. It's been her greatest wish ever since Robby and I split. She wants me to be with another football player, then she can date Brogan, and we can double date every weekend.

Sometimes it's like my best friend lives her life in a romance novel.

My phone dings again, but it's not with a message from Dani.

Unknown: Can I trust you, Pen?

Huh. No one calls me Pen. I don't really allow it. Penny still sticks with some, considering it's what everyone used to call me in elementary school.

I get another message.

Unknown: Can I tell you a secret?

Me: Depends on what it is. Some things I might not want to know...

Clutching my phone, I wait for the next message.

Unknown: Maybe it's better if I tell you in person.

My mouth drops open. No freaking way.

Me: I'm not going to meet you or whatever. I don't even know you. What if you're the one who murdered Gretchen?

My mystery texter actually sends me a row of laughing emojis.

Unknown: I didn't kill Gretchen, even though you might think I did.

Frowning, I stare at my phone's screen. Why do I feel like I've had this conversation before?

Unknown: Meet me Saturday 9 am at Sweet Offerings. I'll tell you more then.

Despite that nagging inner voice inside my head telling me I'm crazy to even contemplate meeting my mystery message sender, I show up at the Sweet Offerings Bakery and Coffee Shop at eight forty-five Saturday morning. Maybe I can spy on this person and figure out who it is before I actually meet with them. And then I'll never meet with them.

Instead, I'll go straight to the cops and rat him or her out.

I sit in my mom's car in the parking lot across the street, watching Sweet Offerings' front door. My mom couldn't understand why I wanted to borrow her car when I have my own, until I made up some lie about being out of gas and how I really couldn't stand the thought of a lecture because oh my God, I'm still in mourning over Gretchen and everything sends me right over the edge.

She bought it. Her expression had gone straight to sad and forgiving and she handed over the keys to her little black Mercedes like she was giving me a grand prize.

"Don't park too close to other cars," she told me before I left. Like that's all she cared about.

Depressing as that thought is, it might be true.

I'm still tired from last night. We played an away game at another school almost two hours south, and we had to ride the bus both there and back. I didn't collapse into bed until well after one in the morning, so getting up to meet someone I don't even know at nine on a Saturday morning kind of sucks.

But I'm too curious not to go. So here I sit, wearing an old navy blue hoodie with the words "Bonita Cheer" in white across the chest. I have the hood on, my hair tucked beneath it, and I'm slouched low in the driver's seat, never taking my eyes off the bakery's door.

It's mostly old people walking their dogs who enter and exit the shop in a constant stream. Three women sit out front at a tiny round metal table, huddled close with their hands curved around their paper coffee cups like they're freezing. The sun is out, but it's cold, though it'll warm up later this afternoon. Another typical fall Saturday in Cape Bonita. Soon the tourists will come in. The day-trippers who want a little slice of seaside heaven before they have to go back to the grind. I love my hometown, I really do, but sometimes it feels fake. Like it's there to make other people happy but not necessarily me.

Does that make sense? Probably not. But I've always sort of felt that way.

I check my phone for about the zillionth time but have

no messages. That's because everyone I know is still sleeping, and I'm jealous. I'm afraid my mystery coffee date is not going to show up.

I was really hoping he or she would, too. Not because I wanted to run to the cops and rat them out, but because I'm just genuinely curious. Who is this person who has dirt on Gretchen and Courtney? Is it someone close to me? Someone I barely know? Just because they tell me that I know them doesn't mean I *know them,* know them. It could be an acquaintance. It could be Brogan, since he likes to pull pranks, though doubtful. Or maybe it's some random, quiet person I've gone to school with my entire life. There are more than a few of those I know—

Someone knocks on my window and I scream, my heart feeling like it could jump right out of my mouth. Glancing up, I see Courtney standing there, all bundled up with a to-go cup of coffee clutched in her hand.

I roll down the window, trying to calm my ragged breathing. "Court." I take a shaky breath. "Hey. You, uh. You scared me."

"What are you doing out here this early?" She's wearing a black knit cap, her shiny blond hair curling around her face. Her cheeks are pink from the cold and even without a lick of makeup on, she's stunning.

"I could ask you the same thing." I smile at her.

"Had breakfast with my mom." Her smile fades. "She's worried about me, so she dragged me out of bed at seven thirty and demanded we come here." Courtney looks around before returning her gaze to mine. "What are you doing? Are you meeting someone?"

"No, I'm contemplating if I should run in and grab a muffin or not." Sweet Offerings is well-known for their amazing muffins.

It's the only excuse I've got.

"You should totally grab one. The pumpkin spice is to die for. You only live once, right?" She smiles again and waves. "I gotta go. My mom's waiting. Bye, Penelope!"

And then she's gone.

I sag against the seat and take a deep breath. Is Courtney the one I was really supposed to meet? Or…what if she met with my mystery date first? What if this person is totally playing all of us?

Grabbing my phone and keys, I climb out of the car and slam the door, then jog across the street until I stop just in front of the coffee shop. I peer through the glass windows, looking for a familiar face among the crowd of people inside, or even a young face. Any face that stands out to me and tells me it's the person I'm supposed to meet.

"Didn't think you'd show, and here you are, early even. You actually beat me."

I go completely still. I know that voice. Slowly, I turn around to find…

Cass Vincenti standing in front of me, dressed all in black and a smug smile on his face.

"What are you doing here?" I ask, trying to remain calm.

He tilts his head to the side, his dark gaze drifting over me. "I could ask you the same question."

That's almost exactly what I said to Courtney. Oh my God. Did he overhear our conversation?

"I came for a pumpkin spice muffin. I hear they're to die for."

"Then let's go inside and grab one." His gaze meets mine, his brown eyes sparkling. He looks really pleased with himself. "My treat."

He heads for the door, and I follow him like a robot, entering the café when he holds the door open for me. The line to order is long, and I stand there, Cass next to me, the both of us acting like it's completely normal to run into each other and hang out.

I watch him from the corner of my eye. He's got on black Adidas track pants with the white stripes along the side of his legs, a black sweatshirt, and those stupid faded Converse shoes. His dark brown hair is an absolute mess, like he just rolled out of bed and came straight here. His cheeks are covered with faint black stubble, and his eyes look sleepy.

Unfortunately, he catches me checking him out and grins. "Rough night. I was still sleeping not even fifteen minutes ago."

"Nice," I say, my voice dripping with sarcasm.

"Uh-huh." His gaze roams over me, lingering on spots that make me vaguely uncomfortable. "What about you? You have a rough one, too?"

"Why do you ask?" I snap, but it doesn't faze him.

"You look pretty beat." His eyes lock with mine and I send him a major eye roll before I turn away.

"You're extra charming this early in the morning," I tell him.

He chuckles. "Sorry. Guess I'm not used to seeing you like…this."

I look at him again. "Like what?"

"I don't know. So…normal. And cute, with your hood on and stuff."

My cheeks go hot at his calling me cute, and I push the hood off, trying my best to ignore him. Instead, I stare straight ahead, pretending I'm reading the chalkboard menu that hangs high up on the wall behind the counter. "Are you in mourning?"

"What?" He sounds totally confused.

"The black getup." I give him a quick glance. "Looks like

you're going to a funeral."

"You've seen me at a funeral. I clean up a little better than this." He points at himself with a laugh.

Ugh. Everything he says seems to get right under my skin. I don't know why he's annoying me so much.

"Did you really come here for the muffins, Penelope?" he asks when I remain quiet.

"Sure." I shrug. "Did you see Courtney?"

He says nothing, and when I finally glance up at him, I notice the panic flickering in his eyes. "Did *you* see Courtney?" he finally asks.

I nod, resuming my pretend menu reading. "She said she was here with her mom having breakfast."

"Huh."

"But no local comes here for breakfast this early, especially locals I know," I continue. "This place is either a total tourist trap or for the retired empty nesters who walk their dogs at six in the morning and are dying for a coffee by the time they're finished."

"Rather observant, aren't you?"

I whirl on him. "So why are you here?"

"You know why." His gaze never leaves mine, but at least that smug look on his face has faded away. "You'll just have to trust me, okay?"

CHAPTER ELEVEN

"We can't stay here," I tell Cass as soon as we make our orders. He actually paid for my muffin and coffee, which surprises me.

"What do you mean?" He frowns.

We're standing together waiting for our order along with a small crowd of people, all of them older than us. This doesn't reassure me. What if we see someone we know, from school? What if they see Cass and me together?

No way can that happen. We're not friends, and if someone sees us like this, they might question it. Or worse, spread a rumor about us. I'd rather be safe than sorry.

"I don't think we should be seen together."

"What, am I going to ruin your reputation?" He shakes his head and mutters under his breath. I swear I hear him say, "They're all the same."

"Listen, you send me cryptic anonymous texts, and then you ask me to meet you here. I figure you have information you want to tell me about—" I pause and glance around, making sure no one is paying attention to us. "You-know-who. And I don't think we should discuss said information in such a public place."

"I thought you'd prefer to meet in a public place because you'd feel safer."

"But it's so crowded."

"We can sit outside."

"On the off chance someone we know could walk by and see us together?"

He raises his brows. "Am I really that detrimental to your reputation?"

"My reputation has nothing to do with this!"

"Keep your voice down. People are staring," he says out of the side of his mouth.

Just before he starts to laugh.

Oh my God. He's totally making fun of me, and this is serious. I smack him on the arm, shocked at how hard his muscles are, and he sends me an amused look. One that says, *Aw, the little girl is so funny when she tries to hurt me.*

Ugh. He's probably as strong as the jocks on the football team.

The barista behind the counter sets a white paper bag and two to-go cups on the counter. "Cass! Your order is ready!"

He grabs the bag and cups, handing mine over. "What's your suggestion, then?"

We walk together, and I follow him out of the café. "My car is parked across the street."

"So is mine."

"We'll sit in my car."

"Or mine."

I shake my head. "It's mine or this conversation is over." I want to be in control of the situation. What if I get in his car and then he locks me inside before taking off somewhere? No way do I want to be completely alone with him. I can't risk it.

Despite his easy use of the word, I don't trust him.

"Your car, then." He sounds irritated.

I really don't care.

We cross the street and I stop at my mom's Mercedes, hitting the keyless remote to unlock the doors.

"This isn't your car," Cass says as he stops to stand beside me.

I glance up at him. I'm average height, around five foot four, but he's also really tall—like well over six feet. "It's my mom's." It's kind of disturbing that he knows my car.

"I'm driving my grandma's car." He points toward a silver Lexus SUV. "Well, now it's mine, but it used to be hers."

"You live with her, right?"

"Yeah." That's all he says.

Okay then.

He opens my car door for me and I sit down, setting my coffee in the center console. He hands me the bag of muffins and then shuts the door, rounds the front of the car, and then he's settling into the passenger seat. The moment the door shuts, I realize how close we're sitting together. He seems to take up a lot of space. If I shift a little to the right, my shoulder will brush against his. And I can smell him—like warm boy, soapy clean with the underlying scent of…fabric softener. The sun shines on his dark brown hair and I notice his eyelashes are long and thick.

He's total swoon material, if I'm being honest. Like, seriously good looking. Why haven't I ever noticed him before?

"You're staring." His voice breaks the silence and my cheeks go hot at being caught.

Clearing my throat, I decide to get right to the point. The faster I find out what he wants to tell me, the faster I can get away from him.

"What exactly did you want to talk about?"

Cass takes a sip from his coffee, wincing a little. "Damn, that's hot," he mutters.

Rolling my eyes, I open the white bag and look inside, trying to decide if I actually want to eat one of those muffins or not. "So tell me. How did you know Gretchen?"

"We were...friends."

"Friends?" I look at him, one brow arched. It's what I call my *do tell* look. I practiced it in the mirror for months when I was thirteen, trying to perfect it. "*Intimate* friends?"

"Not in that way, no. Not really. But closer than you'd think."

"Really." My voice is flat. It's hard for me to believe him. I spent a lot of time with Gretchen. Not once did she ever mention Cass Vincenti. His name never even came up in casual conversation.

"I wasn't fucking her, if that's what you're thinking."

"What? No!" He says it so casually. Yes, I hear boys talk all the time. They're lewd and crass and love to shock. But f-bombs aren't the norm for me, especially at nine in the morning.

"What? It's true." He shrugs, then reaches over and slips his hand into the bag that is sitting on my lap. His fingers brush my thighs; I feel them through the thin paper bag, and my skin tingles.

"You care which muffin I eat?" he asks as he pulls one out.

"I like the way you ask *after* you put your fingers all over them," I say snidely, trying to cover up my unexpected reaction to his touching me. Yeah, it was probably by accident, but he threw me.

He laughs. "Man, you're uptight."

His offhand remark pisses me off. He's not the first boy to tell me that. Maybe I am wound a little tight. But I'm busy, like *all* the time. What with school, cheer, the Larks, college applications...I never get a chance to just sit down and relax.

So please. Forgive me if I'm a little uptight sometimes.

"I'm tired." My excuse is lame. I take a long drink from my coffee, not caring how hot it is. It tastes heavenly. "And still caffeine deprived."

"Have a muffin." He waves the one he's holding at me. "It'll make you nicer. Promise."

Rolling my eyes, I grab the other muffin out of the bag along with a napkin, and pinch a bit off the top before popping it into my mouth.

Yum. Courtney was right. This muffin is delicious.

"Who do you think killed Gretchen?"

I nearly choke on my muffin. And I thought *I* wanted to get straight to the point. I cough a little once I swallow, then take another sip of my coffee. "I don't know. Do you have any theories?"

He shrugs. "Maybe."

"Don't be coy," I say. He glances over at me. "Tell me who you think did it."

"All right." He takes a deep breath. "First of all, this stays between us," he murmurs, his gaze intense when it meets mine. "You can't tell anyone else that we met, we talked, nothing. Understand?"

"Yeah." I nod, thankful he's the one with the demands and not me, considering I'm totally agreeing with him. "But *you* can't tell anyone else, either. Got it?"

"Not a problem." He looks away, staring out the windshield. "But if you tell any of your bitchy friends what I said, I'll let everyone know you met me at Sweet Offerings and made a sweet offering of your own," he says, his voice deadly serious.

"Like what?" I frown.

"A hand job."

My mouth pops open. "Seriously?"

"Or I could say a blow job." His mouth kicks up on one side. "Your choice."

"Are you for real right now?" I ask incredulously. "Or are you seriously trying to blackmail me?"

He starts to laugh and shake his head. "I'm totally messing with you."

I raise a brow. "Really?"

"Really." His expression is solemn as he says, "Let's just… promise not to tell anyone about this conversation. Cool?"

Okay, he'd better not be playing me. "All right," I say with a nod.

"Good." He takes a long drink from his coffee and sets it in the center console, moving so slowly, so freaking deliberately, I know he's just messing with me now. If he starts eating his muffin, I might launch mine at his head. "I think Courtney might be involved with Gretchen's murder."

"Too obvious." The words pop out of my mouth before I can stop them.

"I'm being serious, Pen. They *hated* each other." No one calls me Pen. But he just dropped that one so casually, I didn't even think to correct him. "Courtney threatened Gretchen more than once."

"Courtney has threatened all of us, at one point or another. You do realize you just threatened me, too," I point out. "Even if it was, as you claimed, a joke." I mean, he said it was a joke, but what if he really does spread some vicious, nasty rumor about me if I tell someone what we talked about?

Guess I'm keeping my lips shut. That's a chance I just can't take.

He ignores me. "Did you see her at the vigil last week? She said the worst things."

"Court always says the worst things, especially about

Gretchen. She was just saying what everyone feels."

Cass turns so he's looking right at me. "Did *you* really feel that way about Gretchen?"

I sigh and drop my head, staring at the muffin. I don't even know this guy. Why should I trust him? "I really shouldn't be talking to you right now."

"Why not?"

"I don't know you." I look at him to find he's already watching me. "At all. We've never really spoken until now, and it's kind of weird."

"What's weird?"

"That we're talking, but only because Gretchen is dead."

Cass remains quiet for a moment, sipping from his coffee. Taking a bite of his muffin. I drink my coffee, too, but my appetite has fled. This entire situation is making me uneasy. "You don't have to tell me anything, but I need to say this: I think Courtney might've done something to Gretchen. And I want to try and prove it."

"So what? You want to do a little investigating and try to pin this on Court? That's crazy."

"The entire situation is crazy," he mutters, staring off into the distance.

My mind starts to go into overdrive with all the what-if questions. "Did you see her with Gretchen that night? Up at the church?" Our Lady of Mount Carmel isn't too far from where Cass lives with his grandma. Could he have seen the two of them in the parking lot, right before—oh my God—Courtney might've killed Gretchen?

No. Impossible.

When he says nothing, I push a little harder. "Well? Did you? I know you live pretty close to the church. Maybe you saw something that night?"

He turns to look out the passenger-side window. "I saw

nothing. I wasn't even at home when it happened."

"Where were you?"

Cass ignores my question yet again. "Do you know how Gretchen was murdered?"

I slowly shake my head, startled by his change of topic. I let my earlier question go. "No."

"Her throat was slit. From here to here." He gestures on his own throat, starting at one ear and slicing his finger across his neck to the other ear. "A clean cut. She bled out fast."

My heart is pounding. The way he just described it, his voice so flat, his emotionless expression...

"How do you know that?"

He shrugs. "My grandma read it in the paper."

No one reads the newspaper, not even my parents. So maybe he's telling the truth. Or maybe he's...

Not.

"That's awful," I murmur.

"I know."

"Was she..." *Raped?* I can hardly make myself say the word. "Sexually assaulted?"

"No." He shakes his head slowly. "I don't think she was. Actually, I'm not sure."

I swallow hard. As usual, I don't know what to say. The image flashing in my mind is horrific. Gretchen sprawled in the parking lot, her head bent back, her throat open and exposed, glistening with blood.

A shiver moves through me.

"I think Courtney might've done it," he whispers.

"Why?" I shove the muffin back into the bag. My appetite is gone, gone, gone.

"Because." His dark gaze meets mine. "They were fighting over me."

CHAPTER TWELVE

"So tell me." It's Monday afternoon after school, and we're at cheer practice. I'm next to Court and we're all sitting on the field sidelines, our legs stretched out in front of us, upper bodies bent forward and arms reaching. Our coach is screaming at us to *stretch those bodies!* and *work those muscles!* while the football team is running through drills in the center of the field. I can even hear the band practicing on the lower field and I know the varsity volleyball team has finally resumed practice in the gym. It's a busy Monday afternoon and everything feels so normal, so mundane.

Yet it's not. There's this underlying vibe I can't quite describe, but I can feel it. Lurking in the shadows, lingering in the cooling air. So many unanswered questions, a lot of fear, and plenty of paranoia will do that to people. And right now, Cape Bonita Prep is dealing with all of that and more. We're just trying to push forward and pretend everything is okay.

"Tell you what?" Courtney asks as she bends forward,

her face practically between her knees. The girl is freaking limber, but she's also our best tumbler, so no surprise.

"I'm just curious." I hesitate, then decide to go for it. "Who exactly are you hooking up with?"

She sits up straight, glaring at me. "What the hell are you talking about? I'm hooking up with no one."

I try my best to read her face, searching for a sign that she's lying. Is she? I don't know. Her face is like a smooth, beautiful Courtney mask. Not even a flicker of emotion in her eyes. I can't tell if she's happy, sad, or mad right now, and I've known Courtney for years.

Once Cass dropped that particular bomb, about Gretchen and Courtney fighting over him, I immediately started asking questions. One after the other, all of them starting with the word *why*.

Why do you say that?

Why would they fight over you?

Why are you involved?

Why?

Why?

Why?

But he clammed up, grabbed the muffins, and fled from my car before offering a solid answer. Good-bye and good riddance, I told him mentally. Who the hell did he think he was, anyway? Asking me to meet him with the cryptic anonymous texts, spinning all sorts of elaborate tales, and then refusing to answer me? Whatever. I think he's full of crap.

But I pondered over what he said for the rest of the weekend, unable to wrap my head around any of it. Would Gretchen and Courtney seriously fight over *him*? And is that enough motive for Courtney to want to *murder* Gretchen? What exactly did the three of them do anyway?

Ugh. I couldn't even bring myself to think about the many possibilities.

"Who was the guy Gretchen supposedly stole from you?" I ask her.

The irritation on Court's face is clear. At least I'm seeing some sort of emotion. "There are too many of them to mention." She looks away from me and heaves a big sigh.

"Who was the last one, then? The one that sent you over the edge?" When she turns to glare at me, I explain further. "The one who made you act crazy at the candlelight vigil."

"I acted *crazy* at the candlelight vigil because I was *upset* over Gretchen's *murder*." Her eyes are blazing with anger. "Everyone deals with grief differently, Penelope. We all can't be cold and unfeeling like you."

Ouch. I rear back. "Is that what you really think about me? That I'm cold and unfeeling?"

"You're the one calling me crazy. How do you think that feels?" Courtney leaps to her feet, resting her hands on her slender hips as she stares down at me where I still sit on the grass. "What's up with you, huh? Why are you questioning me about stuff that's really none of your business? I don't ask you who you're hooking up with."

That's because I'm not hooking up with anyone. And I've always been an open book with my friends when it comes to my love life. I have nothing to hide. I'm not sneaking around with guys. I never really have.

But I say none of that. There's no point. I need to keep this casual. I don't want to raise her suspicions.

"I was just curious." I stand as well, brushing bits of grass off my legs. "You seemed so...mad at Gretchen, even after she died. You said some really mean things when we found out, and at the vigil. I was worried about you. We all were. Once I started thinking about it, I wondered who she supposedly stole from you, and why you were so upset."

"He's no one. Just…a guy. A stupid guy." She says it so dismissively. I know she wants to quit talking about it, about him. "A guy who's not even in my life anymore, okay? So let's just drop it."

"Okay. Fine. We'll drop it."

She glances around, her gaze lingering on the football players. They're all yelling and grunting like a bunch of cavemen as their coach shouts orders at them. I remember last year, when I was with Robby and I used to watch like some breathless groupie as they practiced. Robby would always puff up his chest and strut around on the field like he was the king of the team. Which he sort of was. His ego was massive—sometimes it felt like I was more of a prize for him to show off versus a girl he was truly interested in.

"I've moved on and found someone else, anyway," Courtney says offhandedly.

"Really? Who?" It's only October. How many guys is Court trying to go through by the time we graduate?

"I can't tell you." Her gaze meets mine once more. "If you knew, you'd run off and tell someone else."

"What? How old do you think I am? I don't run off and tell anyone anything." I'm slightly offended she'd even say it.

"You'd tell your best friend," she says pointedly.

Oh. Well, crap. That means Courtney is hooking up with…

"Are you messing around with *Brogan*?" My voice squeaks. We all know how Dani feels about him. She's been panting after Brogan since we were sophomores. He teases her, acts like he's interested, and then completely shuts her out. He runs so hot and cold, and I swear that's half of the allure for Dani. He makes her crazy, and she freaking loves it.

"Ssshh! Be quiet!" Courtney steps closer to me, her voice

low. "He's been texting me for the past week. Well. More like sexting me."

According to Dani—and Lex—and me—Courtney sexts everyone. Including Cass. "Who started it?"

Courtney looks offended. She even rests a hand on her chest like some scandalized grandma. "He did."

"He did what? And who are we talking about?" Lex magically appears, a smirk on her face, and I wonder how much of our conversation she overheard.

"Nothing and no one." Courtney flashes her beauty queen smile and dashes off to go stretch with…

Dani.

Ugh. Now that's messed up.

"She's been weird lately," Lex observes.

"I think we've all been sort of weird lately," I tell her, plopping onto the grass once again. I need to stretch. My entire body is tight, especially after that tense conversation with Courtney.

Lex joins me, spreading her long legs into a wide *V*. "You're right. Murder has a way of making people behave strangely."

I send her a look. "You watch too many episodes of *CSI*."

She shrugs. "What? I'm just stating a fact. Everyone's been jumpy lately. It's freaky, thinking there might be a murderer in our midst."

It's always strange to me when Lex and I get along so easily. Like right now. Makes me wonder if she's up to something. But what?

"Do you think it was someone who goes here? A student? Oh God, maybe even a teacher?" I ask incredulously. The police are implying it's a stranger, and I like to think it was, too. It's easier that way. You don't want to believe someone you know could've done this.

"I don't know. I have no clue. The police are certainly keeping quiet. They're releasing no details, and that either means they have a suspect or they don't know shit." Lex looks over at me. "Did they ever call you back in for questioning?"

I slowly shake my head.

"Me neither. Everyone's saying it was an outsider. Some freak transient stranger who somehow came across Gretchen at the church and killed her. A murder of opportunity."

We're quiet for a moment and I wonder if I should tell her my theories. The things that keep me up at night, racing through my head so I can't fall asleep. Lex is smart. Even though she drives me crazy most of the time, I know she probably has some interesting theories, too.

I decide to go for it.

"It makes no sense, though," I point out. "First, Gretchen's not even Catholic, so why would she be at that particular church? Second, supposedly she got a text saying there was an emergency Larks meeting and that's where she was going."

Lex's eyes go wide as she sits up straight. "What are you talking about? I've never heard about an emergency Larks meeting."

Oh. Crap. Maybe I wasn't supposed to say that. "The detectives told me when I talked to them," I admit.

Her eyes are wide as she stares at me. "Do they think you're the one who texted her?"

"I didn't! It wasn't me! I never called an emergency meeting that day."

Lex rolls her eyes. "Calm down. I know you didn't do it. But I asked if the cops *thought* you were the one who sent that text," she repeats. "Have they looked over Gretchen's phone records?"

"I don't know. I haven't talked to them since the day we

found out Gretchen died." I hate how defensive I feel when we talk about this stuff. "When I talked to them, they asked me if I did, and of course, I said no."

"Right. And since you haven't talked to them about it again, I'm guessing they figured out you were telling the truth." Lex tilts her head, the sun glinting off her long dark hair, making it shine. "So you think Gretchen was lured out to the church by some random stranger? Because that sounds pretty bogus to me."

"I know. But there's no other reason for Gretchen to be there."

"Unless she was meeting someone she knew?"

"The detectives told me her mom received a text saying she was going to the emergency Larks meeting and she'd be home later," I say.

"She could've lied. She always lied to her mom."

"That's what I told the cops."

Lex stares off into the distance, her eyes squinting against the waning sun. "I wouldn't put it past her. Her mom is totally overbearing and a complete control freak. Always wanting to know what Gretchen was doing and who she's doing it with." Lex smirks. "If she only knew."

"If she only knew what?"

"What Gretchen really did—her and Courtney both, really. Gretch was a hot mess, Penny, and we know Court is one, too." Ugh, she called me Penny on purpose. "Messing around with the wrong people. Maybe Gretchen finally did something totally awful to someone and they decided to get their revenge by killing her."

"That's ridiculous," I protest weakly.

Lex just watches me and I can't help but think who she's referring to.

Courtney.

CHAPTER THIRTEEN

W ell, I really knocked their socks off by killing the pretty girl, didn't I? Not that they care that the bitch totally deserved it. Because she so did.

Trust me. I know.

They are all talking. They are all speculating. It's all anyone in this stupid town can discuss. The rumors are flying around school. They're even flying around the town. The residents are interrogating the cops, demanding answers to questions the police department isn't ready to answer. What are they going to do? How are they going to stop this? There is a murderer in their ritzy, special little town and they don't like it.

They want answers. Now.

They want the killer stopped before he strikes again.

Well, good fucking luck with that, peeps.

It's dark and I'm still at school. It's like I never leave this place, though no one seems to notice me here. Everyone is long gone, even the creepy janitor, Brick.

Yes, his name is really Brick and he's about as dumb as

one, too. And he's also a leering pervert who likes to spy on the girls by lurking behind dark corners and listening in on their conversations when they don't know he's around. But you see, they *do* know he's around most of the time, and they actually make up conversations about blow jobs and messy sex in the backseat of their boyfriends' cars and weekend slumber parties where the girls wear tiny T-shirts with no bras and skimpy panties and have pillow fights.

They make up all these crazy, over-the-top stories and he eats them up. He walks around campus all day long whistling and smiling, probably trying to hide his boner as he relives those glorious bogus stories of pretty teen girls and the dirty, secret things they do when they think no one else is paying attention.

But he's not our murderer, so let's not get distracted by Brick and his twisted story.

Let's focus on me.

I'm out at the football field, sitting in the stands. There is one single light on, across the field in the visitor stands, but it's just enough to illuminate the area. Plus, the moon is full, wispy white clouds passing over it every few minutes. The breeze coming off the ocean smells of salt and brine, and I hear the low murmur of the lighthouse foghorn in the far distance. It's a perfect Cape Bonita night, and I'm taking advantage of it.

The metal bench I'm sitting on is so cold my ass is going numb, yet still I wait. I fidget and check my phone again. She's almost fifteen minutes late, but she'll show up.

They always show up.

When I finally see her in the distance, headed straight toward the bleachers, straight toward me, I sit up straight and shove my hands into the front pockets of my thick jacket. I curl my fingers tight around the knife handle, the smooth wood fitting perfectly in my palm.

It is my lifeline. My security blanket. I don't want to use it tonight, but I can already sense she's not going to give me much choice.

They're stubborn and dumb. They seem perfect and beautiful and driven and smart, but they all end up disappointing you in the end. Trust me.

"Oh. It's you." She sounds disappointed and I stare at her face, taking in her sharp features. She is not classically beautiful like Courtney is, not vibrant and bright like Gretchen was.

No, this girl is the complete opposite of Gretchen, with her long dark hair pulled into a tight, high ponytail and her wide-set, dark eyes, her perfect slashing eyebrows, and those high cheekbones that look like they could cut glass. She's tall and slender and she carries herself like a dancer, with perfect posture and those long legs, always walking on her toes like she's about to go *en pointe* and pirouette away at any given moment.

"Were you expecting someone else?" I ask her calmly. She hates when people are calm. She always wants to be the calm one so she can do and say something just to rattle the shit out of you.

"Honestly? Yeah. I was hoping." She shrugs and slips her hands into her pockets, chomping loudly on her gum. So freaking rude. These girls are supposedly perfect, but all of them are rude bitches. Every single one of them.

And this one is no different, despite how beautifully she's put together. She's wearing a fitted black leather jacket and a pair of black leggings that make her legs look like matchsticks. She doesn't have much meat on her bones.

"Want to go grab some dinner together?" I ask, as a test. For once, I'd like to rattle her.

"Now?" she asks incredulously. Like I just asked her to go rob a bank.

"Yeah, now."

She wrinkles her nose. "I don't eat dinner. You know this."

Right. That's because she has an eating disorder. She believes no one else notices. That we all think she's just naturally skinny. But that's a crock of shit. She's delusional.

"Why'd you ask me to meet you out here so late anyway? What do you want?" Her tone is snotty. She sounds completely put out. "It's fucking freezing," she mutters under her breath, a little shiver moving through her.

"I thought we could talk. I've missed you." Truth, though I hate to admit it. It's like I ask for their abuse whenever I encounter one of them.

She squirms, clearly uncomfortable. "We were friends for like two seconds over the summer and you act like we spent every waking moment together."

"I can't help it. I thought we were friends, and when we're at school, you totally ignore me." It's true. She walks right by me in the halls with a blank expression, like she's not even aware of me.

But I'm always aware of her.

"Please. We are definitely not friends," she practically spits out.

"That's all I wanted. Why is that always too much to ask for?" I rise to my feet and take a step toward her. She's standing on the aisle steps, her hands still in her pockets. It would be so easy to push her over. She's completely defenseless like that. I'd give her a shove and she'd tumble to the bottom of the steps. Maybe she'd hit her head on the sharp corner of a bleacher, cut herself wide open. All the dirty work would be done for me, just like that.

Ha. I couldn't get so lucky.

"Well, I don't want to be *your* friend. I don't know how many times I have to tell you that. I wish you'd just let it go. Yeah, I was nice to you when we were younger, before you got all messed up. And yeah, we tried to be friends again last summer, but that didn't work out, either. You're too weird, not to mention pathetic." With that pleasant last statement, she turns to leave, her hands still in her pockets, her shoulders perfectly straight.

I hate her. I hate her so much. Yet I still crave the friendship. The approval. And that makes me hate myself even more.

Without a word, I rush toward her, throw my hands out. They make contact with her sharp shoulder blades and I don't even hesitate.

I shove her as hard as I can.

She screams, tumbling down the steps, head over feet, just like you see on TV or in the movies. I stay still and watch, holding my breath as she keeps rolling, until finally she lands on the concrete walkway at the very bottom of the steps. Her hands are still in her stupid pockets, like she didn't even bother to try and break her fall, and her right leg is bent at an unnatural angle. My gaze goes to her face and I see the giant gash on her forehead. Her eyes are full of fear and pain and rage. All directed at me.

"What did you do, you fucking asshole!" She sounds like she's in shock. I bet I did surprise her, and nothing much gets past this girl. "You *pushed* me!"

"I did not," I call from where I'm standing. I sound so calm I impress myself. "You tripped and fell."

She tries to move her leg and winces in agony, a low moan escaping her. I bet she broke her leg. Maybe even her hip. I'd bet big money her bones are extra brittle, too.

They probably snapped, just like that. "I felt your hands on my back, you fucking liar! You did this on purpose!"

I just smile. What can I say? She won't listen to me. She's already made up her mind.

She fumbles for something in her pocket, grasping and tugging and becoming out of breath the more she struggles, before she finally pulls out her phone. She sucks in a deep, sharp breath. "I'm calling the cops, you psychopath! You're going down for this. You're going down!"

Oh hell no, I'm not.

I run down the steps, the metal clanging loudly from my pounding feet as I whip the knife out of my right pocket. It gleams in the darkness, the moon shining on the silver blade, and her eyes go wide just before I reach her. I grab her by the front of the jacket, thrust my face in hers, and smile, then bring the knife so the point is nudging her just beneath her chin.

"Don't," she whispers, her eyes filling with tears, her lips trembling. "Don't, don't, don't. Please don't do this."

I say nothing. There's nothing left to say. She can see it in my eyes, just like I can see it in hers.

She knows it's done.

She knows *she's* done.

I'm so tired of being pushed aside. I'm over it.

Over.

It.

CHAPTER FOURTEEN

I'm getting ready for school when there's a frantic knock on my bedroom door, just before my mother bursts inside, her face flushed and her eyes wide. She's still in her robe and her dark blond hair is a wild tangle about her head.

"I'm almost ready, okay? I'm not going to be late to school, so stop freaking out," I tell her before resuming my morning makeup ritual in front of the lighted mirror that sits on my vanity. We battle at least three mornings a week, Mom riding my ass, nagging at me that I'm going to miss the first bell, until I finally leave. It's like she enjoys getting all stressed out.

Mom and Dad both wanted all three of us to be perfect, Mom especially. Her demands can be exhausting. Sometimes I want to chill, you know? What's wrong with being late to first period? Not that I've ever skipped a class or been late, ever. Mom would lose her mind. So would Dad.

"Those detectives are here," she says, sounding breathless. "Spalding and Hughes, the ones who interviewed you right after Gretchen died. They want to talk to you again. Right now. Supposedly another dead body has been found this morning—at the *school*."

I drop my eyeliner on the table and swivel around to stare at her. "What did you just say?"

Mom nods, tucking a strand of hair behind her ear. "Someone else has been murdered. Another student, I think. I saw it on the news. On the ticker tape thing they run on the bottom of the screen? 'Dead body found in the football stands at Cape Bonita Prep,' it said."

Rising to my feet, I go to her on shaky legs. "Who was it? Did they say?"

"I don't know." She shakes her head and then reaches for me, drawing me into her arms. I cling to her, my face pressed against her shoulder, breathing in her familiar smell. A hug from Mom always comforts me, but not now.

Instead my mind races, and I can't seem to catch my breath. It happened again? Someone else is dead? "But why are the cops here for me? What do I have to do with this?"

"I don't know," she repeats, grabbing hold of my shoulders and pulling away from me so she can stare into my eyes. "Let's go talk to them."

When we enter the living room, Spalding and Hughes are waiting for me, pacing in front of the giant window that faces the street, both of them clearly agitated. Their suits are even more rumpled than the last time I saw them, and the exhaustion is plain on their wan faces.

"Miss Malone," Detective Spalding says, keeping up the polite facade. "I hope you don't mind if we talk to you for a few minutes."

"What's going on?" My voice is shaky and I settle heavily into the overstuffed chair Mom directed me to.

"Another body was found. This time at the high school," Hughes says gruffly. His body practically vibrates with frustration. "Early this morning, by a jogger who likes to run the track."

My mouth drops open. Even though Mom already told me, I still can't believe it. My entire body is numb and I feel like my heart is beating so hard it's going to burst out of my chest.

"Is it someone from school?" Mom asks.

Spalding nods, his expression grim. "Someone your daughter knows," he tells my mother, though his gaze is locked on me.

"Who is it? Who? Who?" I sound like a stupid owl, but I can't help myself.

He hesitates for a moment before he finally admits, "Alexis Nguyen."

I slump against the chair, my head spinning. "I was just with her yesterday," I tell them. "She can't be dead."

"She is." Spalding sits on the couch across from my chair and leans forward, his expression earnest. Probing. "Tell us exactly when you saw her yesterday and what you two talked about."

I recap everything. Cheer practice. How Lex and I talked about the murder and how it's set everyone on edge. Though I don't mention Lex's suspicions about Courtney. That was pure speculation. "She seemed fine. Like her usual Lex self."

"What time was practice over?"

"Four thirty."

"And you didn't have a Larks meeting afterward?"

I shake my head. "No."

"You didn't leave with her? See her leave with someone else?"

"No. I saw her get into her car alone."

Spalding scratches something down on his notepad. "You two were close?"

"Not particularly," I admit.

Hughes seems to jump on this statement. "Why not? You didn't like her? She didn't like you? You two were sharing the same boyfriend or something ridiculous like that?"

"Hey," Spalding chastises, sending Hughes a stern look.

I pause, wondering how I should approach this or how much I should reveal. No way can I bring up that Lex is— *was* my enemy. My nemesis. That sounds crazy. That makes me sound...

Guilty.

"We were...friends, but we weren't as close as I am with Courtney and Danielle," I tell them.

Hughes says, "Alexis Nguyen was a Lark."

I nod.

"So was Gretchen."

"Yes, she was. They both were," I whisper. "So?"

"You do understand that you're connected to both of these deaths." Hughes sends me a pointed look.

"I'm not the only one," I point out.

"But it sounds like you disliked both Gretchen and Alexis." Hughes hesitates, his gaze sharp as he glares at me. "A lot."

I open my mouth to protest, but Mom barrels in front of me, blocking my view. "That'll be enough, gentlemen. If you have any more questions for my daughter, you'll need to do so through our attorney. Now I'd like to ask you to please leave my house."

Reluctantly, and with some grumbling, the two men finally stand up to leave, Hughes calling out, "We'll be in touch, Penelope!" but Mom closes the door before he can say anything else to intimidate me. She turns the lock with a firm *click* and returns to the living room, rushing to the overstuffed chair where I'm sitting so we can be together, wrapping her arms around me.

The second she hugs me, I can't stop the tears from falling. I cried a little bit over Gretchen's death, but now that Lex is gone, too? Two girls who are very close to me, who were Larks, who I've known forever…I can't believe this is happening. This doesn't feel random.

Their deaths feel planned. Almost like these girls were targeted.

Oh God.

What if I'm next?

"I'm so sorry, darling. I can't believe it. First Gretchen, now Alexis is gone," Mom murmurs against my hair, stroking my back. "This is all so terrifying. I don't know what to say."

I sniff against her robe. "Are you really going to call your lawyer and have him represent me? Or will Daddy be my lawyer?"

"Your father isn't in criminal law, but he knows plenty of qualified attorneys who can help us. Don't worry about it. They'll know exactly what to do and what to say. You're still a minor, even though they'll try to tell us you're close enough to being an adult, since you're seventeen, so they'll try to talk to you alone. And we can't allow those detectives to question you by yourself. They'll badger you for hours, breaking you down until you finally confess that you did it," Mom explains.

I lift away from her, my entire body shaking. "I would never do that. Because I didn't do it!"

"I'm not saying you would, darling." She pats my back. "But there are too many documented cases out there of innocent teenagers confessing to something they didn't do because of stubborn detectives who interrogated them for hours until they finally cracked."

God. How awful. I can't imagine what that would be

like. "I didn't kill Gretchen, Mom. I didn't kill Lex, either. I promise I didn't."

"I know you didn't. I never thought you did." She runs a hand over my hair, trying to smile. "But do you know anything, anything at all? Did you see something happen? Hear rumors at school or from your friends? Is there something you're not telling me?"

I think of Cass Vincenti and what he told me. I haven't talked to him since we met Saturday morning. He hasn't texted me, either. We pass each other in the halls at school but don't make eye contact. And he ignores me in physics while I do the same to him. It's best we leave this alone—or so I thought until Lex.

But maybe I should go find him. Get his opinion on all of this.

"Penelope? Talk to me," Mom says, interrupting my thoughts. "Your father and I are worried. And now with another one of your friends murdered..." Her voice drifts and a visible shiver moves through her. "It's not safe at school. It can't be."

"You can't keep me from going to school—" I start but she cuts me off with a look.

"We can do whatever we want if it keeps you safe," Mom says firmly. "What exactly is the school doing in order to ensure the students' safety, hmm? Because so far, they're doing a terrible job."

"Gretchen wasn't killed at school, and it looks like Lex w-was k-killed last n-night." I'm stumbling over my words because the tears are coming now. I collapse against my mother, burying my face against her shoulder as I cry in earnest.

She offers me comfort, running her hand up and down my back, whispering into my hair, asking yet again if I remember anything. If I saw anything. My mind drifts, and I remember what Lex said to me just yesterday and how she suspected Court. But who wouldn't, with her irrational behavior?

I lift away from Mom's shoulder and meet her concerned gaze. She wipes the tears away from my face with her fingers, a gentle smile curving her lips. "Were you going to say something?" she asks.

"Um, well. People are saying things about—" I falter, trying to contain the sob that wants to leave me. "About Courtney."

Shock washes over Mom's face, but then she blinks and it's gone. "Courtney? *Really?* Don't tell me you think she's involved."

"I don't know. I doubt it. There are always arguments between us, but would Courtney go so far as to try to kill someone?" No freaking way. It seems impossible. "She was mad at both Gretchen and Lex, though. Well, everyone's always irritated with Lex." And Gretchen, if I'm being truthful.

"You should tell the police that," Mom says softly.

"I don't want to be the one who gets Courtney in trouble," I whisper.

"Darling, if she's involved, she's already gotten herself in trouble, right?" Mom tries to smile but it looks more like a grimace.

I nod and duck my head, diving back into her embrace. I can't take this. Two girls dead. Two Larks. There is no coincidence here. I think the cops realize it, too.

I just hope they figure out who the killer is before another girl—another Lark—is murdered.

CHAPTER FIFTEEN

Soon after the detectives left my house, a mass text was sent out from the school, saying classes were canceled. The entire campus is being treated as a crime scene, and both the local police and outside investigators—that's how they were described in the text—were there.

Within minutes of the notice going out, I started getting texts, pretty much from every Lark member. I asked my mom and then invited them all over, figuring we were better together as a hive mind than stuck at our homes and freaked out all by ourselves.

This is how, by eleven on a Tuesday morning, the Larks are in my bedroom. Dani and Courtney sit on my bed with me. The juniors are sprawled across my floor, and every single one of them looks scared out of their mind.

"Do you think we're being targeted?" asks Grace, the quietest Lark of the bunch. She gives off a shy boho vibe during the weekend when she doesn't have to wear the school uniform, with her flowing sweaters and flower headbands, and how she always smells like incense. Her parents run a gift shop called Spellbound, and it's full of candles, handmade potpourri, crystals, and—you guessed it—incense. "The Larks?"

I say "no" at the same time Courtney says "yes" and I shoot her a warning look before I address the younger girls. There's no need to get everyone riled up. We're already on edge, not that Courtney cares.

"I don't want to set you all off in a panic. As of this time, I don't think our group is being specifically targeted, and the police don't think so, either." I have no idea if that's true. "I will say, though, that it's strange, how Gretchen and Alexis have been…murdered. And they're both Larks. It doesn't *feel* like a coincidence, but I don't know…"

Kayla is Grace's best friend, the straight arrow to Grace's peace and love vibe. She's sitting up so straight it looks painful, and she's the only one out of all of us who is wearing her school uniform. Plus, she's an organizational freak. She puts me to absolute shame, which makes me think she might be a good presidential candidate for the Larks, too. "If there's a pattern, then I think the killer is going after the seniors first."

"Way to reassure us, K," Courtney says with a laugh.

Dani is openly crying, the poor thing. I want to hug her, but I need to keep it together. Be the example everyone else needs right now. "Why would you say something like that, Kayla?" she asks, her voice shaky. "I would never say that to you. Now you make me feel like I'm going to be next! Or maybe Courtney will be. Or Penelope! And we can't lose Penelope!" Danielle sounds like she's borderline hysterical.

"You're not next," I reassure her with a gentle arm rub. I send a subtle glare in Kayla's direction but she just blinks at me in return, then flips her long, thick black hair over her shoulder with a loud sigh. "None of us are *next*. Not if we stick with one another and stay safe," I tell them all.

"And how do you propose we do that?" asks Maggie, throwing her hands up in the air. "Stay safe? We can't be together twenty-four-seven, so what do we do when we go home? Or participate in extracurricular activities and have to stay late after school?"

All the juniors nod and murmur among themselves, sending me the occasional furtive glance before they hurriedly look away. There's a divide happening. The juniors against the seniors, and I know what they're thinking.

At least all the juniors are still alive. They're not the initial target.

Us seniors are.

I withhold the sigh that wants to escape. Maybe it wasn't such a good idea to have them over. I thought I could act like some sort of den mother and reassure them all that we were safe. That I would take care of my Lark babies still left in the nest. Yes, we've lost two, and we shall mourn them properly, but I was going to vow we weren't losing any more, no matter what.

But that's a promise I can't keep. I didn't count on seven anxious, paranoid girls looking at me like I need to solve their problems with a snap of my fingers, girls who can't be consoled. And that's what I've got, all of them sitting in my room and staring at me like I have life's answers.

Wish Mom would hurry up and finish making those brownies. Chocolate cures all ailments, and these girls need as much chocolate as they can get. So do I, really.

"Maybe..." Alyssa's voice sounds clear and strong, and the other girls shut up when she starts speaking. "Maybe we should temporarily disband. We're paranoid and scared, and what if this killer really is targeting the Larks? If we break apart, we could become less of a target."

She sounds like such a leader, even when she has to deliver bad news.

"But if we break apart, even temporarily, then we're doing exactly what they want us to," Maggie cries. "They want to split us apart, so why should we give them that satisfaction? It makes no sense. Now is the time for us to stay strong and stay together."

"We're stronger together than we are apart," Dani agrees with a little hiccup, just before she grabs a Kleenex and blows her nose.

"According to who?" Courtney asks, her voice tinged with amusement. She even has a smile on her face, like this entire situation is one big joke. "Seriously, there is no way *all* the Larks are being targeted. Who gives a shit about you girls anyway?" She waves her hand at the junior Larks on the floor, causing all of them to gasp indignantly. "No offense, but you guys are nothing with us here blocking your path. For all we know, it's one of *you* trying to off us so you can take charge. Like you, little Miss Type A with the stick up your ass." She's pointing at Kayla, whose mouth is hanging wide open. "You're just dying to take over Penelope's spot, aren't you?"

It's difficult enough to become a member of the Larks, since only a chosen few are selected. The organization has been a part of Cape Bonita Prep for years, and many of the girls who are former Larks members have gone on to some of the top colleges in the country, including my sister Peyton, who's at Stanford. I've heard stories about the juniors practically destroying each other with vicious rumors just to become president.

Me? Considering my older sister was president her senior year, it was practically a given that I would be, too. Not that Courtney, Gretchen, and Lex didn't all fight hard for the position. The only one who didn't try for it was Dani. And I think that's because she was too afraid of the rest of us to make an attempt.

We're a fairly intimidating bunch, if you haven't already figured that out. Not that I like to group myself with the mean girls. This last year I've tried to distance myself, only because I was tired of their attitudes. Time to grow up and move on, you know?

"She's probably the only one capable of the position next year," Grace says, earning dirty looks from the rest of the juniors—except Kayla. "She's the perfect one to step into Penelope's shoes."

"Hey, let me get through my year first," I joke, though my voice is a little shaky. "We still have a long way to go."

"See? She's dying to replace you, Penny. I knew it." Courtney scowls at Kayla, who scowls right back.

"Oh my God, *stop,* Court. You're not making any of this better." I reach over to grab her arm, but she jerks out of my hold.

"Neither are you, letting them cry and sob and act like the world is coming to an end. What sort of leader are you?" Court glares at me, then casts her smile at everyone else like she's the queen and we're her servants. They all just glare at her in return. "I know exactly what we need."

"Oh, please, Court. Tell us," I say, my voice dripping with sarcasm.

"A party!" Courtney claps her hands and bounces on the edge of my bed. "I'm serious! We need a party to lighten the mood. Maybe we could have the party tonight. What do you think? All of this down-and-out, we're-all-gonna-die talk—it's getting old. I'm over it."

"We can't have a party," I whisper. "Lex just *died.*" I think of her family. I think of the detectives, the school, Mr. Rose and Mrs. Adney. Our families. What would they think if we had a party in celebration of Lex's death?

Oh hey, I know. They'd think we've lost our minds.

"I know she just died. Do you really think Lex would want us moping around, crying over her? Hell no! So we'll have a party this weekend. It'll be a celebration of her life. And a celebration of Gretchen's life, too! A big bash will be the perfect kickoff into the afterlife they'd want," Court says with a shout and a fist pump.

No joke.

Like, she's serious right now. I can barely wrap my head around her behavior. Fist pumps and parties and life celebrations? Court has clearly lost her mind.

"I really don't think it's a good idea—" Dani starts, her voice hesitant, but Courtney interrupts her.

"You never think *anything* is a good idea. What's wrong with having a party and cutting loose? We've been so tense these last few days. You need to relax. Plus, I'll invite all the boys, including *Brogan,* Dani." Courtney offers up Brogan like he's a rich, decadent dessert and Dani's on a strict no-sugar diet.

Dani's eyes light up and I know she can't help herself. She can't resist Brogan. It's almost pitiful, especially when I know Courtney is secretly sexting and most likely hooking up with Brogan on the side.

I should warn Dani before she really makes a fool of herself over this boy. But how do I break it to her? She's crushed on Brogan for years. We've told her time and again he's not that interested in her and she still pursues him. I don't know if I want to be the one who tells her that Brogan is sexting one of her closest friends.

But who else will watch out for her?

Ugh.

"You want us to have a *party*? A blow-out bash in celebration of Gretchen and Lex? Really? Are you guys for real?" Alyssa asks incredulously. Her protest surprises me. She's the one who tends to go along with everything we suggest, and she rarely—if ever—argues. But this is good. She's showing us she has a backbone. "If we have a party, don't you think people will think the Larks are...tacky, especially if we have one so close to Lex's...*murder*? It's totally disrespectful."

"They'll think we're awesome because they need the escape," Courtney points out, as if she's ever so logical.

Please.

"Before we commit to throwing a party, we really need to think it through," Alyssa continues, Grace and Kayla nodding in agreement.

"Personally, I think it's a great idea!" Maggie leaps to her feet, a big smile on her freckled face. With her hair in two French braids and wearing a pair of black leggings and a PINK sweatshirt, she actually looks pretty cute today. "We can charge to enter and call it a fund-raiser. That way we raise money and can donate to a charity that was near and dear to Lex's heart—and Gretchen's, too. What do you think?"

Okay, let's be real for a minute. It may be totally tacky and disrespectful to party it up so soon after both girls' deaths, but I do have to say Maggie's fund-raising suggestion is a good one. Meaning, it's the perfect thing to say to the school, because they're going to step in on this one considering we're a school club. And they'll probably tell us we shouldn't or flat-out can't do it.

"We can have the party at my house," Courtney says, a smug smile curling her lips. She's confident the party plan is going to happen, which is typical Court behavior. Once she gets an idea in her mind, nothing seems to stop her. "My parents are going out of town for a two-week European vacation and they leave this Thursday. They won't have a clue what's going on."

Courtney's house is huge, with twenty bathrooms, I swear. She also lives up on Hot Springs Road, in an ultra exclusive gated community where like, Oprah has a giant mansion. Everyone will want to come to Court's party. I don't think even a couple of murders will stop them.

"How much should we charge to get in?" Dani asks.

I shoot her a look. Dani almost always takes my side. We used to joke that we shared a brain. I was the rational side and she was the silly side. Those are the roles we've always taken together, so I'm surprised she's going for this. We're a team. We always agree on stuff, especially when it comes to the Larks. "Do you really think this is a good idea?" I ask Dani, who's blinking at me like I've just surprised her with my question. "Having a big party this weekend like everything's normal? Lex *died* today."

"Actually, Lex died last night," Courtney points out.

Oh my *God.*

And how exactly does she know that?

Dani offers up a weak smile and shrugs. "Come on, Penelope. It might be fun, to relax and let loose. Don't you think?"

"No, I don't think," I bite out, wondering when I became the only rational one in this group. "It's an awful idea. What about their families? We're going to look heartless."

"No, we aren't," Court says. "We're going to look like we care, because we do. It's a terrible tragedy, what happened to our friends." No surprise, she actually stumbled over the word "friends." "What we're doing is for the good of the student body."

Please. Since when does Court care about the student body?

"Maybe we should vote on the party thing?" I ask, looking around the room, hoping to spot some support.

All I see are blank faces staring back at me.

"But this isn't an official Larks meeting," Dani says softly, wincing when our gazes meet. She has this pleading look on her face, one I usually cave to, but not this time. "Can't we just make this happen?"

"We should probably put it to vote," I say firmly, not giving in. I'm the president, for God's sake. What I say goes.

Right?

"Does it have to be an official, declared meeting in order for us to make a decision on the Larks' behalf, Penny?" Courtney asks, her tone snotty.

Trying my best to control my frustration, I turn to everyone and say, "All in favor of having a party in honor of Alexis Nguyen at Courtney's house this weekend, raise your hand."

Every single one of them looks at one another before they all raise their hands, except for Alyssa.

Oh. And me.

Crap. We are obviously outvoted.

"You're not for the party, Penny? How disappointing." Courtney makes a *tsk*ing noise.

I ignore her. "All not in favor, raise your hands."

They all drop while my and Alyssa's hands go up.

Courtney claps like she just won the grand prize. "This is great! What day should we have the party? Friday or Saturday?"

"Saturday. The boys have a game Friday night," Dani answers.

"It's a bye week," Grace practically whispers, tugging on the stretched-out sleeve of her sweater. She won't even look at anyone and I wonder how for this party she really is. Or if she's just going along with the majority because she thinks that's the right thing to do. "They aren't playing again until next week."

"Then let's do it Friday! The sooner the better," Courtney says, throwing her arms up in the air and wiggling around like she can barely contain her excitement. And that might be true. Court loves nothing more than getting her way. "They might have Lex's funeral on Saturday so Friday works out better anyway."

Right. Because it'll be so great when the majority of the school population goes to Lex's funeral hungover and strung out.

"We shouldn't do this," I murmur, though no one's listening to me. Though it has to be said. I can already feel the guilt washing over me. I don't want to have this party. It seems cold and callous and awful and…

Wrong.

"How much should we charge?" Dani asks again.

"Five dollars a head, and all proceeds will go to Lex's favorite cause," Courtney says and Maggie nods, like they're a pair or something.

"What was her favorite cause?" I ask them.

Courtney shrugs. "I don't know, but we'll figure it out! Won't we, Maggie?" Maggie is practically bouncing up and down like she's a puppy, and I scowl at her. Has she become Courtney's minion? It's like I'm slowly losing control over the group and Courtney's becoming the one they look up to.

"You guys, really—" I start to say but Courtney interrupts me.

"God, lighten up, Penelope!" The look on Court's face is pure disgust. "We have to do something to shake the blues. I can't stand how somber everyone is, how we're all scared to even talk to each other, or even look at each other. It's like we've all turned into a bunch of zombies, and I hate it! It was bad enough with one dead body, and now we have *two*. We have to party on and overcome this!"

I don't have the heart to tell her just how insensitive she's being right now. It's like she can't even see how crazy it is to have a party only a few days after someone's death—in honor of that someone's death. The entire situation has turned into some sort of a bizarre three-ring circus.

A knock sounds and then Mom pushes open the door, a tentative smile on her face as she scans the room. "Okay, ladies. Who's in the mood for warm brownies?"

Every girl leaps to her feet and files out of the room, following my mom to the kitchen. I climb off the bed along with Courtney and Dani, and Courtney chases after the girls, demanding that they make more plans.

Dani grabs hold of my arm and stops me, her gaze serious when it meets mine. "You really don't want to have this party, do you?"

"No. Of course I don't." I slowly shake my head, ignoring the disappointment on her face. I'm disappointed, too. She needs to know this. "It's not right, D. Two of our friends are *dead*. They were *murdered*. It looks really bad, to have a party with kegs and weed in supposed celebration of them. It's weird."

"I know." Dani sighs, her shoulders slumping. "But how can we stop her? Courtney is loving every minute of this."

"Anything to take the attention off the dead girls so everyone can focus on her," I say bitterly. "Can't you see it, Dani? Court wants all the attention, all the time. Who cares if her friends are dead? Let's party!" I raise my hands and wiggle my fingers, full on jazz hands with a fake smile on my face.

Dani shakes her head. "You're right. I totally get it. So let her be her own demise then, Penny."

"But don't you see? We'll *all* be dragged into it because this party is being held by the Larks. In everyone else's eyes, we're supporting it. And I'm the president. In the end, I'll look as bad as she does," I remind her.

"But I don't know how to get us out of it now," Dani says, her voice small.

Now it's my turn to sigh. "I don't either."

CHAPTER SIXTEEN

Funny, how my murderous rampage kept us off campus for two days. Most of my fellow students are thrilled—no school! They don't even think about what happened to make them cancel school. They don't focus on the gruesome aspects of our unexpected mini vacation in the middle of the week.

The cold, hard facts are that someone we all know is dead. Someone they supposedly love and miss. But Alexis Nguyen was a total bitch—worse than Gretchen, and that's saying a lot, because Gretchen sucked. The one positive thing about Lex is that you knew what you were dealing with. Yeah, she could be a bitch, but at least she owned it.

Gretchen would try to be nice every once in a while, like she had an attack of conscience or something. Maybe her parents or her shrink encouraged her to try and redeem herself. I have no idea. But the facade always wore down; she could never keep it going for too long. And her true colors would eventually shine.

The police swarmed the school these last two days,

searching through every classroom, the lockers, the gym, the faculty lounge, the administrative offices…everything. Cell phone records were subpoenaed. I heard they spied on everyone's social media, calling people in for questioning when they saw something suspect.

They even brought in FBI specialists to assist in the investigation, though they keep that info on the down low. They don't want to alarm the fine citizens of Cape Bonita that they might have a potential serial killer in their midst. That sort of rumor would make everyone lose their minds.

I'm sorry, but I know that killing two girls does not make me a serial killer.

Yet.

I need to kill at least one, preferably two more. Considering that's part of my plan, I'll be a bona fide serial killer soon. Going down in his-tor-y for ridding the world of a bunch of bullying bitches, how great is this? People at school will put me on a pedestal for killing off the mean girls. My hard work deserves a reward. I'm like the female Dexter, I swear.

Killing them was so easy, now that I look back on it. Gretchen and Lex pretty much asked for what happened to them. And they screamed and carried on, indignant in the face of their death. Especially Lex, whose situation was a little more difficult. It lasted a little longer, and I suppose I should've felt bad about her suffering.

But I didn't.

Next time, I want a challenge. I *need* a challenge. Someone who proves a little more difficult. Maybe even someone unexpected, though she will still have to stay within my theme.

And I do have a theme—you notice that, right? Everyone would have to be blind or an idiot if they can't figure it out.

Am I scared they'll figure me out? No. I've been pretty clean, kept a low profile. No fuss, no muss, and I wipe everything down. Or wear gloves. Or change my clothes, get rid of my clothes, whatever needs to be done. No blood evidence. No fingerprints. No witnesses. And I tell no one.

A secret's not a secret if you tell someone, and guess what? No one knows what I'm doing. Not a soul. This is my biggest secret.

I plan on keeping it that way.

CHAPTER SEVENTEEN

The first morning back in school after being off for two days is going as well as expected. Everyone's extra quiet—I'm sure the teachers love this. It's not easy, acting like everything's fine when it's so not. The police presence is everywhere on campus today. Uniformed officers seem to be everywhere I look, and there were a couple of local news trucks parked out in front of the school when I first got here this morning.

But I try my best to put on my confident face and pretend everything's okay. I might be dying a little inside—because seriously, it's hard to fake normal when everything is so not normal—but I'm trying. I really, really am.

By third period I'm exhausted from smiling at everyone and I give myself permission to be my regular self for a while. I hide behind my propped-up physics book while Mrs. Emmert drones on about pendulums and Galileo, slowly rubbing my neck as I stare at my notes for so long, the words start to lose focus.

A folded piece of lined paper lands on top of my desk,

right in the middle of my notebook. I glance over at Cass—yes, he still sits next to me, and no I can't change my seat yet—but he's not even looking in my direction.

I unfold the paper to find one line written across the center.

How you holding up?

Should I answer him? I sneak another look in his direction but he's totally focused on Mrs. Emmert's lecture.

Please. He must know I'm studying him.

I write the words *why do you care?* quickly, fold the paper, and toss it back to him, immediately upset with myself for being so rude.

Too late now.

He taps his pen against the edge of his desk again and again, maybe trying to draw my attention? But I don't look over at him. I rest my left elbow on my desk and prop my head on my fist, blocking out Cass completely because really, we shouldn't be talking. I don't want to talk to him. I want nothing to do with him.

The folded note is back on my desk within minutes, and I stare at it for a long moment before I exhale and unfold the paper.

I was just checking on you. I know this must be hard, what happened to Gretchen and now Lex. I wanted to make sure you were okay.

His words are…kind. Since this has all started, no one has asked if I'm okay. Oh, my parents have, but more because they have to and they're concerned for my welfare. I know they care, but they're parents. They're *supposed* to care.

No one else has checked on me, and it feels…nice. Even if it is Cass Vincenti who's doing the asking.

I decide to answer him.

I'm all right. It's been really hard, and I don't

know what's going on, but I'm holding up as best I can.

   How are you?

When Mrs. Emmert's back is to us as she writes on the white board, I look over at Cass to find he's already watching me, his dark eyes meeting mine. I hold my hand out with the note and he takes it from me, his fingers brushing against mine, making my skin tingle.

Weird.

I try to concentrate on what Mrs. Emmert is saying, but I can't. All I can focus on is Cass sitting next to me, the scratch of his pen as he writes on the paper we're sharing, the way a lock of dark hair falls across his forehead as he hunches over his desk. I'm blatantly watching him now, slumped in my seat, the book hopefully hiding my face, and I glance over the top edge, watching Mrs. Emmert just as the note lands on my desk once more.

Anticipation fills me as I open the paper, which is ridiculous. This is Cass. And we're passing notes back and forth like we're lovesick twelve-year-olds.

I want to talk to you. Meet me by the bathrooms in ten?

Glancing up with a frown, our gazes meet. *How?* I mouth at him.

Watch me, he mouths back, just before he raises his hand.

"Yes, Cass?" Mrs. Emmert asks wearily when she spots him.

He drops his arm. "I forgot I need to go to the main office."

Mrs. Emmert frowns. "Why?"

"My grandma left something there for me to pick up." His expression is completely solemn as he adds, "It's personal."

A few of the jocks start snickering, but Cass ignores them. So does Mrs. Emmert.

"Go ahead," she says, making a shooing gesture with her hands. "But don't take too long."

"I won't," he promises her as he gathers up his stuff, shoves it all into his backpack before he whispers to me, "Get a hall pass in like, five minutes."

Then he flashes me a smile and leaves.

His departure disrupts the classroom and Mrs. Emmert gives up for a few minutes, going over to her desk to take a few swigs from her Dr Pepper. Courtney whisper-shouts from where she's sitting two desks over, her eyebrows raised when I ask her what's up.

"What's up with you? Suddenly getting all cozy with Cass?" Court smirks. "Decided to give the dark side a try or what?"

Panic makes my stomach twist. Did she see us passing notes? "What do you mean?"

"He whispered something to you before he left." Her smile is small, and vaguely evil, if that's even a thing. "I saw him. And he smiled at you. He never smiles at anyone."

He doesn't? "Oh, he said everyone in this class is a bunch of assholes, and that made me laugh because it's not a lie, you know?" I laugh again, though it sounds fake, not that Court notices. She laughs, too, and nods, dramatically rolling her eyes when Mrs. Emmert claps her hands and demands our attention.

Not five minutes later I'm ducking out of class, the hall pass clutched in my hand as I make my way to the bathrooms. I glance around the empty hall, looking for Cass, but I don't see him anywhere.

Maybe we're not going to be able to talk after all. Why do I feel disappointed? I don't trust him. I don't even really know him. One chat in my car after a string of ominous texts doesn't form a friendship.

I'm about to push the door into the girls' bathroom

when I hear something.

"Psst."

I look over at the boys' bathroom to see Cass holding open the door, already inside. He takes my hand and yanks me in with him, shutting and locking the door behind us.

"Hey!" I protest as I shake his hand off mine. "Why'd you lock it? Won't someone try to come in?"

"I want to have a private conversation with you." Something about the way he says private makes me want to shiver, and not in a bad way either.

"What if someone tries to open the door?" And why am I so fixated on the door? Because I don't want to think about why I'm alone with Cass in the boys' bathroom in the middle of third period? This has gotten really weird.

"If someone does, we stay quiet until he leaves." He shrugs, shoves his hands in his front pockets, and watches me. "So you're telling me the truth? You're really okay?"

I nod, glancing around the bathroom. I've never been in here before, and it looks just like ours, with the exception of the three urinals hanging on the wall. "I don't mean to be rude but…why do you care? It's not like we're close friends or whatever."

"Hate to say it, but that sounded kind of rude to me," he says with a faint smile, and I can tell he's joking. And that he's not afraid to call me out on my crap. "I don't know. After we talked, I felt bad for telling you all that stuff."

"You felt bad?"

"I didn't mean to put theories in your head, you know? You're friends with those girls, and here I am, coming at you with accusations against Courtney."

True. "Do you still think she's involved?"

"Honestly?" Our gazes meet. Hold. His expression is serious. Like, deadly serious. "Not really."

I tilt my head. "Why?"

"It's too obvious. *She's* too obvious. I don't think the person who killed Lex and Gretchen would act like Court does."

"So you think the same person killed both girls."

"Definitely. Don't you?"

"Of course."

"Who do you think did it?"

I shrug. "I have no idea. Who do you think did it?" This conversation is kind of bizarre and feels like we're getting nowhere.

"I have some new theories." He says nothing else, and I figure he's silent on purpose.

"Is that why you dragged me into the boys' bathroom, then? To tell me you have new theories?"

"I just wanted to make sure you're okay," he says, his voice soft.

But I'm too frustrated to pay attention to his soft voice and warm brown eyes. Forget it. I'm sort of mad now, and I don't really understand why. "Why do you care if I'm okay? Why do you care at all? You don't even know me."

He takes a step back, clearly offended. "I don't know, considering how defensive you're acting."

"Defensive?" My voice is rising. As in, I'm yelling. "You say words like that and I feel like you're accusing me of something."

He shrugs. "Take it as you will."

I stare at him for a moment, wondering if his new theory involves...

Me.

"You're an asshole," I tell him before I stomp toward the door and turn the lock so I can rush outside. He doesn't follow after me.

And he never comes back to class, either.

CHAPTER EIGHTEEN

I'm angry for the rest of the day, and I'm glad I don't spot Cass at lunch, because I'd probably rip into him and call him all sorts of names. I know that sounds crazy, but I can't help my feelings. It's like my emotions are all over the place, all because he called me defensive.

Maybe I am defensive. Maybe I'm on edge. Maybe I'm scared someone is watching me and might try to off me next. Gretchen and Lex were both strong girls. Stronger than me, at least physically. I probably couldn't fight off this creep if he came at me and tried to kill me.

Or she. It could be a she. It could be anyone.

We sat in the library for lunch, just Dani and me in a quiet corner, sharing a Fiji water and a packaged salad her mom keeps on hand for days when we don't leave campus. And right now, they're not letting anyone leave. We're all prisoners trapped at Cape Bonita, since the teachers and administration don't want to let us out of their sights.

I'm glad to be alone with Dani, considering I don't want to deal with anyone during lunch. I don't want to listen to

Courtney and everyone else talking about the party this weekend, which is bullshit. That's all it is, complete bullshit. I'm over this entire thing. People pretending they care about Gretchen and Lex when really they just want to party.

But I'm no better. Not really. Do I miss Gretchen and Lex? I would never, ever wish them dead, and I'm sad they're gone, but I wouldn't say I miss them. Which sucks, right? I'm an awful person who doesn't care. That's how I feel. I remain pretty quiet throughout lunch, letting Dani jabber on about all kinds of stuff. She doesn't even realize I'm being abnormally quiet and I'm sort of glad. This way, she won't question me too much.

Right after lunch, though, I'm called into Mrs. Adney's office. The second time in less than a month, which isn't cool. People are starting to talk. And if it's those detectives wanting to interrogate me again, I'm going to freak out. They really should focus their energy elsewhere, not on me. I know nothing.

Well. Not really. Cass's theories are overblown. And I have no idea who might've done this. So I'm just keeping my mouth shut.

It's probably best.

When I show up just outside Mrs. Adney's door and see who else is in her office, I figure out quick what this visit is all about.

"Hi Mrs. Adney." I stop in the open doorway and smile at her. She scowls in return. "You wanted to see me?"

"Sit down." She waves a hand toward the empty chair between where Courtney and Danielle sit.

I do as she demands, shooting Dani a sympathetic smile.

Yet I don't even bother looking in Court's direction. I'm still pissed at her about this Friday-night party thing. We haven't really talked beyond that one minor moment in physics class, when she gave me crap over Cass. The last real conversation I had with Court was when she left my house Tuesday morning with two of my mom's homemade brownies wrapped in a napkin and tucked inside her Gucci purse.

"My three senior Larks. How are you all doing?" Mrs. Adney settles into the chair behind her desk and studies us with that hawk-like gaze of hers. I do my best not to squirm in my seat, but Dani's sitting next to me, wiggling her butt like she's ready to leap out of her chair at any second. Courtney, on the other hand, is totally relaxed, slumping down like she doesn't have a care in the world.

"It's been very difficult. We can't believe both Gretchen and Lex are gone," I say, my voice barely above a whisper.

"Right. You girls are *so* torn up, you're planning on having a party to celebrate the loss of your friends this Friday night."

Courtney opens her mouth to argue, but Mrs. Adney shuts her down with only a look. "I cannot *believe* you girls would plan something like this. I thought you knew better. All three of you are considered leaders; girls look up to you. You're leaders of one of the most coveted and respected organizations in this school. Yet you plan something so incredibly insensitive and downright callous, considering what's happened to our school these last few weeks. Don't you think so, Courtney?"

Court sits up straight, her expression serious, even a little sad. She knows how to put it on when she needs to. "I know we're supposed to be in mourning, Mrs. Adney. And we are, I promise. What's happened to CBP and to the Larks is awful. A total tragedy, and those girls will be missed, most of all by me." I come this close to reminding her of her awful speech at Gretchen's candlelight vigil, but I keep my mouth shut. "But sometimes, even in the absolute darkness of tragedy, we need to let loose and remember that we're still alive. We need to strive toward the light."

Oh my God, is she for real? The girl is ballsy, I'll give her that.

"To be honest, Courtney, I'm particularly concerned by your behavior." Mrs. Adney shakes her head. "I think we should have a meeting and get your parents involved."

I'm silent, deathly still. So is Dani. I can't believe Mrs. Adney is saying this in front of us, and I think Court feels the same. Her face is red, like she's going to blow at any moment, and I grip my chair handles so tight my fingers ache.

"Mrs. Adney." Courtney tries to smile but it's shaky. "You don't have to do that. My parents don't need to be involved."

"Too late. I've already called them. But we'll discuss that privately in a moment." Mrs. Adney turns to look at Dani and me, her gaze narrowed. "Penelope and Danielle, I'm disappointed and surprised the both of you would support something like this."

I don't want her to call my parents, either. No way. "The issue was discussed, and we brought it to vote during a casual Larks get-together, but I voted against it," I tell Mrs. Adney. I can feel Courtney glaring, her anger radiating toward me in palpable waves, but I ignore her. I want Mrs. Adney to know I never supported Court's idea, and I refuse to go down with her. "I'm worried over who we might end up offending."

"Right. Like the girls' families." Mrs. Adney stares hard at Courtney. "This is not the time to have a party. You know this."

"I can do whatever I want as long as I'm not on school grounds," Court says defiantly, crossing her arms in front of her chest. "You can't stop me."

"The Larks is a school organization—"

"Fine, then this particular party won't be sponsored by

the Larks," Courtney says, looking pleased that she was able to talk over Mrs. Adney. "I'm the one who's sponsoring this fund-raiser for Lex and Gretchen. Who will want to stop me when I'm doing a good deed? I'm sure my parents will support it."

Court has to be bluffing. She just told us she could have this party because her parents will be out of the country. If they find out about the planned party—and you know Mrs. Adney is going to tell them—they're going to shut her down fast.

Mrs. Adney sighs heavily before she turns to stare down Dani. "What about you? How can you explain your part in this atrocity?"

"Um, well. I thought…" Dani shrugs and looks down, twisting her hands together in her lap. "I thought it might be fun, you know? We could have a little party and relax after all the seriousness of the last few weeks. It's been really stressful for everyone, especially the seniors. I haven't been able to work on my college applications as much as I've wanted to, what with everything going on."

"Uh-huh, sounds very stressful. While the Nelson and Nguyen families have lost their daughters forever." Mrs. Adney slaps the edge of her desk so hard it makes all three of us startle. "I would strongly advise against having this party, Courtney, and I'm going to say the same thing to your parents. But as you stated, if you want to host this special little get-together on private property and as long as the Larks aren't associated with it, then I can't stop you."

Courtney looks terribly pleased with herself, despite Mrs. Adney calling her parents. She just won that battle.

"I would suggest, Penelope, that you avoid going to the party. You, too, Danielle." Mrs. Adney nods once. "You're dismissed. Go back to your class. And don't dawdle!"

The moment we hustle out of the main office, Courtney is in full-on attack mode.

"Way to make me look like a total shithead, Penny. Thanks for the support," she says snidely.

"Hey, you know how I felt about this situation. I never wanted to have this party. I've said that from the start," I remind her. "It was all your idea, I just got outvoted."

"Yeah, but you didn't need to tell her that you voted against the idea. Now I look like a total bitch, and Mrs. Adney is trying to keep you out of the party when I'll need your help!"

I shrug. She wants me there so I can *help* her? Screw that. "I never planned on going in the first place. So I wouldn't have been much help."

Courtney comes to a stop, as does Dani. "What did you just say?"

We're standing in the middle of the empty hall, most everyone tucked away in their classes. "I didn't want to go. I still don't want to go. So." I take a deep breath. "I'm not going."

"Fine. You're not invited." Courtney sniffs. "I don't want you there. If you show up at my front door, you'll be turned away."

"Good." I tilt my head up, hoping I look like I don't care. I really don't. There's just hoping you don't make an ass of yourself, and then there's social suicide. And I feel like Courtney hosting this party is flat-out social suicide.

"Penelope," Dani starts, and I turn to glare at her, shutting her up.

"Since when did you turn into such a righteous little bitch, Penny?" Courtney asks.

"Since when did you turn into such an attention-seeking whore, Court?" I break out into a big smile, keeping my voice disgustingly pleasant. "Oh, that's right. You've been keeping that up for years. Nice to see you've been staying consistent! Even Mrs. Adney said so."

Um.

Wow.

I can't believe I just said that.

But…it's the truth. I've always kept quiet and let the girls act like they usually do. So they're bitches to everyone, so what? That's what I would tell myself. I sort of fell into their ways, though I tried to be kinder. My older sister was no better. She wasn't just queen bee at the school, she was also queen bitch. When we were younger, she terrified me most of the time.

She's better now. But am I? Or am I just a queen bitch, too?

No one is laughing. No one is gasping or yelling, either. We're all three just staring at one another like we're having some sort of face off, and in a way, I suppose we are.

I refuse to look away first. Seems like Courtney feels the same way. It's finally Dani who breaks the tension.

"I hate it when you guys fight," she says softly.

"Too late. We're fighting." I raise my brows and pin my gaze on Court. "You really think you're going to have a blow-out bash for two dead girls and people will actually show up?"

"Better than sitting at home and doing nothing about it. Maybe we could bring out the killer with this party. Did you ever think of that?" With a huff and a flounce of her tiny plaid skirt—she likes to roll up her waistband to show off more leg—Courtney stalks down the hall toward her class, never once looking back.

"Is she for real?" Dani asks the moment Courtney's out of earshot. "Do you really think she's having this party to lure out Gretchen and Lex's killer?"

I shrug, kind of pissed I didn't think of the idea first, since it's a good one. I can admit it. Though it's scary, too. What if Court's party does bring the killer out? What then? The way Courtney's acting is totally reckless. "Maybe. I don't know. She's crazy to do something like that, though it's also kind of smart. I doubt she's the one who came up with it."

"Who would?"

"I don't know." I shrug. "Maybe the cops?"

"You really think so?" Realization dawns all over Dani's expressive face. "You think Court is *working* with the cops?"

"Who knows?" I can't imagine Courtney willingly working with the police department, but stranger things have happened. "I'm so confused with everything going on, I don't know what to think anymore."

"Me neither," Dani mutters as she looks around.

"I have a confession." When Dani turns to look at me, I admit, "Now I sort of wish I *could* go to that stupid party. We need to stick together."

Despite how risky it would be to show up, I do want to go. Is that dumb? Probably. I shouldn't bother, especially if I'm by myself. What if something...

Happens?

I don't want to risk it.

"You're right. We should stick together. I can get you in if you really want to be there," Dani says with a slow smile. "She said you'll be turned away at the front door, but she never mentioned anything about the back door."

I return her smile. "That definitely has potential."

. . .

I'm in bed when I get a Snapchat text from Cass. I don't remember adding him, but I must've, so I open it up, curious to see what he says.

Cass: You still mad at me?

I can't help but smile. He's pretty unapologetic, isn't he?

Me: Sort of.

Cass: Will my saying sorry help?

Me: Maybe.

I receive a selfie pic of him making an exaggerated sad face, with a pouty lower lip and everything. The caption on the photo says: SORRY PEN.

The smile that stretches across my face can't be helped. It comes easier, too, considering no one is around to see me. I take a selfie of me in mid eye roll, a slight smile on my face, and include a caption.

Me: You're forgiven.

Cass starts texting me again.

Cass: Good. I don't want you mad at me, Pen. I like you.

I frown when I read his response. I don't get this guy. It's like he came out of nowhere and wants to attach himself to my side. It's kind of…weird. And intriguing. But he's weird and intriguing and mysterious. Totally not my type.

So why am I…attracted to him?

Me: Why do you like me? I don't get it.

I send the text before I can second-guess myself and then drop my phone on the bed, covering my face with both hands. I'm quietly freaking out and wishing I had someone to talk to. Dani would try to convince me I've lost my mind—and maybe she's right. Court would laugh her ass off and blab to everyone at school that I have a thing for Cass. And I can't tell my parents, not that I really talk to them about this type of stuff anyway. Plus, Dad would probably suspect Cass is the killer and trying to get close to me—which is just ridiculous. While Mom would ask if he played any sports. She has a thing for jocks, like I used to.

Ugh.

Dropping my hands, I grab my phone and check if Cass replied.

He did.

Cass: You're beautiful and smart and funny. Why wouldn't I like you?

Me: Are you being for real right now?

Cass: Are you being insecure right now, Pen? I didn't know you had it in you.

Me: What's that supposed to mean?

Cass: You're a confident girl at school. It's like nothing bothers you.

Me: Things bother me. My friends being murdered bothers me.

Lots of other things bother me, too. Like how it's starting to feel like my friends aren't really my friends at all, with the exception of Dani. How fast everything's changing yet I somehow still feel the same. How everyone's scared and tense and nothing is normal and I hate it.

I really do.

Cass: They were my friends too.

I frown at the words he typed, wondering why neither Gretchen nor Lex ever mentioned Cass to any of us before.

Me: Were you guys close?

Cass: Sort of. I'll tell you more about it next time I see you.

I don't reply for a moment, too stuck on what he said. He'll tell me more? I'd love to hear it. I don't know anything about him. Nothing at all save for the few rumors Dani mentioned to me. Oh, and Court. He's a total mystery. One I'd like to get to know better.

But on the down low. I don't want my so-called friends knowing about this. They'll just give me endless crap.

I receive another Snapchat from Cass, and this time it's a photo of him. I can tell he's shirtless but I don't see much, just his shoulders and up. He has tan, smooth skin, fresh-shaven cheeks and sleepy eyes. His hair is tousled and it looks damp. Like he just got out of the shower.

Hmmm.

He captioned the photo, too.

Good night, Pen.

He included a star emoji.

I send him a pic of myself back, my eyes closed and my head against the pillow like I'm already asleep.

Night, Cass.

CHAPTER NINETEEN

Friday afternoon, I'm leaving school and headed toward the parking lot when I sense someone is walking beside me. When I turn to see who it is, I come to a sudden stop.

And so does Cass. "Hey," he says easily when I just stare at him. "Do you have a minute? Can we talk?"

It's weird to have him face-to-face again after Snapchatting last night. He wasn't in physics today, and I figured he didn't come to school at all. "Sure," I say, glancing around. "What's going on?"

He glances around, too, as if he just had the same thought. "Could we talk somewhere private?"

"I don't know. I need to get home…" Why am I acting like this? Like I don't want to talk to him when I really do?

"Just for a few minutes." He steps closer, and I tilt my head back to meet his gaze. He is really tall. Why doesn't he play on the basketball team? Or maybe he does and I never paid attention before? If he did, that would make my mom happy.

Geez, what am I thinking? That Cass will meet my

parents and I want their approval? Clearly I'm getting ahead of myself.

"Please, Pen," he says when I don't answer him.

I give in and start walking, waving at him to come with me when he doesn't. He falls into step behind me and I find an empty classroom, slipping into it, and he follows.

The door shuts and I turn to face him, taking a deep breath before I ask, "What's up?"

"Getting right to it, huh? No casual how are yous or bland observations about the weather?" He smiles, but I don't. "Okay, then. I was wondering if you'd, uh, go with me to Courtney's party tonight."

My heart trips over itself at his request. Is he asking me on a date? "No."

Cass frowns. "Really? You don't want to go with me?"

I shake my head, flustered by his question, which never happens. "No, it's not that. It's just... I'm not going." Should I tell him my plan to sneak in?

His frown deepens. "Why not? It's a Lark event, and you're the president."

It's weird, to hear him talk about the Larks. "It's not officially sponsored by the Larks. It's Courtney's deal." I don't bother explaining to him the reasons why that is. I don't want to bore him.

"You two are friends."

"Not at the moment."

Cass frowns. "Why is it you Larks never seem to get along?"

I say nothing. Why deny it when he's right?

But wait a minute—how does he know that?

"Is that what you wanted to talk about?" I ask when he says nothing else.

"Yeah. I'm just— There's no way I can convince you

to come with me?" He makes a cute little face, and I'm tempted to give in.

But I can't just walk into Court's party with Cass. That would cause all sorts of drama.

Wouldn't it?

"No, sorry. I can't go." I feel bad. I should tell him the truth.

"It's just..." His expression turns serious. "It's not because of me, is it?"

I soften toward him. I don't want him to think I don't like him, because I do. Though I can't quite figure him out yet. "It's not you. It's—it's Courtney. I didn't want her to have this party. We fought about it and now she doesn't want me there. So it's this mutual stand-off type of thing between us."

"Ah, gotcha," he says with a nod, though he looks confused. But Courtney and I have fought like this off and on for years. It's just our thing.

And for once, I'm totally over it.

Cass shuffles his feet and I glance down at his Converse. I don't know how he gets away with wearing them, since they're not part of our uniform. "Maybe we could sneak into the party then."

I frown. "What?"

"The two of us together, we can sneak into Courtney's house and spy on everyone. Watch what they're doing and see how they act." He steps even closer to me, and I can feel his body heat radiating toward me. I can smell him, too. That same mixture of clean boy and fabric softener and the faintest hint of cologne. "I have a feeling the person who murdered Alexis and Gretchen might be there tonight."

I try my best to look like what he just said meant nothing to me, but deep down inside, I am totally flipping out. He's repeating exactly what Courtney said about the party. Using it to bring out the killer, which is freaking scary. "If that's the case, what if the cops are there?"

"So what if they are?"

"Then we should let them do their job and not interfere."

"But maybe they're not so great at doing their job. So far, they haven't done much. I'm not impressed." He sends me a look. "Don't you agree?"

I don't bother answering him. "Do you really want to go to the party if the killer could possibly be there?"

I don't want to, but I feel like I have to. Dani will be there, and I want to protect her. And I really don't want to be alone tonight, either.

"Hell yeah, I do."

His answer is no surprise.

"Mrs. Adney doesn't want the party to happen."

"Of course she doesn't." He smiles. Actually looks excited at the prospect. "Come on, Pen. Sneak into the party with me. It'll be…fun."

That is the last word I'd use to describe this party. "It'll be awful. We shouldn't be having a big party when they just died. It's so disrespectful." I feel like I keep repeating myself, yet no one is listening.

"Think if we actually caught the killer, though. We'd be heroes." His eyes are sparkling and his body is practically vibrating with excitement. "It'll be the coolest thing ever."

He sounded so young when he said that, like a little kid. I wonder what he was like when he was kid. When exactly did his mom murder his dad? Is that story even true? And how long has he lived with his grandma?

These are all questions I want to ask him, but I don't know how.

"You really want to do this, don't you?" I ask softly.

"Yeah." He hesitates. "Plus, I've never been to Courtney's

house before. I want to check it out."

"Right. Though you two have hooked up multiple times." At his shocked look, I forge on. "You basically said that to me when we met at Sweet Offerings. Remember? You said Courtney and Gretchen were fighting over you and all that."

His expression turns to stone. "It was nothing. Definitely not multiple times."

I roll my eyes, exasperated. "Really? Because you made it sound like it happened a lot." When he just stares at me with a blank look on his face, I'm tempted to kick him. "Seriously right now? And come on, the two of you are practically neighbors. I have a hard time believing you've never been to her house."

"Will you go with me to the party or not?" He runs a hand through his hair in frustration, glaring at me. He went from giddy little boy to brooding angry teen in ten seconds flat.

"Fine, I'll go." I can't believe I just said that. And maybe I don't want to go with Cass after all. He's being weird.

He smiles that transforming smile that turns him from average good-looking boy to swoon-worthy hotness, and I steel myself, repeating the words *must resist, must resist,* in my head. "I'll pick you up at your house. Say around nine?"

"No, you don't have to do that." I do not want to introduce this guy to my parents. Not yet. I haven't had a boyfriend since Robby and I broke up right before last summer, and Mom still asks me if I'm ever going to "get back in the saddle." I don't even know what she means by that, but it sounds gross and slightly perverted.

"Don't suggest that we meet at the party, because I want to make sure you're safe," he says.

I frown. "Safe?"

"Yeah. I want you with me the whole night." When I give

him a doubtful look, he continues. "I'm serious. I don't want you to leave my side. So I'm picking you up at your house."

"What if I pick you up?"

"I guess you can, but I'm driving to Courtney's." He pauses. "With you." Another pause. "Together."

He's rather demanding. "You are so not."

"I am," he says, his voice firm. "That's the only way I'll agree to you picking me up. Otherwise, I'll come get you at your house."

"No way." I shake my head. "I'll come get you."

"At nine?"

"Yes. At nine."

"Awesome." He smiles. "I'll walk you out to your car."

I don't protest because I think I know what he's doing. He's making sure I'm safe, which I can totally appreciate. I walk beside him out to the parking lot, my car parked in its usual spot at the far end of the lot, close to the street. But I see another car parked next to mine. It's a dark, nondescript sedan, and I know without seeing them that the car belongs to Detectives Spalding and Hughes.

And then I do see them, the both of them leaning against the hood of their car. The moment they spot us, they stand up straight and start to make their approach.

They pop up at the worst times, I swear.

"Miss Malone," Spalding says with a nod. "Mr. Vincenti."

We both stop, Cass immediately going tense. "Hi," I say.

Cass says nothing.

"Didn't realize you two knew each other," Hughes says, sounding amused. He even smiles at us. "You guys friends?"

"Yeah," Cass croaks, then clears his throat. I send him a quick look, but he never takes his gaze off the detectives.

"More than friends?" Hughes pushes.

"No," I say firmly, only because I don't want the detectives to think otherwise.

Spalding is all pleasant smiles. "Okay then. We wanted to ask you a few questions. The both of you," he says, his gaze landing on Cass.

"I'm afraid I can't talk to you unless we're in the presence of my attorney," I say with a polite smile.

Hughes scowls. Spalding lets it slide. "Not a problem. We'll just talk to Mr. Vincenti here."

"What do you want?" Cass asks, his voice tight.

"First off, do you know anything about this party tonight at Courtney Jenkins's house?" Spalding glances over at me. "I hear it's a Larks thing."

"It's not," Cass says easily. "Courtney is having the party, not the Larks."

I'm so glad I told him that.

"Are you going?"

"What does it matter?"

Spalding turns to me. "Are *you* going to the party?"

I slowly shake my head but don't say a word.

They both stare at us, trying to…what? Break us down? I have no idea. But I don't say anything else and neither does Cass, and I'm totally impressed. I'm starting to realize that the best defense is not to say anything at all.

"Word of advice," Hughes starts, looking thoroughly pissed. "Don't go."

"We'll take it into consideration," Cass says sarcastically.

The detectives look at each other and then silently head for their car.

Cass doesn't speak again until they're long gone down the road. "Assholes," he spits out.

"They're not so bad." Ugh, why am I defending them? They *are* assholes.

"Yeah, well, it's easy to say that when you have a powerful

lawyer backing you up and allowing you to keep your mouth shut." He shakes his head, looking bitter. "They brought me into the station a few nights ago and questioned me there for hours."

I'm surprised. "Really? Why?"

"My number showed up on Gretchen's cell phone records." He says nothing else.

And I don't know what to say either. Really, I want to press him for more info.

"Did your number show up on her phone records recently?" The question pops out of my mouth like I have no control.

"We talked." He looks away, like he can't meet my gaze. "We were…friends."

I'm wondering what his definition of "friends" is.

"Okay, well, I should get going." I smile but it feels fake, so I let it fade quickly. "See ya tonight."

"See ya." He shoves his hands into the front pockets of his khakis. When he doesn't walk away, I glance around the empty parking lot.

"Where's your car?" I ask.

"I didn't drive today. Rode with someone else."

"Who?"

"Uh…" He gives me a helpless look. "Courtney."

Seriously? "You weren't in class this morning, but Court was."

"Are you saying you missed me?" His brows shoot up. He looks genuinely surprised, all the earlier tension leaving his body.

"I definitely noticed you weren't there," I admit.

"So you did miss me." His eyes flash. He looks very pleased at my answer, and my cheeks are going hot. So embarrassing. I need to change the subject quick.

"Do you, uh, need a ride?"

His smile is easy and his eyes still sparkle. "That would be great. Thanks."

We get into my car and leave school, turning left so we head up toward Hot Springs Road. We climb and climb, talking about the last few days at school and how crazy they were. He's surprisingly easy to talk to, and I start to forget that he's a suspect. Crap, I'm a suspect, too, so who am I to judge?

I keep sending him quick looks, trying to notice every little detail. I like how he slouches in the passenger seat, his long legs bent, his thighs spread wide in that way boys sit. He never once looks at his phone during our entire conversation, and I remember how when Robby was with me, he would check his phone fifty times in approximately two minutes.

It was annoying. I never felt important to him. He could never cut off communication with his friends, his bros, other girls…

Yeah. That was Robby's biggest problem. Other girls. He liked them way too much. I was never enough for him.

Cass gives me directions and tells me where to turn as we go. His house is right on Hot Springs Road, and we're high above town. The road winds through the quiet neighborhood that's on the outskirts of town, climbing higher up the mountain, and we pass gigantic estate after gigantic estate. Some of them so big, you don't even see the house, it's set so far back on the expansive property.

When we finally arrive at his house, Cass asks me to pull into the driveway and so I do, stopping just in front of the ivy-covered garage. I put the car in park and turn to my left, sucking in a breath when I see the view spread out before me.

Nothing but glittering, deep-blue ocean as far as the eye can see. It's gorgeous, the sun shining on the waves and making the water sparkle like it's covered with diamonds. "Wow, what a view," I say.

"Pretty nice, huh?" he asks. I turn to find him leaning over the center console, his face terribly close to mine. "When you look at it every single day, you don't even realize how beautiful it is anymore."

"Really?" My voice squeaks and I clamp my lips shut. I don't want to make a fool of myself in front of him. I need to play it cool, like this is no big deal. I'm in a car with Cass. I'm at his house. Just another Friday afternoon, right?

Right.

Cass nods, his gaze flickering to the water. "You always take for granted what you have, know what I mean?"

Now it's my turn to nod. He's right. If I lived here, I wouldn't care about the beautiful view, either. We have a minor ocean view from certain rooms in our house, but I don't even notice.

"So I'll see you tonight?" he asks, his voice huskier than usual. It feels very intimate, sitting in my car with him in front of his house, staring at the ocean and with him so close.

I nod again, then realize I should probably say something. "Yeah. Nine o'clock. I'll be here."

"You'll remember how to get here?"

"Definitely. It wasn't that difficult to find." I smile at him and he smiles back, his eyes soft, his face almost...

Kind. And cute. And maybe even...

Sexy.

"See you in a few hours," he says as he reaches for the door handle.

"See you," I say weakly, watching as he climbs out of my car, slams the door, and slings his backpack over his shoulder. He gives me a little wave as I pull away and I wave back, not restraining the slow smile that spreads across my face.

I start plotting and planning what I should wear for my date/not date with Cass tonight the entire drive back home. Better to focus on my outfit than the fact that a serial killer might come to the party, too.

Yeah. I can't stop thinking about that, either.

CHAPTER TWENTY

I trash my closet as I search through it, trying to come up with an outfit for tonight. I'm tossing sweaters and shirts and jeans and shoes all over the floor, muttering under my breath in frustration, until I finally find something that's stylish and cute without looking like I'm trying too hard.

Once I have my outfit selected, I take a quick shower and then try to figure out how I want to do my shoulder-length brown hair. I decide to just quickly curl the ends, giving it those beachy waves that are so popular right now and Courtney is so good at doing.

Ugh. I frown at my reflection. Why am I thinking about Courtney now? But then again, how can I not think about Courtney? We're going to her house tonight. My date is a guy she's hooked up with.

I fight the tiny flicker of jealousy that lights up within me. How far did she take it with Cass? All the way? Has she had sex with this guy?

God, I really hope not.

And yeah, I'm not examining that thought too closely,

thank you very much.

Grabbing my phone, I open up Snapchat and send Dani a quick text.

Me: Tell me what you know about Cass Vincenti.

I start to do my makeup as I wait for her reply.

Dani: I don't know much. He's kind of mysterious.

Me: Right. But do you have any clue who he's been with?

Dani: Like r u talking girls?

I roll my eyes.

Me: Yes.

Dani: Hmm…

I'm rubbing tinted moisturizer into my skin when I hear back from her.

Dani: Listen. I know some stuff, but I was sworn to secrecy.

Me: By who?

Dani: By Gretchen.

My best friend has been withholding information?

Me: What did she say?

Dani: I swore I would never tell.

Oh. My. God.

Me: Dani! I don't mean to be a total bitch, but she's dead. What is she going to do if you tell me her secrets?

Dani: Fine. Fine. You're right. I'll tell you.

She leaves me open on read and doesn't respond for another five freaking minutes. I'm practically dying from anticipation when I finally hear from her.

Dani: Whenever G's parents caught her drinking or whatever, they made her attend a bunch of AA meetings as punishment. 1 night, Cass was at a meeting. Like, for real.

I frown.

Me: Really?

Dani: Yeah. Supposedly he had a serious problem a while ago, but he's clean now. And he really wanted to help Gretchen. That's how they got so close.

Me: Did they hook up?

Dani: Not that I know of, but you know Gretchen. So yeah, they probably did and she didn't tell me.

I drop the phone on the counter and stare at my reflection. I almost wish Dani hadn't told me about his problems. He's a recovering addict? Was it just alcohol? Or did he have a drug problem, too? I've heard some rumors. And how am I supposed to ever bring that up? I can't, so I have to sit here with the knowledge and pretend I don't know this very intimate detail about his past.

For all I know, he might still have a problem. And what if he does? What if he's some drunken druggie who'll lose his shit tonight at the party and make a fool out of himself? And me?

A shuddery sigh escapes me. I need to think positive. Cass has been nothing but nice to me, if at times a little too enigmatic. I've never seen him act high or drunk, and he wanted to come to this party with me to protect me. I have to remember that.

Not everyone is out to get me.

I finish putting my makeup on, lightly spritz my curled hair with hairspray, and then go to my closet, where I clean it up somewhat before slipping on the outfit I'm wearing tonight. I'm keeping it simple with a black oversize sweater and skinny jeans paired with black knee-high boots. I put on a long pendant necklace and the diamond earrings my parents gave me on my sixteenth birthday. Staring at myself in the full-length mirror on the back of my closet door, I think I look pretty good, considering all that I've gone through the past couple of weeks.

There's a knock on the door and I step out of my closet just in time to see my sister Peyton step inside the room. Her face is pale, her brown hair pulled into a messy bun on top of her head, and she's wearing a UC Santa Cruz hoodie that our brother got her for Christmas the year he started there and a pair of battered jeans with dark gray Uggs on her feet.

Typical college attire, when my sister used to dress to perfection every single day in high school. I'm still not used to sloppy Peyton, but I'm so glad to see her, I don't really care.

"Penny!" She lunges toward me and envelops me in a fierce hug, pulling away to stare at me, her hands clutching my shoulders. "Sorry I haven't been able to come home until this weekend. Midterms were killing me."

"It's fine. I'm just glad you're here." I smile and hug her again. I love my sister, especially now that she's out of high school. We used to fight like crazy and still do on occasion, but for the most part, we get along. "How are you?"

"I'm good, but don't worry about me. I want to know

what's going on with you and at school." Peyton frowns. "First Gretchen and now Lex is dead? What's happening? Has anyone been arrested? Are you scared to go to school?"

We go sit on my bed and I explain everything as best I can, including when the detectives questioned me and how Courtney's having a party tonight. I even tell her about my encounter with the detectives earlier in the parking lot, when I was with Cass. She's frowning by the time I finish, her eyes full of concern.

"Who exactly is this Cass guy?" she asks.

"He's someone I go to school with. We're in physics together." I shrug, going for nonchalant, but my sister has always been able to read me like a book.

Peyton smiles and nudges me in the shoulder with hers. "You like him?"

I shake my head, then shrug. "Kind of."

Okay fine, I do.

I totally do.

"Is he on the football team?"

She sounds just like Mom.

"No, he doesn't really play sports, that I know of." I shrug again. "He's just a guy, you know? Kind of quiet, keeps to himself."

"One of those secretive, mysterious types? They can be very appealing," Peyton says with a naughty grin.

"Stop." I shove her shoulder and she falls away from me with a laugh.

Thankfully, she drops the subject. "And so this big, crazy party at Courtney's tonight—you're not going, are you?"

"Well…" I let my voice drift, and I wince when I see the scowl on Peyton's face. "I wasn't going to, and Court told me she didn't want me there."

"Why?" Peyton's frowning, but I'm sure she gets it. She

went through the same drama during her high school years.

"You know how it is." I shrug. "Cass told me we should crash it. Dani said she could get me in."

"Will that make Court angry?"

"Probably, but isn't she always angry?" I smile, but Peyton doesn't smile back. "I don't agree with her having this party. I think it's wrong because of what—what happened."

"You mean Gretchen and Lex?" Peyton's voice is low, almost a whisper, and she looks really sad.

I nod. "I can't believe they're gone."

"Me either." She looks away, her gaze contemplative. "Listen, Penny. I don't want to tell you what to do, but I don't think it's smart to go to that party. And I know for a fact Mom and Dad won't let you go."

"They know about it?"

"Well, yeah. Mom said the school sent out one of those automated texts warning parents about the party and how they shouldn't let anyone go."

Oh. My. God. I'm never going to be able to leave the house. How am I going to do this?

"It's just a party," I say weakly, pressing my lips together when Peyton sends me a look.

"Yeah, at the house of a girl who you're currently fighting with. And considering it looks like the Larks are being targeted, I don't think it's smart to go out tonight."

"It's not like I'll be alone," I mumble, looking down at the ground.

"It doesn't even matter because Mom won't let you out of the house anyway." Peyton rises to her feet, that smug expression on her face irritating the crap out of me. "You get to stay home tonight. It's for your own good, little sister."

With that, she walks out of the room, shutting the door behind her.

I flop backward on my bed, staring up at the ceiling. I can't believe the school sent out that text message. Rolling over, I grab my phone off my bedside table and immediately send a Snapchat text to Cass.

Me: I'm a prisoner in my own home.

Cass: What do you mean?

Me: Did you hear about the text alert the school sent out about the party? My parents got it. I don't think they're going to let me go.

Cass: Have you asked them?

I frown up at the ceiling. No, I haven't. I snap a quick selfie pic, set it to three seconds so he can't check out my date outfit for too long, and caption it BRB before hitting send.

Climbing off the bed, I leave my room and head out to the living room, where Mom is sitting watching the evening news. And great, they're talking about Lex and Gretchen.

Mom hits pause on the DVR the moment she sees me. "Penny. You look pretty."

"Thanks." I smile weakly. "Dani and I are going to the movies."

Peyton is slouching on the couch, glaring at me silently. I send her a pleading look.

"Really?" Mom arches a brow, holding her phone up. "I got an interesting text from the school earlier."

"Yeah. Right. About Court's party?" When Mom nods, I continue. May as well face this head-on. "I'm not going. Court and I got into an argument and she doesn't want me there. Which is fine by me, because I don't want to go. It's really awful that she's doing this."

"I should think so." Mom sniffs, her upper lip curled in disgust. "And her parents are okay with it?"

"They're out of town." Turns our Mrs. Adney was never able to get a hold of them and tell them about Courtney's plans. They ignored her calls because they were already on the plane and on their way to their vacation destination.

"She's always been a girl who likes to push people's buttons." Mom shakes her head, her worried gaze meeting mine. "Promise me you're not lying about going to the movies with Dani."

Shit. "I'm not lying," I say with the straightest face possible.

And unbelievably, Peyton doesn't say a word.

"You'll come home right after? What are you going to see? And what time is the showing?"

"Um." It takes me a second, but I rattle off the name of a movie I really did want to see, along with a realistic time. I hope Mom doesn't double check me. I feel horrible about breaking her trust, but everyone is making such a big deal about this.

Plus, I want to spend more time with Cass.

"I might spend the night at Dani's," I tell Mom after I grab my purse and phone from my room and come back out to the living room. "Where's Dad?"

"At a dinner with business associates. I begged out of it so I can spend some time with Peyton." She sends me a sad look. "I was hoping to spend time with both my girls tonight, but looks like you're skipping out on us."

Thanks for laying on the guilt, Mom. "We can hang out tomorrow, right? How late are you here till, Peyton?"

"I go home Sunday." Peyton stands and walks toward me, her gaze direct. "Call me or text me if anything happens, okay?"

The silent message she's sending with her eyes tells me she's got me covered, but she doesn't like it. But crap, she owes me big. I don't know how many times I covered for her in the past. Over some real crazy stuff, too. Outrageous parties that got busted by the cops and people were arrested. That one time she went skinny-dipping with her boyfriend in the ocean and beach patrol caught them. She almost got a public indecency charge for that one. I lied to Mom and Dad every time, telling them she was at one of her friends' houses.

My sister envelops me in a hug, whispering close to my ear, "Be careful," before she releases me. I hug Mom and then I'm walking out the door, a free woman for the night.

I remember to text Dani real quick and let her know about my movie lie so she can cover for me in case Mom contacts her.

The night air is cold, and I shiver, coming to a stop by the driver's side of my car. It feels like someone is…

Watching me.

Slowly, I glance over my shoulder to find our neighbor across the street standing in his driveway, his annoying little dog running circles in the lawn. Mr. Yamaguchi is watching me, his hands in his front pockets, that beat-up old fisherman's hat he's always wearing propped at a weird angle on his head.

I lift my hand in a half-hearted wave and call out, "Hi, Mr. Yamaguchi."

He waves back just as his dog notices me. The little jerk comes to a stop and starts yapping ferociously, like he can take me down. "Good evening, Penelope." Mr. Yamaguchi pauses. "Nice night for a party, isn't it?"

Unease slips down my spine. Does he know about Courtney's party? How could he? He's, like, eighty years old. "I'm going to the movies," I tell him. Why, I don't know.

To cover my alibi?

"Have fun with your boyfriend," Mr. Yamaguchi yells over his still yipping dog.

I don't bother telling him I don't have a boyfriend. I don't bother saying anything else to him at all.

Instead, I hop into my car, back out of the driveway, and head toward Cass's house.

CHAPTER TWENTY-ONE

As I'm driving to pick up Cass, I realize I don't have his phone number.

Well, I have that number he texted from anonymously, but when I tried it earlier, I got no reply.

I tried texting him on Snapchat but he never responded. Once I get to his house, I park in front of the garage just like I did earlier this afternoon and check my Snapchat. No reply from Cass. So I sit there and wait for a few minutes, hoping he will see my car lights and come out to meet me, but he doesn't.

Crap.

Reluctantly, I turn off the car's engine, climb out, and go to the front door, nearly tripping on a cracked part of the sidewalk. There's a fog bank hanging over the ocean tonight, so I can't see it. Instead there's an eerie white glow that has settled over the water, the moonlight casting it in a silvery sheen.

A single porch light is on, but it's dim. Up close, I can tell the house needs a new coat of paint. And the ivy covers almost all the exterior walls, giving it a cool, hushed feel. I hit the doorbell but nothing happens, so I knock on the door instead.

"Coming!" shouts a little voice from inside.

I'm guessing that's his grandma.

The door swings open and I glance down to see a white-haired woman barely five feet tall. She's wearing a black velour Juicy Couture tracksuit, something my mom ran around town in ten years ago, looking very casual chic.

But that was ten years ago, so…

"Hi!" the woman greets me brightly. "Well, aren't you a pretty thing."

"Um, hi. Is, uh, Cass home?"

She smiles and opens the door wider. "Why, um, yes. He, uh, is. Would you like to come in?"

She is totally making fun of me, but not in a mean-spirited way.

I hope.

"Sure, thanks." I walk inside and she shuts and locks the door behind me. We're in the living room, which is dark and cluttered with all sorts of books and knickknacks. The TV is on, a giant flat screen that takes up almost the entire wall, and it casts everything in an artificial blue glow.

"What's your name, pumpkin?"

"Penelope." So I guess he hasn't talked about me to his grandma. Huh.

"Lovely name." She beams. "I'm Sue."

"Nice to meet you, Sue." I take a step and almost fall over a stack of books sitting next to a recliner. I dodge left, stumbling a little before I right myself and stand up straight.

"You okay there, sweetie?"

I nod, brush my hair out of my face. "Yeah, thanks."

"Have a seat." She waves at the recliner and I sit down,

shocked when a longhaired white cat jumps up on my lap, its claws digging into my legs. "Oh, that's Millie. She's a real sweetheart."

The cat looks at me and meows in reply. I smile and nod, trying not to freak out over the fact that I now have a ton of white cat fur all over my black sweater.

Where the hell is Cass?

"Cass will be out in just a minute," she tells me, like she can read my mind. "He only just hopped in the shower a few minutes ago."

Now she's put images in my head. Of Cass in the shower, which is…not good. It's sort of uncomfortable, considering I'm sitting here in front of his grandma while thinking of him naked.

Yeah. So not cool.

"You go to school with Cass?" she asks as she settles into the recliner next to mine. A black cat jumps into her lap and I wish it was in mine instead of this white one, who's settled right in and started cleaning her hind quarters. Gross.

"I do. We have physics together," I tell her, smiling politely before I glance around the room. It's very homey and cozy, though it also looks like it hasn't been thoroughly cleaned in about fifteen years. Not that the room is dirty, it's just so cluttered. There's stuff everywhere. My mom would lose her shit in here. And then she'd immediately start cleaning everything out like she was on an episode of *Hoarders*.

"Tough class," Sue says with a nod. She reaches out and pets the black cat so hard, it meows in protest. "You going on to college after high school?"

"Definitely. Though I'm not sure where yet."

"Do you have an idea where you want to go?"

"UC Santa Cruz maybe. That's where my brother goes. Or

Cal Poly." I'd rather go to Cal Poly. I love San Luis Obispo. "Or maybe even UC Berkeley."

"You should stay on the coast. It's nicer by the ocean." She smiles, still aggressively petting the cat. There are sparkly rings on every one of her fingers, and they catch the light as her hand moves up and down that cat's back. "Cass is going into the military."

"Really?" I'm shocked. I can't imagine him being the type.

"Well, he doesn't really want to, but I think it would be a good idea, and he always wants to please his grandma. If he joins the military, then he won't end up like his daddy." She shakes her head and I lean in closer, disturbing the cat on my lap so that she looks right at me with her bright blue eyes and meows in irritation.

"What do you mean?" I ask casually.

"Oh, that's another story for another time." She waves her ring-covered hand. "Bless his poor soul. If he hadn't met my daughter, then maybe he'd still be alive and able to take care of his son."

Wow, she's throwing it all out there, and I've barely been here five minutes. "Does Cass have any brothers or sisters?"

"Yes, he has a younger sister who has a different mama. They live in Iowa. He never sees her." Sue shoves the cat off her lap, who yowls at her as he scurries out of the room. "Damn cats are a pain in my ass."

I look at the cat on my lap, who's now cleaning her face by licking her paws. It's kind of cute. "We don't have cats at my house. We just have a dog." Roy, who's a total dork and only loves my dad.

"Oh? That's a shame. Cats are such lovely creatures."

And this woman is a total contradiction.

"So you mentioned a brother. Is it just the two of you?" she asks.

"I have an older brother and sister," I tell her, and she nods enthusiastically.

"A nice big happy family then? Your mama and daddy are still together?" she asks.

"Yes, they are." This entire conversation is just weird. I remember when Robby and I first started dating and he brought me to his house. His dad checked me out in a vaguely perverted way and his mother acted like I was stealing her precious baby boy. She treated me like the enemy the entire time we were together, and I bet she still blames me for the breakup.

"That's so nice," Sue says with a big smile. "I wish Cass could've had that. I did the best I could, what with my Don gone after all these years. I had to raise my grandson on my own, all by myself." She lowers her voice, like she's about to share a big secret. "His mama is *never* getting out of prison. It's me and him against the world."

I open my mouth, just about to ask about his "mama," when Cass enters the room, his face full of alarm and his hair still damp from the shower.

"Pen," he breathes, looking completely freaked out that I'm sitting in his living room with a cat on my lap and chatting up his grandma. "You're early."

"Not really." I shake my head. "I got here just a little after nine."

He yanks his phone out of the front pocket of his jeans and checks it. "Shit," he mutters before he looks up at me. "Sorry. Guess I'm the one who's running late."

"I tried to Snapchat you, since I don't have your number," I remind him sweetly.

"Aw, Cass, why aren't you giving this darling girl your number? Shame on you," his grandma tells him good-naturedly.

"Sorry." I swear he's blushing, but it's hard to tell with

how dark it is in the room. "Give me a minute and I'll be ready to go."

"You should show her your room!" She stands and plucks the cat right off my lap. "Go on, check it out. Cass has the nicest room in the house."

"Gram…"

"Go, go. Just don't get into any funny business," she says, then bursts into laughter.

Okay. Now I'm the one blushing. We're both blushing. Cass tilts his head toward a hallway and I follow after him, the both of us silent until we walk into his room.

"I'm sorry," he says after he halfway closes the door. "My grandma doesn't leave the house much, so when she meets someone for the first time, she tends to get a little out there."

"Oh, is she homebound?" She seemed to move around just fine, but you never know.

"Nah, she's just antisocial. Claims she hates people." He chuckles and goes to his closet. "Let me grab a sweatshirt and then we'll go."

I glance around his room, not noticing anything unusual or particularly special. It's your average teenage boy's room, though a little on the larger size, with a giant king size bed dominating the space. The furniture is dark oak and looks old, but it works. There are Japanese anime posters all over the walls and I study them, then look over at Cass.

He's got a sheepish expression on his face. "I used to be really into anime."

"Used to be?" I take in all the posters yet again.

"I still sort of am, but I don't have time to watch them anymore, or to discover any new ones. When I was thirteen, fourteen, I was obsessed."

"Clearly." I'm smiling, and he smiles, too.

"I wanted to go to Japan. Still do."

"Is that why you plan to join the military?"

His smile fades. "Who told you that?"

"Your grandma." When he stares at me blankly, I continue. "You know, the woman you live with."

"I haven't mentioned the military to her in a long time. In years," he finally says with a slow shake of his head.

"Well, she thinks that's what you plan on doing once you graduate high school."

"Not even close." He hesitates. "What else did she say?" he asks with a wince, like he's afraid to find out.

"Um, she mentioned that you have a half sister you never see and that your mama is never going to get out of prison," I tell him, a little embarrassed on his behalf.

He covers his face for a brief moment before dropping his hands and staring up at the ceiling. "She really said that?"

"She did."

"So humiliating," he mutters before he lowers his head, his gaze on mine. "You know about my mom."

"Only rumors."

"Right. You know the standard 'his mom murdered his dad' rumor, then."

I nod. "Yeah." This is incredibly awkward, talking about the rumors that involve him, *with* him.

"Someday I'll tell you the full story." He grabs a black — surprise, surprise — sweatshirt off a hanger from his closet and slips it over his head, tugging down until it fully covers him. "Ready to go?"

"Why does your grandma say your room is the best one in the house?" I ask.

"Oh. Because of this." He goes to the window and pulls back the curtains, revealing the fog-shrouded ocean view. "Tonight's not so great though, what with the fog."

"So you have the best view right out your bedroom

window." I walk over to the window and stare outside. I see my car, the moonlight gleaming off the white paint. See the houses, the city lights below, and the fog that's slowly creeping into town. The fog seems lit from within, almost like it's glowing, and an ominous shiver moves through me.

I'm suddenly scared to go to Courtney's house. I'd rather stay here with Cass. Or maybe I could take him back to my house and we could watch movies with my sister and mom. That would be risky because they'd both probably interrogate him and I'd have to make up some lie about why Dani and I aren't at the movies after all, but I'd rather face their questions than go to Court's stupid party.

"I definitely have the best view." He stops right beside me and I turn to look at him. His gaze drops to the front of my sweater and he frowns. "You have cat hair all over you." He reaches out and starts wiping at my chest, his fingers brushing against my breasts, and I freeze.

He freezes, too, his fingers hovering for the briefest moment before he drops his hand. "Sorry," he mutters. "I didn't mean—"

"It's okay," I reassure him. "Really. No big deal."

His cheeks are flushed. "You want a lint brush? I have one in my bathroom. Always gotta have it if you live here, what with all the cats my grandma has."

"How many are there?"

"Eight."

Yikes.

He grabs me a lint brush and I attack my sweater, taking off as much white cat hair as I can. Once that's done, he guides me back out to the living room with a hand resting lightly on my lower back.

It's like I can feel his fingers pressing into my skin, making me hyperaware that he's touching me. Which is strangely exciting, because he's Cass Vincenti and he's kind of weird. So is his grandma, what with their jumble of a house and all the cats.

But every time he looks at me with those dark, mysterious eyes, my heart speeds up. And I can't help but appreciate how different he is—because he is *so* different. The complete opposite of Robby and every other boy I've dated in the past.

"Grams, we gotta go," he announces.

"Penelope." She pops out of the recliner and rises to her feet, the white cat falling off her lap with a snotty meow. She approaches me and rests her jeweled hands on my cheeks, making me suck in a breath. Her palms are ice cold. "It was so lovely to meet you. You're a treat. Cass, be a gentleman with this young lady tonight, okay?"

"Okay, Grams," he says, amusement tingeing his voice.

She drops her hands and pulls me into a hug. All I can smell is her overpowering perfume, and I try my best not to cough. "Have fun, you two. Be safe!"

He leads me outside and toward my car, holding out his hand when he stops by the driver's side. "Keys?"

I'm reluctant to hand them over. "You really want to drive my car?"

"I definitely want to drive." He runs a hand along the top, his long fingers seeming to caress the car. Now I'm actually feeling jealous, which is so stupid. "Let me drive, okay? I don't know what sort of situation we're going into."

"You don't trust my driving abilities?" I'm teasing him, but I'm also sort of offended. Because seriously, he doesn't trust my driving abilities?

"I'd rather be in control tonight," he says, his expression, his gaze serious. "Like I said earlier, I don't want anything to happen to you."

"Why me?" I ask, like I can't help myself. "I really—I don't get it."

He takes a step closer to me, his gaze dropping to my lips for a lingering moment. Like he might want to kiss them. And I sort of want him to, which is crazy. Totally crazy. "I told you," he says, his voice low. "I've liked you for a while now. I never thought you noticed me."

I don't want to tell him I didn't, so I say nothing. The crazy thing is, Gretchen's murder has brought us closer together. And I'm starting to realize he's a nice guy. An interesting guy. "You're very sweet," I tell him.

Cass smiles. "No one's called me sweet before."

I'm sure. "So you're not going to let me drive?"

"No." He slowly shakes his head. "I want to be in control of tonight. In case something crazy goes down. That way I can keep you safe."

How can I protest that? He's being protective. I kind of like it. I'm all about being an independent woman, but sometimes, a girl needs a partner. Someone to help her.

And I'm thinking tonight, Cass can be my partner.

I hand over the keys and drop them in his open palm. "Here you go."

He grips them tight and smiles at me. "You ready?"

"As I'll ever be," I say as I heave out a big sigh.

"You look pretty," he murmurs as his gaze sweeps over me. "Sorry about the cat fur, though."

I start to laugh. "Your grandma's cute."

"My grandma's crazy."

He leads me over to the passenger side of my car and opens the door for me. I climb inside and let him shut the door.

Nerves bubble in my stomach, but I try to ignore them. We're going to be just fine tonight. It's no big deal.

As long as we stick together.

CHAPTER TWENTY-TWO

We head up Courtney's long, winding driveway and Cass whistles low, shaking his head. "I know all the houses in my neighborhood are big, but Courtney's house is—huge."

That's an understatement. The Jenkins house is beyond impressive. Twenty thousand square feet, so many rooms you can get lost inside trying to find your way around. They have a full-time staff that will attend to your every need, including a chef. There are two pools, a tennis court, an indoor basketball court, and a massive garden where her mother grows her grand prize–winning roses. Her mother is obsessed with roses.

Courtney says that's because her mom is such a prickly bitch.

There are parking attendants working the party, so Cass reluctantly hands over my keys to the valet, giving me a look as he does so. "You okay with this?"

I shrug. "Do we have a choice?"

We watch my car drive away before we slowly start to

approach the house, me busy Snapchatting Dani in the hopes she'll get us in through the back door while Cass openly gawks at the beautiful landscaping.

"This place looks like a park," he says.

"You act like you've never been to one of these houses up here before," I tell him, my gaze glued to my phone.

"I haven't," he says. I look up at him with a frown. "What? It's true. I don't get out much."

"Why?"

He shrugs. "I don't know. Most people who live around here consider my grandma and me outcasts. They don't always treat us that great."

"Really? So like, your neighbors are mean to you?" I know a bunch of rich snobs live up here, but I figured they embraced everyone in the neighborhood.

"They're not mean. They just…ignore us. It hurts Gram's feelings." His expression turns sad. "That's why she doesn't go out much."

"That's awful," I murmur just as my phone buzzes with a Snapchat from Dani. I open it up to see a photo of her and Brogan Pearson, their cheeks pressed against each other's and a giant smile on her face.

It's captioned, **LOOK WHO'S MINE TONIGHT!**

Ha. Wonder if Courtney knows about this.

I send Dani a quick reply.

Me: I'm here with Cass. Will you let us in through the backyard?

She answers me immediately.

Dani: Casssss???? Wowowowowow.

I send her another message.

Me: Will you let us in?

Dani: Yeah but hurry up! I don't want to lose Brogan.

"Let's go." I take Cass's hand and lead him up the walkway until we reach the house. I avoid the front porch, which is packed with people from school, and dart around the side of the house, my fingers clutched tight around Cass's. His hand is warm and his fingers and palm are calloused. People pass by us and I catch them looking at our linked hands. I'm sure they'll be talking about us come Monday morning.

Great.

I see Dani bouncing around near the back door that leads to the kitchen. She's got on a tiny floral print dress with a flouncy skirt, and every time she hops, her skirt rises higher. Brogan is right behind her, clutching a beer in his hand and tilting his head to the side. I know he's just waiting to catch a glimpse of her panties.

Ugh. Perv.

"There you are!" Dani exclaims as she runs toward us. Her eyes are bright, her pupils huge, and I can tell she's already a few cups in. "Who's your date?" she asks as she eyes Cass up and down. "Wait! That's right! It's Cass Vincenti! What are *you* doing with my Penny?"

"We came together," he says, holding up our intertwined hands.

"Oh! My God!" She grabs hold of me and I have no choice but to let go of Cass's hand as she pulls me into a hug. "You bad girl you, totally going against type," she whispers in my ear.

"Stop." I shove her away from me and we're both laughing. "Where's Courtney?" I want to avoid her as much as possible, which means I need to keep tabs on her whereabouts at all times.

"She's in the rec room. Don't worry about her." Dani trips over her own feet, and Brogan magically appears by her side, cupping her elbow so she doesn't fall on her face. "She's too busy talking to all of her subjects."

I frown. "Her subjects?"

"You know, she's now the queen and we're all her subjects or servants or whatever? Yeah, that." Dani grabs the beer out of Brogan's hand and drains it.

"Hey," he protests, sounding truly irritated.

"Go get another for us!" She turns and grabs Brogan, giving him a loud, smacking kiss on his cheek. "Please?"

"I'll be right back." He looks at Cass and flicks his chin. "Want anything, dude?"

"No thanks, Bro." The worst thing about Brogan's name is everyone can call him Bro and it works because he really is a Bro. It's kind of lame in that macho, bromance/dude way. "Want me to come with and help out?"

I send him a look, one that I hope says, *what about us sticking together?*

"Nah, I got this. Want a drink, Penny?" Brogan asks me.

"I'll take a beer, please." I wonder if Cass refused a drink because he's a recovering alcoholic. Or maybe he did drugs and now he's completely sober? I wish I could ask him, but when is there ever a right time to ask that type of question?

Oh hey man, just wondering when exactly you fell apart and became an addict? Curious minds want to know.

"Be right back," Brogan tells us before he lays a sloppy kiss on Dani's lips and then walks away.

"He is sooooo great," she says dreamily as she turns and watches him saunter into the house. "And he has the best butt."

Cass clears his throat, and I can tell he's trying not to laugh.

"Hey." Dani points at Cass, her eyes narrowed. "Don't laugh. You've got a great butt, too."

Oh. My. God.

"Thanks," he says amusedly, his gaze meeting mine. "Maybe you should lay off the beer, Danielle."

"No thanks, *Dad*. I'm perfectly happy getting my drink on." Her eyes go wide when she sees the crazy look on my face, and I swear, she's about to cry. "Oh wow, I am so, *so* sorry for calling you *Dad*, because like, you don't have a dad, since your mom killed him. And that's just terrible! I had no business calling you that. Do you forgive me, Cass? Do you?" She walks over to him and drapes herself all over his front, her arms going around his neck as she presses her face against his chest. "Forgive me, Cass? Please?" Her voice is muffled against his sweatshirt.

He slowly disentangles her from him and hands her over to me. "I forgive you, Dani. I swear."

"Thank goodness." She slips her arm around my shoulders and gives me a side squeeze before she points with her free hand around the backyard. "So many people! I wonder how much money Courtney has raised for the charity tonight?"

"What charity? Come on. You know she's going to pocket it all," I say with a catty smile.

"Noooo." Dani shakes her head. "She wouldn't do that. That's sooo messed up."

"Well…" I let my voice drift and then the both of us start laughing.

"Yeah, she's totally messed up," Dani agrees, smiling in Cass's direction. "Hey Cass."

"Yeah?"

"Why is your name Cass?"

Dani gets even sillier than normal when she's drunk.

"It's the name my parents gave me," he answers.

"Like your dead dad gave you that name?"

I could slap my hand over her mouth but it wouldn't be a good enough muzzle.

"Yeah, like my dead dad." At least he has a sense of humor. And plenty of tolerance for drunk girls.

"Is Cass short for something?" Dani asks.

"Nope, I'm just Cass," he says with a smile, his gaze briefly meeting mine. I smile back, giving him a helpless look. I can't defend her. She's flat-out silly when she's drunk, saying whatever first comes to her mind. As in, there's no real filter.

"I'm going to call you Just Cass from now on, okay?" Dani laughs. "Okay, Just Cass?"

"Sure."

"Maybe we should go into the house," I suggest. The backyard is crammed full with people and it's getting cold out here. There are giant heat lamps scattered throughout the large back patio, but they're still not giving off enough warmth. A wind has kicked up, and it's going to bring the fog toward the mountain soon, I'm sure of it. And once that happens, the temperature will drop fast.

"Let's wait for Brogan to come back first with our beers. Then we'll go inside." Dani frowns at Cass. "You really didn't want a beer?"

"I don't drink," he tells her easily.

"Right, because you're a former addict or whatever." Dani waves a careless hand, waving her equally careless statement away. "Look! There's Brogan! Brooooooogan!" She pushes away from me and makes her way toward Brogan, greeting him with a big hug and almost making him drop his beers.

I turn to look at Cass, noting how pale his face is. His gaze meets mine, his expression solemn, his mouth a straight, thin line. He says nothing for a moment, and neither do I.

"You want to go inside?" I ask.

"Do you? Or do you want to get your beer from Brogan?" He nods toward where Brogan and Dani are standing.

"Maybe it's best if I'm sober tonight," I tell him, my voice low, my gaze on his. I wish he knew that I understood, that I wouldn't pressure him or ask about the addiction problem. Though I am curious. I wish I could just ask him what's going on and that he would be honest with me.

But we don't know each other well enough. Not yet. I don't feel right in asking him such invasive questions.

"It probably is best," he murmurs, reaching out to brush a stray strand of hair away from my face. I suck in a breath when his fingers lightly skim my cheek and then he's smiling at me, a soft, intimate smile that I've never seen from him before. "I know you're dying to ask me like a million questions after what Dani said, but we'll talk later, okay?"

I nod, unable to speak. My throat is too thick with some foreign emotion I can't identify.

Cass leans in so close, his mouth is by my ear. "I want to go inside and find Courtney's room," he whispers. "Will you take me?"

I nod again. "What are you looking for in there?"

"I think she's hiding something." His mouth brushes against my ear, making me shiver. "I think she's more involved in this whole thing than she's letting on."

Could that be true? I have never truly suspected Courtney. I know she hated Gretchen and most likely Lex, too. But did she hate them enough to actually kill them?

I don't think so.

"What exactly do you mean?" I pull away so I can look him in the eyes. "Do you think Courtney is…the *murderer*? You told me earlier you thought she was too obvious to be the killer."

He glances around to make sure no one is paying us any attention before his gaze returns to mine. "Maybe she's too obvious on purpose. I don't know. But I want to search her room. See if I can find anything."

"What are you hoping to find?"

"Evidence. Clues." He grins and looks excited, a little reckless. "Whatever." Taking my hand, he pulls me toward the back door. "Come on, Pen. Live on the edge with me."

CHAPTER TWENTY-THREE

I wait for Cass by the back staircase, the one that leads up to the private bedrooms in the west wing of the house. Yes, this house has actual wings, and I sort of got lost at first, which is why I was smart not to drink tonight.

Dani is so trashed, and it's barely ten. We left her in the backyard with Brogan, the both of them cuddled up on a plush lounge chair, Dani's head lolling on Brogan's shoulder as he chugged yet another beer.

I have to remember to go back outside in a little bit to make sure she's okay, even though Brogan promised that he'd watch over her. For the most part he's a decent guy, just annoying, but he's also messing around with Courtney on the side. I don't want him to hurt Dani.

And I don't know how to stop it.

Later I should probably tell her what I know about Court and Brogan, but I can't do it now. I need to help Cass.

Speaking of Cass, he went in search of Courtney to make sure she's still downstairs, before we head up to her room. The only reason he left me alone is because I told him I would be okay as long as there was a bathroom nearby that I could lock myself in. Besides, how long could he take? He's currently headed for the rec room, where Dani said Court was holding court over her subjects.

I frown just thinking of Courtney acting so haughty, like she rules the world. Makes me realize I was never the queen bee of school. Just because my sister was doesn't mean I am.

No, I'm pretty sure that's Courtney's title.

Court's taking this feud between us way too seriously, trying to divide everyone on either her side or mine. More than a few girls have walked by me with a sneer on their faces as they looked me up and down. Like I'm nothing but trash.

I've never had that happen before.

Dani sends me a Snapchat and I open it up to find a photo of her kissing Brogan and a bunch of heart eyes and kissy-face emojis.

I take a selfie of me making a mean face and send it to her, with the caption SMH.

That's directed right at Brogan, not that he'll get it.

I get another Snapchat, but this one isn't from Dani. It's from Cass, and it's a photo of Courtney wearing a tight white shirt and extremely short black shorts, dancing on the pool table in the rec room with her hands up in the air. He drew a red arrow pointing at Courtney's head and captioned the photo:

THE WICKED WITCH OF THE WEST IS IN HER ELEMENT, SO WE'RE GOOD.

Smiling, I send him back a quick response telling him to hurry and then shove my phone into the back pocket of my jeans.

"Hey, Penelope. What are *you* doing here?"

I turn to find Maggie and Alyssa standing in front of me, tentative smiles on their faces.

"Hi, girls." I smile, but it quickly fades when I notice the strange way they're watching me. "Everything okay?"

"Um, yes. It's great!" Alyssa smiles brightly, but it doesn't quite reach her eyes. "Are you having fun?"

"Time of my life," I say just as enthusiastically.

Maggie is staring at me like I'm a bug under a microscope. "I thought you weren't coming tonight."

"I changed my mind." I shrug.

"Courtney is telling everyone that you weren't invited. And that she didn't want you here." Her voice drops to a whisper. "But I guess she was lying?"

"No, she's right." I keep the smile in place, though deep inside I'm white hot with anger. Court's actually *telling everyone* she doesn't want me here? "I decided to come anyway."

"You're so brave to show your face at her house," Alyssa murmurs.

My smile is gone in an instant. "Why do you say that?" I snap.

"Because she's saying the worst things about you, Penelope," Maggie starts, but clamps her lips shut when Alyssa jabs her in the ribs with her elbow.

"Like what? What is she saying?" When they remain silent, I get even angrier. "Tell me!"

"She complained that you're a lunatic who's losing control of the Larks. How you're freaking out over all the girls dying on your watch, and that you feel responsible. And she warned that if you don't watch it, you're going to be the next one dead, since you're the biggest bitch of all." Maggie takes a deep breath after she rambled on, like it took everything within her to tell me the nasty rumors Courtney is spreading.

"Oh my God, she is such a *bitch*!" I spit the last word out, so mad I can hardly see straight. No wonder Gretchen and Lex hated Courtney so much. She's awful.

I hate her, too.

"We just thought you should know," Alyssa squeaks out, stepping back when I glare at her. "We're so sorry."

Cass chooses that moment to make his appearance, frowning when he catches me seething. I'm so pissed I'm surprised there's not steam coming out of my ears. "You okay?" he asks me, slipping his arm around my shoulders and pulling me close to his side. I try not to focus on how warm and solid he is, but it's like I can't help myself. I sort of melt into him.

I shake my head as Alyssa and Maggie scurry off. Not that I can blame them for wanting to leave. "Courtney's spreading rumors about me," I tell him.

"Who cares?" He steers me toward the stairs and we start walking up them. "She's a bitch. Forget her."

"I can't, Cass." I try to wiggle out of his grasp and he lets me go. "She called me a lunatic and said I deserve to die just like Gretchen and Lex did!"

He pauses at the top of the steps and I stop with him, his gaze meeting mine. "She said you *deserved* to die?"

I nod, my anger dissipating and being replaced with frustration. Sadness. I swear, if I start crying, that's going to make me even madder. "I hate her!"

"Come on. Don't let her get to you." He interlocks his fingers with mine. "Which door is hers?"

"Last one on the left."

Cass practically drags me over to the door, and I can't help but think the little smirk he sends my way when he discovers the door easily opens is cute. Even through my anger over this entire situation, I still find him attractive.

I don't know what this says about me.

We enter the room quietly, and I hear Cass suck in a breath.

"What the hell? This room is *huge*," he says. "It's as big as my freaking house."

"I know. She's spoiled rotten." I go to her bedside table and turn on the lamp, illuminating the room with soft light.

"You think we should have that on?"

"It's better than using the flashlights on our phones. What if someone sees the beams of light flashing around in the darkness? Talk about suspicious," I tell him.

"You're right." He rests his hands on his hips and surveys the room. "You want to help me search through her stuff?"

"Gladly." This is some sort of revenge thing on my part, but I don't care. I'm so done with her, it's not even funny.

"Cool. I'll start with her desk."

"I'll dig through her bedside table." That's where I tend to hide my most private or secretive items. Not that I have much. There are a few actual handwritten notes I saved from middle school boyfriends that I put in a special envelope and marked private, because at fourteen I wasn't that subtle. Old jewelry that were gifts from exes that I don't want to wear but can't part with, either. There's even a book Dani gave me when I turned sixteen that's called *Mastering the Female Orgasm*. She thought it was hilarious, but once I started reading, I found it fascinating.

Yeah. Private stuff you don't want anyone else to find, you know?

I open the top drawer and find it full of old receipts, a bunch of Eos lip balms, a TV remote, a fan remote, and a tangle of old iPhone chargers. I rifle through all of it, digging until I reach the bottom. Broken earrings, a photo of me, Court, and Gretchen from our freshman year, wearing our cheer uniforms and standing by the sidelines.

Pulling the photo out, I stare at it. We look happy. Young. Carefree. Now Gretchen is dead. Courtney is a total bitch. And I'm searching through Court's stuff like some sort of thief.

I shove the photo back into the drawer and feel around some more, pulling out a tiny, carefully folded piece of notepaper. I unfold it, blinking as I try to read the small handwriting.

You are so hot and sexy as fuck I love to look at your naked body you don't show it to me enough when are you going to send me pictures again? I want more

Whoa.

"I think I found something," I say quietly.

Cass turns away from the desk, his eyes wide. "What?"

I hold out the piece of paper and he takes it from me, his eyebrows shooting up as he reads it. When he's done, his gaze meets mine. "Who do you think wrote it?"

"I don't know." I shrug, and he hands the note back to me. "It could be old. Or it could be recent."

"Is she hooking up with anyone right now that you know of?"

"I thought *you* were hooking up with her."

"I'm not." He shakes his head. "I mean, we sort of did. We kissed once. A long time ago. But it was nothing."

"Nothing? Really?" I stand, clutching the note in my right hand so tight I'm wrinkling the paper. "You told me you two hooked up, when we met at the coffee shop and talked in my car. You said Gretchen and Courtney were *fighting* over you, so that doesn't sound like nothing, you know? You made it sound like you were…I don't know… hooking up with both of them?"

"They were fighting over me, but not over that kind of

thing. It's just—" He sighs and tilts his head back, staring at the ceiling. "I know stuff about them. Both of them. Stuff they wouldn't want to get out."

I watch him, my heart beating in my throat as I wait for him to continue.

"What do you know?" I ask when he doesn't say anything.

He looks down at the floor. "What Dani said earlier? It's true."

"About being an…"

"Addict. Yeah." His gaze finally meets mine, and his eyes are so dark, they're almost black. "So was Gretchen. And so is Courtney. That's what they were fighting over. We'd all see each other at our meetings, and they got jealous if I spent more time with one than the other. I would talk to them, and listen to them when they complained about their problems. No one else got them but me."

"What, so they didn't want to share you when you guys had your special powwows during your weekly meetings?" My voice is sharper than I intended, but this is some crazy crap.

"Don't make fun of us," he snaps back. "This shit is hard. You don't know what it's like."

"Right, so being an addict is Courtney's excuse for also being such a bitch?"

Cass shakes his head. "I never said that."

"It doesn't matter. We're getting off track." I look down and carefully refold the note I'm holding with shaky fingers. "I know that Courtney is currently messing around with Brogan Pearson."

"Wait a minute. Are you serious?"

I shove the note in my back pocket. I assume it's from him. "Yeah. They're sexting each other. She admitted that much to me. I'm guessing they're doing more than that, but

I don't have proof."

"What about Dani? Does she know?"

"Courtney doesn't give a shit about anyone as long as she gets what she wants." I raise a brow. "You haven't realized that yet?"

Cass is watching me carefully. Too carefully. "You're mad at me."

"No shit."

Sighing, he looks away, his gaze seeming to search the room. "Let's just finish looking through this stuff, and then we'll leave."

"No, I'm ready to go. I'm over this." I shove all the crap back into her bedside table drawer as haphazardly as I found it and slam the drawer shut. "You with me?"

"Come on, Pen. Don't act like this," he says, his voice pleading as he makes his way back to her desk. "Just…give me a few more minutes."

I stare at his wide back as he bends over the desk and resumes his search through one of the drawers. But I can tell he's not getting anywhere. All he's pulling out is a bunch of old schoolwork and notebooks. "You totally conned me into coming to this party with you."

His back goes still. "I didn't con you."

"You so did."

He glances at me from over his shoulder. "You wanted to come tonight."

"I really didn't. I was disinvited. Remember?" Oh, I'm just saying this like I want to start a fight. What's wrong with me?

"You said you wanted to help." He stacks all the stuff he pulled out of one drawer and shoves it back in before he moves on to the next one. "And now what? You're pissed because I have a secret past with Gretchen and Courtney?

Don't tell me you're jealous."

"You're an asshole," I throw out at him, and I get the satisfaction of watching him flinch.

"You're just upset because Courtney's talking shit," he mutters. "Why don't you go sit on the bed and chill out."

I do as he says, annoyed at him. Pissed at myself. He's right. I did want to come this party with him. And I sort of wanted to do it as a big F U to Courtney, too. And I am mad that she's talking shit about me, and that he has this intimate past with girls I wish he'd never met.

But are we even on a real date here? Does he really want to be with me? Or did he bring me because I could take him to Court's room so we can search it and hopefully wouldn't get caught?

I feel kind of skeevy just thinking about it. I'm lowering myself to Courtney's level. She would totally do something like this without a second thought. Hell, she'd probably think it was her right, to dig up information on other people.

Taking a deep breath, I remind myself to chill and check out my Snapchat, my mind on the note in my back pocket, on the things Courtney said about me, on Dani and how she's totally being played. Everyone sucks. The school year has hardly begun, and it's already a complete disaster. I wish I could graduate early. I'd shut down the Larks, quit cheer, and escape to the college of my choice, which will hopefully accept me with wide-open arms. I'd never have to come back to stupid Cape Bonita, ever. We could convince my parents to sell the house, retire, and move somewhere awesome.

And I am firmly planted in dreamland right now, let me tell you.

The more I watch Cass digging through the desk drawers, the madder I get. He totally brought me here to get into her room. That's it. Besides, he's not even finding anything.

I'm the one with the only interesting discovery. I want out of here. Screw Cass.

Voices come from down the hall. A girl shrieking and yelling, "No! Stop! Put me down!"

I look up just as Cass whirls around, his hands full of papers and bullshit from the desk. "That was Courtney," I whisper.

"Are you sure?" His eyes are wide and panicked.

Nodding, I rush toward him and help him shove everything back into the desk, slamming the drawer shut with a gentle *thud*. I can hear the voices drawing closer, Courtney laughing and sounding like a drunk idiot, accompanied by a low, male voice repeatedly telling her she likes it.

"Closet," Cass whispers, and I follow after him, quietly shutting the door. My breaths are coming fast, as are Cass's, but we have to keep our mouths shut. If Courtney finds us lurking in her closet, we are so dead.

"Be quiet," I tell Cass, though I can't really see him, it's so dark inside. But the front of the closet door is slotted, allowing in shards of light, and I can sort of make out his face. "Try not to breathe so loud. If she hears us, we're done for."

He nods and swallows hard, as if he's trying to control himself. I lean back, my head against the wall, my butt wedged in between a pile of shoes. Cass sits opposite me, his long legs bent at the knees and his feet planted on the floor.

The bedroom door swings open and I lean forward, squinting through the door slats so I can see who's with Courtney.

"I could swear I didn't leave the light on when I left," Courtney says almost to herself, striking fear into my already overworked heart.

But she forgets all about the lamp in an instant.

"Put me down, Bro!" She's pummeling Brogan's back with her fists, laughing and shaking her ponytail. "And stop putting your hands all over my ass!"

I look at Cass, who's suddenly sitting right next to me and is also peering through the slats. We both roll our eyes.

This is probably going to escalate fast.

CHAPTER TWENTY-FOUR

"Where's Dani?" Courtney asks after Brogan drops her onto her giant bed. I swear it's custom-made, the mattress has to be bigger than a king and outfitted with the fluffiest, pinkest comforter I've ever seen.

"She's passed out. I left her on the lounger outside. Put a blanket over her and everything. A bunch of junior girls were sitting on the loungers by her. Some of those Lark girls you don't like." Brogan's still standing by the end of the mattress with his hands on his hips and his back to us. I wish I could see his face. "You should be happy with me. I got Dani totally wasted just like you told me to."

"Good." I can hear the smugness in Courtney's voice, and it makes my stomach turn. She's so mean. She knows how much Dani likes Brogan, how she's been after him for what feels like the majority of our high school lives. And she actually told Brogan to get Dani wasted on purpose?

I wish I could call her. Text her. But I don't want to make a wrong move and let them know we're hiding out in the closet. So we're stuck here while Courtney is with Brogan in her room. I know something is about to go down.

Ew. And we're trapped in the closet. We won't have to watch but we'll still have to hear everything.

Double ew.

"I have a theory," Brogan says, his voice serious, which is a surprise. Brogan's rarely, if ever, serious.

"What is it?" Courtney scoots toward the top of the mattress, her back pressed against a gigantic pile of pillows. I can see her face, the amused tilt of her lips, the way she's hungrily watching Brogan.

Who is currently pulling his shirt off and dropping it onto the floor.

I cover my eyes but keep listening.

"I think you like me because I like Dani." He hesitates, like he's afraid to mention the next theory. "I bet you're one of those girls who always wants what you can't have."

I drop my hands from my face. Wait a minute. He actually *likes* Dani? Then what the hell is he doing with Court?

"You don't really like her," Courtney says in that blasé way of hers. "You just like the *idea* of Dani. How she chases after you like a hyperactive puppy dog, always wanting to please you and tell you how great you are. She's your biggest fan and you love it."

"Yeah." He chuckles. "I do kinda love it when she makes a big deal about me. She's just so into me, you know? Who wouldn't love that?"

I roll my eyes and send a look to Cass, who quirks his lips.

"But after a while, doesn't all that adoration get... annoying?" Courtney asks. "Old? Cloying—"

"What do you mean?" Brogan interrupts.

Courtney growls irritably. She hates having to explain herself. "She suffocates you, Brogan. She doesn't understand that sometimes, a guy just wants to get off, you know? And that's it. That's all you want. Your needs are simple."

"Hell yeah, they are. I'm a simple dude." I can hear the sound of his zipper going down. "All Dani wants is me to be her boyfriend. Like, she wants a real relationship. But maybe I don't want that. Why's everything gotta be so serious all the time? I just wanna fuck, you know?"

"I do know. I know exactly what you mean. And all I want is for you to get naked with me." Her voice is low. Seductive. She makes what they have seem so easy. What horny boy wouldn't be drawn to that? Drawn to her? "So get in my bed, Bro. Let's get naked together." She hesitates, and I swear I hear Brogan swallow extra loud. "You know you want me."

Okay. That's it. I can't take it. I send a panicked look in Cass's direction, and he backs away from the closet door, so I do the same. He straightens out and reaches into the front pocket of his jeans, pulling out a pair of ear buds, then waves his hand at me to scoot closer to him.

So I do, curious to see how he's going to solve our problem. I can hear Courtney and Brogan kissing, and the loud, wet sounds of their mouths connecting over and over again? It's gross. I like sexy scenes in movies, don't get me wrong, but I don't want to see this sort of stuff live and in person, with two people I know and go to school with five days a week.

It's like watching Courtney and Brogan's own personal porn video come to life.

No, thank you.

Cass slips his head under his sweatshirt and thrusts his hands under it, too. I see his phone light up through the dark fabric and I realize what he's doing. He doesn't want Courtney or Brogan to see the light coming from his phone. He's tapping away at the screen, then he plugs the ear buds into the jack. His head pops back up through the neck hole and he pushes the hoodie back, resting his index finger against his lips.

I don't think we have to be deathly quiet any longer. Those two aren't paying attention to anything else but each other.

"Come here," Cass says in the softest whisper. "Get really close to me."

I do as he asks, until I'm pressed up next to his side. He hands me an ear bud and I take it, putting it in my left ear. He slips the other ear bud in his right ear and then he turns on some music.

I've never been so thankful for a bunch of loud, alternative, angsty music in all my life. I concentrate hard, focusing all my attention on the music, and I realize quick we're drowning out the sounds of Courtney and Brogan hooking up. Cass smiles at me and I return it, startled when he leans in close and whispers in my ear bud–free ear, "You like it?"

I shrug and whisper back, "Sort of."

"I can change it. I have a few different playlists." His mouth is so close to my ear again, I swear his lips brush the sensitive skin. I shiver, my shoulder pressing into his chest, and then he's grabbing me by the waist, hauling me onto his lap.

"Ssh," he whispers when I go tense. I can tell he knows I want to protest, but it's only because I'm scared. "Relax. We don't want them to find us."

I sit in his lap, his arms encircling me, making me feel protected and safe. I try to concentrate on the music that's still playing, but all I can focus on is Cass's warmth and strength. The width of his chest, how thick his arms are, how my butt is perched on his thigh. We are sitting so close it would take nothing for me to wrap my arms around his neck and push his head down so our lips would meet.

But I don't do that. I can't. I don't have the guts, and besides, I'm still sort of pissed at him for using me to get inside her room. I really don't fully trust him, either.

The music is turned down and then Cass's mouth is right at my ear.

"I'm sorry for what I said earlier," he murmurs. "I was a total jackass."

"You were," I agree, making him chuckle. "But so was I."

"You still have that note on you? The one you found?"

"I do."

He stares off into space. "Wonder who wrote it."

"You think it was Brogan? They kept talking about getting naked." And the note mentioned getting naked, too.

"Maybe. Or maybe it's someone else." His arms tighten around me.

"Did you ever get naked with Court?"

His gaze meets mine, his eyes intense even in the darkness. "No."

"How about Gretchen?" My voice rises, and Cass rests his finger over my lips for the briefest moment before removing it.

"Becoming…intimate with each other would've been a huge mistake, and I tried to avoid it. We were messed up enough on our own. We didn't need to enable each other."

He sounds like a psychologist. "Did they want to get with you?"

"I don't know." He does this half shrug that jostles me even closer to him. "Maybe. Maybe not."

He turns up the music just as the current song ends and a new one begins. This one is slow, the lyrics sad. I recognize the song but don't remember who sang it, and we remain quiet, the both of us listening until I hear a low groan come from the bedroom, followed by a feminine whimper.

I immediately lift my head, my gaze meeting Cass's and we make faces at each other. "So gross," I whisper.

"Yeah." His gaze drops to my lips and lingers there. "Hope they don't take too long."

"Knowing Brogan, he's probably incredibly selfish. He'll be finished in a few minutes." This reminds me of my orgasm book, which, of course, makes my cheeks go hot.

"You don't think he'll care if Courtney gets off or not?" I know he's repeating the same things Court just said, but it's still embarrassing. Which is dumb, because I'm a girl who's tried her best to embrace her sexuality, even if I haven't had much sex in my life (those few times with Robby were super awkward and not that satisfying, at least for me).

Sitting with Cass like this, being so close to him, makes me hyperaware of everything about him. His clean, tinged-with-fabric-softener scent. The sound of his breathing, the beat of his heart. His hair is soft, so are his clothes, and he has angsty taste in music. His shoulders are broad, his thigh is hard beneath my butt, and his chest is firm.

I like him. Despite being angry with him earlier, I can admit that I'm attracted to him. And I think he's attracted to me.

"I'm pretty sure the only person Brogan wants to get off is himself," I mutter under my breath, ducking my head.

Cass chuckles, the warm, deep sound making me shiver. "Most guys are selfish assholes."

"Even you?" I look up to find he's already watching me.

He nods slowly, his gaze dropping to my lips again. "Even me."

"I bet you're not that selfish," I whisper. I am totally flirting with him.

"Oh, I definitely am. Watch me."

And then he does the craziest thing.

Cass leans in, his mouth drawing close. So close, I can feel his breath tickle my lips. I part them, ready to say something, anything to break the sudden tension that's crackling between us, but his mouth lands on mine in an instant.

I suck in a breath, shocked by the jolt of electricity that rushes through my blood when his lips touch mine. We're already completely wrapped up in each other. It feels... natural to kiss him.

His arms tighten around my waist, pulling me into him. I circle my arms around his neck, my fingers sliding into his hair. It's thick and soft, the ends curling around my fingers, and I tunnel my hands deeper into it, savoring the hitch in his breath when I do so.

Our mouths are still connected. We kiss and kiss. Soft, innocent kisses at first, and then I part my lips, and he does too. Our lips linger, the kisses last longer as our breaths accelerate, and then his tongue is there, tracing my lips, circling mine...

It's the hottest kiss I've ever experienced, the both of us trying to be quiet as we secretly make out while hiding in Courtney's closet. His hands go to my waist and he readjusts me so I'm straddling him, and I wrap my legs around his hips. We're chest to chest, his bulky sweatshirt is totally in my way, and I wish I could tear it off him so I can get closer.

But I settle for this. We're kissing for kissing's sake. There's no end game, no trying to get into each other's pants or get each other off, as Courtney so eloquently put it. And it feels so good, to get lost in Cass's arms and lips for a while, to forget about my troubles, to concentrate on the delicious slide of his tongue against mine, his hands in my hair, the race of his heart and the heat of his skin.

Plus, it's Cass. We're giving in to the chemistry that seems to simmer between us every time we're together. There's something between us I'd like to explore, despite all the extra baggage that seems to come with this boy. His dead dad and his murdering mom and his weird grandma with the cluttered house and the cats. His mysterious ways and addiction problem—all of this adds up to a guy I should avoid at all costs.

I don't want to, though. I like him. I think he likes me.

"Are they still in the room?" I ask minutes later, when I finally tear myself away from his lips.

"I don't know," he murmurs against my neck just before he starts kissing it. His lips are warm, his teeth graze my sensitive skin and make me shiver. I clutch him close, frustrated by the stupid hoodie he's wearing, frustrated that we're curled up together in Courtney's stupid closet when I wish we could be somewhere else. Anywhere else...

"Should we check—" I start, but he cuts me off.

"Sshh." Cass gently places his mouth on mine, his teeth tugging on my lower lip, making me whimper in surprise. "Forget them," he whispers just before he kisses me again.

Well. More like he devours me. I can't even blame alcohol for what I'm doing with him at this very moment. I am completely sober. And I am also shoving my hands beneath his hoodie and his shirt, so I can touch his bare skin. My fingers roam over the width of his back and he shivers. I skim my nails along his skin and he sucks in a sharp breath. And then his hands are beneath my sweater and he's touching my back, my hips, my waist, my stomach...

I pull away, his hands falling from underneath my sweater, his eyes lit with surprise. His breaths are coming fast again, and so are mine, though for a different and better reason this time.

"I think they're done," I whisper when I realize they've gone silent on the other side of the closet door.

We stare at each other, the both of us quiet as we wait to hear something come from the bedroom. I focus on calming my breathing, my racing heart. I look down, needing to break away from the intensity of his stare, and his fingers trace my hairline before tucking my hair behind my ear.

Glancing up, I find he's watching me, his eyes full of confusion. "What just happened?" he asks.

I frown. "Out there? I don't know. They're not even talking anymore."

"No." Cass shakes his head. "Right here. Just now. Between us. What was that?"

"We, uh. We kissed," I whisper.

"Yeah. We sure as hell did." He runs a hand through his hair, making it stick up all over the place, and I'm tempted to reach out and smooth it back down just so I can touch it. Touch *him*.

But I restrain myself. For now.

"You don't regret that, do you?" he asks me.

I slowly shake my head, hoping that being honest won't backfire. "No."

"Good." His gaze meets mine, his eyes sparkling. "Me either."

CHAPTER
TWENTY-FIVE

Courtney and Brogan finally left her bedroom a few minutes ago, after hurriedly getting dressed, Courtney hissing at Brogan the entire time that he needed to hurry up.

"You're so uptight after we have sex," he told her, sounding like a petulant child. "You talk a good game before it, but you always make me feel guilty afterwards. Sucks, man."

"Oh, grow up," Courtney snapped. "What do you want me to do? Tell you how great you are like Dani does?"

"At least she seems into me most of the time," he muttered. "Not like you."

"You're such a dick." Courtney's voice dripped with contempt.

And with that, they left.

"Well, that was pleasant," I say once they're gone.

"How long do you think we should wait until we leave?" asks Cass.

"I don't know." I move away from him, giving myself much needed distance. I'm still blown away by Cass's expert kissing skills. Fine, I'm completely rattled by it, rattled by *him*. My hands are shaky. My head is spinning. He has great lips—and I can't help but stare at them. They're full and swollen and still damp from when we kissed. His hair is mussed and his eyes are glazed and he's staring off into space, like his mind was just epically blown.

I sort of love that look on him. Makes me proud that I'm the one who did that.

"We should wait at least a few minutes, just in case they're fighting in the hall or on the staircase or whatever," I tell him.

"Yeah. You're right." He nods, still appearing a little dazed. "Gotta make sure the coast is clear."

"Please tell me you're finished searching through her room." I stand and stretch my arms above my head. My legs are achy and my feet tingle, like they've fallen asleep. We've been cramped up in the closet for a while and I'm dying to get out. See other people, get some fresh air.

Hopefully we won't run into Courtney.

"Yeah, you're right. I'm done." He shrugs and glances around. "If she has any other secrets, I don't know where to look for them."

Probably the closet, but I'm not going to make that suggestion. I am so done going through her things. What we did…it wasn't right. We're just lucky we didn't get caught.

After a few more minutes, we exit the closet and leave Courtney's bedroom, sneaking down the back staircase and along the short hall until we're in the kitchen again. The party is still just as wild and loud as it was before we went upstairs, and I head out to the backyard, in search of Dani.

But she's not on any of the loungers where Brogan said he left her. There are a few couples on the lounge chairs snuggled up together and/or kissing and groping each other.

There are two girls cuddled on one, both of them looking pretty wasted and trying to sleep.

There's no Dani anywhere.

"Where do you think she went?" I turn to look at Cass, and he frowns at me.

"Who are you talking about?"

"Dani! Brogan said he left her out here." I wave a hand at the row of lounge chairs. "But now she's gone."

He scans the backyard before his gaze returns to me. "I don't see her. Brogan's over there with his friends." He points. "Maybe you should ask him."

I shout his name and he looks up, grimacing when he sees it's me. I wave him over, thankful Courtney is nowhere to be found. "Where's Dani?" I ask when he reluctantly approaches.

Brogan shrugs. "I dunno. I left her out here a few minutes ago, but I guess now she's gone."

I cross my arms in front of my chest. "You shouldn't have left her alone, Brogan. She was really drunk. Where'd you go anyway?"

His cheeks turn ruddy and he looks away from me. "I did a few shots with some friends, then I had to take a piss. Why, what's it to you anyway? If you're so concerned about Dani, then you should've stayed with her."

I'd give anything to punch him right now. Just sock him right in his stupid face. Courtney was right. He's a total dick. "I thought *you* were staying with her. She was pretty trashed, *Bro*. You shouldn't have left her alone." I give him a pointed look and he flicks his gaze away from mine, guilt written all over his face. "I just want to make sure she's all right."

"When I left her here on one of the chairs, she was perfectly okay. She was just a little sleepy, you know? I asked if she wanted to come with me, and she said no. She was perfectly fine when I last saw her, I swear," Brogan whines.

"If you see Dani, tell her I'm looking for her," I say, my voice dismissive. Brogan hangs his head and walks away from me to rejoin his friends. The moment he's back standing with them, though, they all laugh and I glance up to find them watching me.

Jackasses.

I check my phone for text messages or Snapchats from Dani, but there's nothing. And it's so cold outside, the fog slowly billowing in, making me shiver. Cass puts a hand on my shoulder, startling me, and I turn to face him.

"Let's go inside. You're cold. I bet she's in the house."

"I don't know. Last time I saw her, she was still outside."

"Yeah, and she probably got cold and wanted to get warm inside." He's talking slowly to me, like I might not understand him, and all I can do is nod as he takes my arm and guides me over to the door. "We'll find her, Pen. Don't worry," he murmurs as he walks me back into the house.

I can't help but worry. What if Dani's in danger? There have been too many scary things happening lately. I leave her alone for a few minutes and now she's gone. Where did she go? Who is she with? What if the killer found her…

If something happened to her, I could never forgive myself.

"Will you help me look for her?" I turn to Cass, grabbing hold of the front of his hoodie and giving him a little shake. "Please? I'm worried. What if—"

"Don't worry," he says, his voice soft. "Yeah, let's go. I'll help you. Dani's gotta be here somewhere." He takes my arm and guides me through the crowded kitchen, down the equally crowded hall, the both of us entering the living room, which is absolutely huge. It's almost obscene, how grand their house is. I look around, seeing all kinds of familiar faces, but not the face I want to see the most.

"Is Dani familiar with the house?" Cass asks me as we wander around the living room.

"Yeah, she's spent the night here a lot." I'm not really listening to what Cass is saying. I'm too busy checking everyone, searching for Dani, and getting more and more frustrated—and scared—when I can't find her.

"Maybe she's on the other side of the house?" Cass suggests when we stop in the mostly empty foyer. "Looks like Courtney is keeping the party on this side, so maybe Dani went to find a quiet spot."

"I don't kn—"

A blood-curling scream rips through the air, rendering both Cass and me completely still. We stare at each other, our mouths hanging open as we wait to hear what comes next and oh, boy, does it *ever* come next.

"OH MY *GOD!!!*"

Cass takes off in the direction where the screams are coming from, heading up a staircase that leads to the east wing of the house. I follow after him, the sounds of the continuous screaming getting louder and louder...

We stop at the top of the stairs, Cass holding out his arms like he doesn't want me to get past him. "Hold on, Pen." His voice is weak. I've never heard him sound like that before. "Stay here."

"What? Why? No, let me go." His arm curls around me, his hand braced on my hip and keeping me behind his back. I struggle against his hold.

"Cass! Thank God you're here! Help me! Help meeee! Oh my God! You're too late! You're too late!"

The hysterical voice is familiar. Female. I know it. I know who it is, I know, I know.

"Shit," Cass mutters, shaking his head, a whimper leaving

him. It's gotta be bad. Whatever he's not letting me see, it has to be awful. I push hard against his arm, breaking away from his grip, and the moment I see it, I wish I would've stayed behind his back.

Courtney is crouched on her knees in the middle of the hall, completely covered in blood. It's in her hair, on her face, all over her clothes and her arms and her legs. Her hair and her eyes and her teeth are stark white against the glistening, deep-red blood, and I stare at her, horrified. She looks like she's walked straight off the set of a horror movie. It doesn't look real.

But it *is* real. And that's what makes it even more terrifying.

My gaze hops everywhere, too afraid to look at one particular thing for too long. Courtney is crying as she bends over and picks up a body that's cradled in her lap. A body I didn't even notice at first.

"No, no, no," Courtney cries, rocking back and forth with the body in her arms. She lifts her head and looks right at me. Her eyes bug out of her head. "I didn't do it! I didn't do it! I swear to God, Penelope! It wasn't me!"

She's holding a girl. Her head is thrown back, her throat cut wide open. I only recognize who it is because she's wearing a floral print dress with a short skirt.

It's Dani.

And she's dead.

CHAPTER TWENTY-SIX

I'm screaming the word *no* over and over again. I'm as hysterical as Courtney is, the both of us screaming and crying and yelling and sobbing. More people run up the stairs and Cass tries his best to block their path, but they all barrel past him, coming to a stop when they see Courtney and Dani.

"Dude! What the fuck!"

"Is this for real?"

"Is that Dani?"

"Holy shit, Courtney killed her!"

"Someone needs to call the cops!"

"Call 911!"

They are all screaming and yelling and pointing fingers and making accusations. Most of them run away. A few of them whip out their phones and actually take photos, maybe even video. If someone Snapchats or Instagrams this or worse—slaps a video up on YouTube of Courtney and Dani covered in blood—I will freaking lose it.

Crap, I'm already losing it.

Cass turns us away from the hall where Courtney is at, his body shielding my view. He holds me close in his arms, and I press my face against the front of his soft, warm hoodie. He pulls his phone out of his pocket and calmly calls 911, reciting Courtney's address and reporting that there's been a murder.

"They'll be here soon," he reassures me when he ends the call. He tightens his arms around me and murmurs words of comfort that I'm not really hearing. All I can think about is Courtney covered in blood, holding Dani close to her. Dani's throat ripped open, the cut jagged and vicious, the blood everywhere.

Everywhere.

It's all I can see, the blood. I squeeze my eyes closed and bury my face against Cass's chest, crying uncontrollably. He runs his hand over my hair but stops talking, thank goodness. The words are useless. Meaningless. My best friend is dead. Two other girls are dead, too. All girls I know. Only Courtney and I are left.

And I think Courtney might've done it. I think she killed those girls.

I lift my head away from Cass's chest and stand on my tiptoes, trying to see over his shoulder. Courtney is still in the hall with Dani in her arms, but people are surrounding them, trying to offer help while others are saying don't move and they shouldn't disturb the crime scene.

The cops show up in less than two minutes, Detectives Spalding and Hughes leading the way. Spalding stops in front of us, his expression somber. "I thought we told you not to come to this party."

Cass just glares at him as I start to cry even harder.

"You two stay right here. We need to talk to you."

"How'd you get here so fast?" Cass asks.

"Surveillance. We've been watching the house since the party started," Spalding explains.

"Big help you were," Cass mutters.

"Who found them first?" Hughes yells as he jogs over to where Courtney and Dani are.

Cass sighs, and I can tell he's reluctant to answer. "We did."

"Uh-huh." Spalding shakes his head and whips out his trusty notepad. "And briefly, tell me what exactly did you see?"

"Courtney in the hall, cradling Dani in her arms. There was...blood everywhere." Cass's voice hitches and he clears his throat. "Dani was already gone. I couldn't tell if Courtney was hurt."

Spalding scribbles furiously on his notepad before stashing it inside his front coat pocket. "Don't leave the premises. You understand me? I'll need a statement from the both of you before you go."

"Yes sir," Cass says with a little salute.

Spalding glares at him for a long moment and then he's gone.

It's total chaos after that. A fleet of cops enters the house, and they guide us all back downstairs as they secure the initial crime scene upstairs. EMTs arrive, running a stretcher up the stairs, another team just behind them with another stretcher.

I can't help but wonder where the body bag is. And that starts me crying all over again.

Because I know I'm going to be in a world of shit if I don't tell them the truth, I text my mom and dad and sister to let them know what happened and that I'm all right. My parents want to come to Court's house and get me, but I tell them I can't leave and they essentially have a total meltdown moment, calling me and demanding that I come home as they practically scream into the phone. They're so mad that I came in the first place.

All I can do is sob and blubber incoherently, so Cass takes the phone away from me and eventually calms my parents down. Then he calls his grandma and reassures her that he's fine, that someone was hurt at the party but we're going to be okay. I even hear her yell at him over the phone, "You better take care of that sweet pumpkin Penelope! She's a good girl! Protect her, Cass!"

Any other time I might've laughed. At the very least I would've smiled.

Now I just cry.

We're all downstairs crowded in the living room and kitchen, the cops watching over us, guarding the doors so no one can slip through and escape. Cass and I are sitting on a couch and I'm leaning forward and perched on the edge of the seat, Cass continuously rubbing my back, trying to comfort me. It's like I can't even feel it, though. I'm completely numb, my throat raw from all the crying, my eyes stinging from the continuous tears. I sniff every once in a while and glance around the room—and I swear I can feel them all staring at me. Watching me. Wondering if I know what happened.

They probably think I'm cursed, and I can't help but think I'm cursed, too. That I'm next. I have to be. Thank God they found Courtney before she could kill someone else. Maybe I'm making assumptions, but she looks guilty as hell. Why else would she be holding Dani like that, covered in blood? She hated Gretchen. She hated Lex, too. She has motive. I didn't think Courtney could be a murderer but I guess she proved me wrong.

And Dani. Poor, innocent Dani. I left her alone with

stupid Brogan who abandoned her. If I'd stayed with her, she'd still be alive. Instead I was locked in a closet with Cass, kissing him.

I'm a terrible, selfish human being.

"What are you thinking?" I glance over my shoulder to stare at Cass. I need to focus on something else or I'm going to lose it.

"What do you mean?"

I lean back so I'm closer to him and lower my voice. "About Courtney. Do you think…"

He frowns. "What? That she did it? I don't know. I'm starting to change my mind again."

"Are you serious?" I ask incredulously. "No. You can't backtrack now. What if she did do it, Cass? What if you're right after all? It makes total sense."

"Come on. We don't know if she was hurt, too. I couldn't tell. There was so much blood…" He looks away, his jaw tight, his mouth firm. "Maybe they were both attacked. Maybe she got away just in time."

"Courtney told me she didn't do it. She literally said my name and screamed at me that she didn't do it." Cass's gaze meets mine and I continue. "That's weird. Why would she say that?"

"I don't know." He shakes his head.

"Because she's guilty." I say the words firmly and Cass flinches. "She did it. She killed Gretchen. And then she killed Lex. Now she's killed Dani. My best friend."

Cue the tears again. I had no idea crying this much could be so exhausting.

Cass says nothing and that tells me he doesn't necessarily agree with my assessment, but I don't care. My mind is made up. I think she did it. I think she killed all of them and if she hadn't been caught, I would've been next on her list.

A shiver moves down my spine at the thought.

I remember earlier, when we first got there and Cass left me alone for a few minutes. It wasn't for long, but what if something had happened to me? I can't be alone anymore. It's too risky, too dangerous.

And I can't take any more risks. Not now.

Commotion comes from upstairs and we all glance up to see two EMTs bringing a stretcher down with Courtney on it. Most of the blood has been cleaned up. Her eyes are closed, her face is so pale, and a white sheet has been pulled up to her chin, covering her entire body. She almost looks...

Dead.

A hush falls over all of us as we watch in silent horror. One of the cops guarding the front door opens it for the EMTs and they sweep Courtney out of the house, the door closing quietly behind them.

"Killer!" yells a girl's shrill voice. "Glad she's gone!"

"She didn't do it," someone yells back.

I close my eyes and sag against Cass. I can't take this anymore. I just want to go home.

It goes on like this for a few minutes, people becoming angrier and angrier, throwing out accusations at one another. Until finally the cops step in, telling everyone to get it together and stop arguing. It feels like I'm in a movie or a TV show. None of this should be happening. I wonder if I'm having an out-of-body experience. I swear I'm not actually me anymore, I'm just observing everything happening around me.

Suddenly there's an incessant pounding on the front door, making me jump. The cop assigned to guarding the door scowls at all of us before he turns and peeks through the peephole. "If you're media, get the hell out of here," the cop yells. "This is a crime scene."

"My daughter is in there." Oh crap, that sounds like my dad. "I demand to see her right now!"

The cop slowly opens the door, blocking anyone from walking inside. My dad is standing on the doorstep, an unfamiliar man with him. "Where is she? I want to see her now!" Dad shouts, making everyone turn to look at him.

I want to die of embarrassment. Just melt away into this couch and never be seen again.

"Who's your daughter, sir?" the cop asks wearily. He'd better get prepared. I have a feeling lots of parents are going to start showing up soon.

"Penelope Malone."

All heads turn to look at me again.

"I am here with her attorney. She's not allowed to talk to the police without him present," Dad says to the cop, loudly enough for everyone to hear him.

Way to make me look guilty, Dad. Thanks.

The officer opens the door wider and lets them in. Dad scans the room, his gaze alighting on me, and he comes toward me, grim determination etched across his features.

I hop to my feet and he wraps me in his arms, murmuring against my hair. "You all right, sweetheart?"

I'm so thankful he's not acting angry at me for being here when I said I wouldn't go, I start to cry all over again and shake my head. "D-Dani's d-dead. I saw her, Dad. I saw her."

"This is so awful. I'm so sorry you had to see that, sweetie." He kisses my forehead, and I can feel Cass suddenly standing behind me. Dad goes stiff and lifts his head. "Penelope. Who is this with you?"

Pulling out of Dad's arms, I look over my shoulder at Cass. "He's my friend, Dad. We came to the party together. Cass Vincenti, this is my dad."

"Mr. Malone." Cass steps beside me and holds out his hand, Dad taking it so they can shake. "Wish I could say nice to meet you, but I don't think that's appropriate under these circumstances."

"Totally understand, son." Dad squints in that way he gets when he's really examining someone. "You're the one who brought my little girl to this party, huh? When she wasn't supposed to come?"

"Dad," I protest, but my voice is weak.

Cass sends me a questioning look. I never did tell him I was supposed to be at the movies with Dani instead of here with him. "I did, sir. And I'm sorry. Didn't think it would turn out like this."

The understatement of the year.

We should've known something bad would happen. Didn't Courtney say she was hoping to draw the killer out? Maybe she drew her own self out, right? Which makes no sense. But I'm not feeling the most rational at the moment, so I think I'm allowed to think outside the box.

"You should've stayed home." Dad casts a stern look in my direction. "You lied to us, Penelope."

I swallow hard, unable to speak. My apology won't do me much good. After all of this settles down, I guarantee I'll be in big trouble.

"You're right, sir," Cass says firmly. "I should've stayed home, too. Just know that while we were here, I never left her side."

Well. That's sort of a lie. He did leave me for a few minutes earlier in the evening, but I won't bring that up. Besides, it wasn't long before Alyssa and Maggie found me. So I never really was alone.

"Good to know." Dad dismisses him in an instant and looks at me. "Let's go, Penny."

"I can't leave. I still need to give my statement. The cops said so."

"You're leaving. Now. If they want a statement from you, they can wait until tomorrow morning. You're in my custody and you're my responsibility, so if they have a problem, they can take it up with me," Dad explains.

"I don't want to leave Cass," I whisper, grabbing hold of my dad's arm. "Please, Daddy. He shouldn't be alone right now. Who knows how long any of this is going to take? How long they'll want to keep us here? It could go on all night."

"I doubt that." Dad's face turns red, and I know he's upset. He doesn't like being put on the spot, and that's exactly what I'm doing to him. "Why won't his parents come get him?"

"His grandma lives all alone, and she's—she's homebound." I send him an imploring look. "Please, Daddy. Maybe can we get him to leave with us? If you call his grandma and maybe the lawyer can say he's representing Cass, too?"

Dad pulls me aside, putting some distance between Cass and us. "Are you good friends with this boy, Penny?" he asks, his voice low, almost a whisper. "Can you trust him? This is important, so be honest."

I glance over at Cass, who's making small talk with the lawyer—whose name I don't even know. Cass's face is pale and he looks exhausted, but he's still keeping it up, keeping watch over me. He took care of me the best he could tonight. And I appreciate that. Even when we got in that minor argument, when we searched Courtney's room, when we kissed in the closet and finally found Courtney—he stood by me throughout it all. "I trust him, Dad. I want to help him. It's the least I can do after everything tonight."

Dad sighs and scrubs a hand over his face. "Fine. Tell Cass to get his grandmother on the phone and we'll see what we can do."

"Thank you, Daddy." I kiss his cheek and hug him close, savoring the familiar smell of his cologne. I rarely see him, since he's always working, and being with him right now, during one of the worst moments of my life, makes me feel better.

Dad calls the lawyer over and introduces me to him. "This is Mel Grossman, Penelope."

"Hi," I say as we shake hands.

"Let us chat for a bit before we work on getting you and your friend out of here," Dad explains before he guides Mel a few feet away from where I stand. They both start talking in low whispers, looking over at me every few seconds.

It's disconcerting. Worse, the detectives are questioning Cass, so I have no one to talk to. Dani's gone. Everyone's gone.

The tears come, and I cover my face with my hands, turning away so I'm facing the wall. I don't want anyone to see me.

But I can feel their eyes on me anyway.

CHAPTER
TWENTY-SEVEN

The cops wouldn't let us take my car home. They declared the entire Jenkins property a crime scene, and everything needed to remain in place until the investigators were through. We didn't realize it until we left, but they had the entire house and grounds on lockdown while they went in search of the killer.

They found no one hiding out in the house or on the estate. They do have a huge lineup of people to talk to. Every one of us at that party is a potential suspect. The interview process is going to be a long one.

But I'm fairly certain they have the killer in captivity — Courtney. They took her to the hospital, where she's under both medical and psychological evaluation. This is all according to the local news apps, which my dad was reading when we were still waiting to be released from Courtney's house. Guess they got some decent information, despite the police trying to shut them out.

Dad dropped Cass off at his house and then we went straight home, neither of us talking much the entire drive.

I was emotionally drained and couldn't work up a reason to care about making small talk. Plus the idea of rehashing to my dad what I just went through made me sick to my stomach.

"Do you want to talk?" he finally asks once he pulls the car into the garage and shuts off the engine.

I shake my head, afraid if I say too many words, I might start crying yet again.

"Do you just want to go to bed?" His voice is gentle, and I glance over at him. His eyes are full of worry and pain, and I can tell he's treating me like I'm fragile. Like he's afraid I might break at any minute.

I feel like I might.

"Yeah," I whisper. "Can we talk about this in the morning?"

He nods. "Of course. But we *do* have to talk about it, Penelope. And you'll need to go down to the police station tomorrow and give your official account of what happened as well."

"I know. I'll be better tomorrow." I hope it's true.

Dad walks me into the house, where I'm embraced and cried over by both Mom and Peyton. They want details, descriptions, all of it, but Dad tells them to lay off and that I just want to go to bed. Peyton almost looks disappointed, but she leaves it alone. Mom guides me to my bedroom, where she pulls a small prescription pill bottle out of her robe pocket and pops the top off.

"Give me your hand," she murmurs, and I do as she asks. She drops two tiny pills into my palm and closes my fingers around them. "Sleeping pills. You should take them tonight, after what you went through."

"Thanks, Mom." I'm weirded out that she shared her pill stash with me, but I'm not going to complain, either. Until now, I had no idea how I was going to fall asleep tonight. My brain is full of too many lurid images, blood and Courtney and the savage cut across Dani's neck.

Mom gives me a tight hug and then leaves me alone in my room. I go to my bedside table where a half-full bottle of water still sits. I screw off the cap, set the pills on my tongue, and wash them down.

There's a knock, and then Peyton is sneaking inside my room, closing the door behind her. She rushes toward me and draws me into her arms, holding me close. "I should've never covered for you," she whispers against my hair.

I blubber/laugh at her confession and pull away so I can look at her. "You didn't tell them you covered for me, did you?"

"No." She shakes her head, tears sliding down her cheeks. "But I will, if that helps get you off the hook."

"You don't have to do that, Peyton." I smile at her, so grateful that she's here for me. A few years ago, that Peyton would've told me I'm on my own. She was selfish and awful. But she's changed a lot since going to college. She's a nicer, gentler version of her old self.

Makes me think there's hope for me yet.

"What happened?" she asks as we both sit on the edge of my bed.

I launch into the story, not mentioning Cass and me getting stuck in Court's closet after searching through her room. Or the fact that I made out with Cass in the closet too.

"So awful," she says when I finish. The crying has started yet again and Peyton's joining me. "I'm sorry, Penny. I can't believe what happened to Dani. Poor Dani."

"I know." I shake my head, sniffing loudly. My head is throbbing and I just want to go to bed. "Can we talk more tomorrow? I just...I can't do this anymore."

"Yeah. Sure. Want me to sleep with you?" When we were really little, we used to cozy up together in bed. Like when I had a bad dream, Peyton was always right there, ready to take care of me.

"Maybe," I say with a tiny smile. "I'll sneak into your bed if I need to."

"You can." She hugs me close. "You're always welcome to."

After she leaves my room, I go through the normal motions of getting ready for bed. I change out of my clothes and pull on a pair of sleep shorts and an old T-shirt. Put my hair into a sloppy topknot. Clean my face off with a makeup wipe and brush my teeth. I crawl into bed and yank the covers up to my neck, waiting for the sleeping pills Mom gave me to kick in.

But they don't. Not yet. And while I lay there alone with my thoughts, I realize everything has changed. Everything. I'm not the same girl I was before even this afternoon, if I want to get specific. Gretchen is gone. Lex is gone. And now…Dani is gone.

I don't know what I'm going to do without her. My entire world has been flipped upside down. My friends are gone. Courtney has lost her mind. The entire school is going to be a wreck. The weekend won't heal our wounds. Hardly anything will.

And I don't know how I feel about that.

Realizing quickly the pills aren't going to kick in anytime soon, I grab my phone and start scrolling. There are all sorts of notifications, since I haven't really looked at it since we discovered Courtney with Dani. I see a few Snapchats mentioning the chaos at Courtney's party, but no photos of an actual dead body, thank God. No videos posted anywhere, either. I close my eyes just thinking about it, but all I can see is blood, so I open them just in time to see a new notification flash at the top of my screen.

It's a Snapchat message from Cass.

I open it up and look at the photo he sent me, smiling a little. He's in bed, it's mostly dark, and there's a sad expression on his face. The photo is captioned, CAN'T SLEEP. And there are sad face and sleeping emojis included.

I take a selfie and caption it, ME EITHER, before I send it to him.

We do this for a little while, messaging back and forth, about normal stuff, and it soothes me. He tells me how his grandma kept asking him questions and how the cats wouldn't leave him alone. How he went to his bedroom and stared out the window for a while, but all he could see was fog so he eventually gave up. I tell him about my family wanting to question me and that my dad wouldn't let them. That my sister snuck into my room anyway and I was glad she did. How my mom gave me sleeping pills and I took them, but they aren't affecting me yet.

Our conversation makes me feel normal, like it's any other Friday night/early Saturday morning and I'm Snapchatting with a boy. A boy I could possibly like, who kisses me like he possibly likes me, too. I try to focus on that, on Cass and his lips and the way he touched me, and how he took care of me tonight.

And when my eyelids get heavy and I finally drift off into sleep, I don't even remember it happening. I don't dream, either.

Something I'm thankful for.

• • •

"**P**enny. Sweetie. Wake up." A hand gently shakes my shoulder and my eyes pop open to find my mom standing beside my bed, frowning down at me.

"What's going on?" I croak. My throat is so dry, and my head hurts like I'm hungover. I swallow hard and grimace, and Mom grabs the water bottle from my bedside table and hands it to me. I take a drink while she talks.

"The detectives are here. They want to talk to you about — about last night." Mom stands up straight, wringing her hands together. "I tried to send them away, told them you were still sleeping, but they didn't care. They've already been here for almost an hour."

"What?" I throw the covers back and sit up, hating how my head spins. "I feel awful," I mumble, rubbing my forehead.

"It's the sleeping pills. They can leave you with a bit of a hangover when you first start them," Mom explains, sounding apologetic.

"Let me take a quick shower and then I'll come down," I tell her as I stand up slowly. I want to go back to bed. I want to go back to sleep and forget everything that happened.

Maybe if I sleep long enough, I'll discover everything was just a dream.

"I called Grossman and he's on his way."

I frown at her. "Who's Grossman?"

"Your attorney. I refuse to let those detectives talk to you without him present," Mom says firmly.

I feel stupid that I didn't remember my own lawyer's name. I can't even believe I need to have a lawyer. It's like I'm living in some alternate world. "Don't you think that makes me look guilty, having a lawyer?"

"It's a smart move. Your father is an attorney. He knows what to do." She glances around my room, her gaze full of worry. "You want me to try to send them away again? Your father is at the office, but I can call him and he'd rush right home. He'll take care of this if those detectives won't listen to me." Mom has always deferred to Dad as the heavy in our house. Those are the roles they like in their parental relationship with us. Mom's easygoing and Dad's the strict one.

"No, if Mr. Grossman is coming over here, I guess I can talk to them and get it over with. At least they're here at the house, so I don't have to go to the police station." I stretch my arms over my head and yawn, trying to fight the nerves that are fizzing in my stomach. "Tell them I'll be down in a few."

I take a quick shower and think over everything that happened last night. I want to be as thorough as possible remembering all the details. I don't want to forget a thing.

And I also just want this conversation over and done with.

By the time I'm walking into the living room, twenty minutes have passed, and Detectives Hughes and Spalding are pacing near the massive window that faces the street. Mr. Grossman is in heavy conversation with my mother in the corner of the room.

Hughes is the one who notices my entrance first, and his expression is grim when he sees me.

"Penelope." He nods once.

Spalding turns away from the window to face me. "Hello, Miss Malone."

"Hello." I stop in the middle of the living room, unsure of what to do next. "You wanted to talk to me?"

Spalding waves at a nearby chair. "Please. Sit down."

"Penelope." Mr. Grossman is at my side, guiding me toward the chair. "Consult me before you answer any of their questions, do you understand? Just look my way and

I'll nod or shake my head."

I can't even answer a question without his approval? I guess that's what I need a lawyer for. "Okay."

Mr. Grossman settles into a nearby chair. My mother hovers in the doorway, watching us carefully. When I make eye contact with her, she smiles and fully enters the room, wringing her hands together nervously. "Would you like some coffee, gentlemen?" she asks, like they're here for a pleasant visit. "Or something else to drink?"

"Coffee sounds great, Mrs. Malone," Spalding says.

"I'm fine," Hughes grits out as he studies his phone, tapping away at the screen for a few moments before he returns his attention to me. They're both sitting on the couch across from me. "Let's talk about last night."

I glance over at my lawyer—who nods his approval—before I run through the moment again in the most matter of fact way I can. Mom dashes in and hands Spalding his coffee as I describe Cass and me going up the stairs. She leaves when I get to the gruesome parts, and I suppose I can't blame her. I'm not enjoying reliving the moment either. But I forge on and tell them how Cass spotted them first and tried to shield me. Hearing Courtney scream and swear she didn't do it. How the blood was everywhere, all over Courtney, and the horrific slash across Dani's neck.

"Was she hurt?" I ask once I'm finished. When they both frown at me, I continue. "Courtney. She had blood all over her. Cass wondered if she was hurt, too."

"She wasn't," Spalding tells me, his gaze falling from mine as he studies the floor. "It was…Danielle's blood."

"Oh." I exhale shakily, staring at the coffee table in front of me. I'm trembling, and I take a deep breath, telling myself I shouldn't cry. My eyes still burn from all the crying last night and into this morning. "There was so much blood. Cass thought for sure some of it was Courtney's and she'd been hurt by the killer. Is she still in the hospital?"

I look up to find Hughes slowly shaking his head, not saying a word.

Weird.

"What were you doing before you found Courtney and Danielle in the east wing? Run us through those events," Spalding says.

Mr. Grossman nods, so I do as Spalding requests.

"Well, I went to the party with Cass."

"But you told your parents differently," Hughes interjects.

I stay quiet, unsure if I should admit that or not. Mr. Grossman clears his throat and when we make eye contact, he gives me a subtle nod.

"I told my mother I was going to the movies with Dani. That mass text the school sent freaked my mom out and she didn't want me anywhere near Court's house."

"You went anyway," Hughes says, his tone downright accusatory. "Why?"

Here's where the partial truth sounds silly. "I wanted to spend more time with Cass. I-I like him and I'm pretty sure he likes me and that's why I went." I hesitate, then decide to go for it. "I wanted to be with him."

"Okay. Go on then," Spalding says. "Tell us what happened next."

"I went and picked up Cass at his house, which is in the same neighborhood as Courtney's, up on Hot Springs Road. He drove my car to her place and we got there around nine thirty, maybe a little later. We ran into Dani right away, and she was with Brogan Pearson. They were both drunk, Dani more than Brogan, and they got us into the house."

"Right, because Courtney didn't want you there," Hughes says.

Wow, that was the last thing I expected him to say. He knows everything, doesn't he?

"Yes, she disinvited me."

"Why?"

"Because I was against the party from the start. I didn't want her to do it. I thought it was tacky and wrong to have a party so soon after Gretchen and Lex died, and I told her so. That made Courtney mad."

"I'm sure Courtney was angry you were at her house."

"I don't think Court realized it until—until we found her." I feel shaky. Lightheaded. I don't like thinking about that moment, when we found Dani and Court together.

"Let's switch gears here. Was that normal behavior for Danielle while at a party? Did she get drunk at parties a lot?" Spalding asks.

I don't want to make her look bad, but… "Yeah, sometimes. She liked to have fun, be silly and cut loose. She was always fun at a party, you know? Most of the time she worried so much, it was nice to see her so carefree."

"So she drank a lot." Hughes's voice is flat.

"No, not really." I shake my head, frustrated. "It's not like we partied every weekend."

"What about Brogan Pearson? What was her relationship with him?" Hughes asks.

Oh. Wow. Do they suspect Brogan? There is no way he could've killed Dani, let alone Gretchen and Lex. He's not a criminal mastermind. Not even close. "She's had a crush on Brogan for years."

"And did he reciprocate her feelings?"

"I thought he did…" My voice drifts, and I think of Courtney and Brogan together last night. I need to tell the cops. They're going to ask why Cass and I were in the closet and I'm going to have to come up with some sort of excuse.

No way can I tell them the truth.

Oh, we were playing detectives like you guys! On the endless search for clues, you know, since we don't think you're all that great at doing your job.

Yeah, that wouldn't go over real well.

But I need to tell the truth. I can't keep this from them, especially if they talk to Cass and he tells them what really happened. Lying won't get us anywhere.

Taking a deep breath, I decide to go for it.

"Cass and I were in Courtney's bedroom last night."

"Penelope," Mr. Grossman barks, and I jerk my head up, my gaze meeting his. "We should talk about this first."

"I want to tell the truth. I didn't do anything wrong." I look at the detectives, and I can tell they're dying to ask me at least fifty more questions.

They both frown at me. "Why were you in her room?" Spalding asks.

"Um, because we wanted to…" I cough discreetly, feeling stupid. "We wanted to find a more private spot."

Spalding's eyebrows shoot straight up, and a gasp escapes from Mom. "So you were in search of privacy," he says.

"Yes."

"Just the two of you."

I nod.

"And what exactly happened when you were in Courtney's room?"

"Well, we heard Courtney outside in the hall and so…we hid in her closet." My cheeks go hot and I duck my head. This is so embarrassing.

"Was she alone?"

"No." I shake my head, and I can practically feel them scooting closer to the edge of the couch cushion as they wait for my answer. "She was with…Brogan Pearson."

"Really?" Spalding is scribbling fiercely in his notepad. "So they came into the room, and what happened next?"

"They, um, talked and made out for a while. And then they had sex." I keep my head ducked because yeah, this is no fun, talking about your friends having sex last night when they really shouldn't be together.

"They had sex," Hughes repeats. "But weren't Danielle and Brogan together?"

"Not officially. I don't think they'd even really dated," I say.

"Huh. So Danielle likes Brogan, but Brogan's messing around with Courtney. And Courtney and Danielle are good friends." I lift my head to find Spalding staring right at me. "Sounds a little twisted."

"It is. Was," I correct, my chest going tight. It's like I can't even focus on Dani right now, or I'll start crying. And once that happens, I won't be able to stop. "There's a lot of drama in high school."

"Indeed." I can't tell if Hughes is mocking me or not. "Sounds like these two girls had reason to be jealous of each other."

"I guess so," I say with a shrug. "Though I'm pretty sure Dani was clueless. I don't think she knew Courtney and Brogan were hooking up." I don't mention that I'd known about Court and Brogan because Courtney told me, and I immediately feel guilty.

"But you knew," Spalding interjects.

"Sort of. I only had it confirmed when we were in the closet and Courtney and Brogan were on the bed." I make a little face.

"You knew Courtney and Brogan were communicating, though, right? That they were texting and sending each other naked photos?" Hughes asks.

"I mean, I heard…"

"It's a yes or no question, Miss Malone," Spalding reminds me quietly.

"Gentlemen, what does Penelope have to do with Brogan and Courtney being together?" Grossman asks.

"We're just trying to see what Penelope knows," Hughes explains. "Currently Courtney and Brogan aren't talking to the police."

"Penelope shouldn't be either," Grossman says grumpily.

"I just want to get it over with," I tell him before I turn to the detectives. "I knew they were communicating. Flirting with each other. I didn't know they'd taken it this far."

"And what were you and Cass Vincenti doing while Courtney and Brogan were—otherwise involved on the bed?" Hughes asks.

"We were in the closet."

"Spying on them?"

"No. Not really. I didn't want to see that, and neither did Cass. I didn't even want to hear it." I shake my head. "Cass had ear buds with him. So we shared them and listened to music."

"Is that all that happened in the closet?" Hughes asks, his hawk-like gaze right on me.

I drop my head again, staring down at the plush, cream-colored carpet. "Cass and I…we kissed in the closet."

"And that's it?" Hughes presses.

"What more do you want me to say?" I look up at both of them, glaring. I don't like how they're making me feel guilty. Or maybe those are just my own insecurities popping up. I'm not really sure. "No, we didn't *do it* in the closet, if that's what you're asking."

It goes on like this for another ten minutes before my

attorney shuts them down and escorts them out of my house. He tells me I did a good job, but I don't feel like I did. They informed me they were going to ask to look over my cell phone records, like that's supposed to scare me, but it doesn't. I have nothing to hide.

Mom and I talk to Grossman for a few minutes longer, and Mom even calls Dad and puts him on speaker so he can say a few things, and then the attorney leaves. Within minutes, Peyton's walking into the house. Her cheeks are flushed from the cool weather and she's got a dark-purple fleece jacket on, along with black leggings. Her brown hair is pulled back into a high ponytail and she looks refreshed. Carefree. Like she doesn't have a single trouble in the world.

I envy her. I want to *be* her.

"Hey." She smiles brightly, though it looks kind of fake. "Want to go to lunch?"

Please. That's the last thing I want to do.

"Not really." I shake my head, suddenly exhausted. I didn't realize being questioned by the cops could drain every drop of energy out of you. "I'd rather go back to bed."

Mom says nothing. Neither does Peyton.

They just watch me walk away.

CHAPTER TWENTY-EIGHT

I t's Sunday afternoon and I'm still in bed when I get a text from Cass.

Cass: Are you home?

I reply quickly, thankful someone actually reached out.

Me: Yeah. I've been in bed pretty much the entire weekend. I don't think I ever want to get out of my bed again.

It hit me this morning when I first woke up that Dani was gone, and I couldn't stop crying. My best friend in the whole world is gone. All my friends are dead—except for the last one, and she's a *suspect* in our friends' deaths. The junior Larks are probably terrified they're on the list, too, and not a one of them has contacted me since Friday night. Not a one of them has really reached out to me *ever*. I guess I can't blame them. I was never that friendly toward them, and they knew it.

I have no real friends left.

And then I realized quickly I was being pathetic and I needed to get over myself. At least I'm still alive. Dani, Lex, and Gretchen are dead. Their lives are over. At least I'm still here.

My phone buzzes with a text from Cass.

Cass: Not even to see me?

I smile a little. That was definitely a flirtatious text, and I like it. If Dani were here, I'd ask her what she thought and she'd confirm my suspicions—Cass likes me. I haven't felt this giddy about a boy since my freshman year.

My heart aches just thinking about her. The guilt comes, too, that I can be happy and flirty with Cass while Dani is dead and so are Gretchen and Lex. The contradictory emotions are wearing me out.

Cass sends me another text.

Cass: Did you talk to the cops yet?

Me: They questioned me yesterday morning. What about you?

Cass: I spent three hours this afternoon at the station. I just left.

Me: Are you serious????

Cass: Totally. It sucked.

Me: What did they ask you?

Cass: All sorts of things, I'll tell you when I see you.

Cass: So.

Cass: Do you mind if I come by?

My parents might mind. Dad has been super protective the entire weekend. Mom's been hovering, too, even Peyton. She went back to college earlier this afternoon, having left the house about an hour ago, once we came back from going out to lunch, like she wanted to do yesterday. I got out of bed for that event, but otherwise, I've hardly left my room this weekend. It's become my sanctuary.

I don't want to face reality. Real life sucks right now.

Me: I look awful.

Cass: I don't care.

Me: My parents won't let me leave the house.

I don't know if that's true, but I bet it is.

Cass: If they'll let me stay, I'll stay. We can talk outside, in the living room, in front of your parents, whatever. I just

He leaves it at that and so of course I have to ask.

Me: You just what?

Cass: I want to see you.

I want to see him, too.

Climbing out of bed, I go in search of my mom, and I find her in the kitchen.

"Can Cass come over?"

Mom turns away from the stove, a frown on her face. "Right now?"

"Yeah, right now." I nod.

"You, um…don't look your best." She waves a hand at me. Leave it to Mom to be brutally honest.

I'm wearing holiday themed red-and-white pajama pants and an old black and orange San Francisco Giants hoodie that used to belong to my brother, Peter. He gave it to me when he moved out. I never even took a shower today. So yeah. Me not looking my best is an understatement.

"So?" I shrug. "He just wants to come over and talk."

"I don't know…"

"Mom." I approach her, my expression serious. "Cass and I experienced something awful together. We…bonded after what happened Friday night. I want to see him. He wants to see me. I think he needs to talk and I need to talk to him, too. So please? It's not like we want to go out or anything like that."

She sighs and turns back to the stove, stirring whatever she's got cooking in a giant pot. "Fine. He can come over. Do you want him to stay for dinner? I've made enough."

"I'll see what he wants to do, but yeah. Probably." I walk up to her and kiss her on the cheek. She rarely wanted Robby over for dinner, and we were together for nine months. Not that I was interested in having him around my parents, either. "Thank you for letting Cass come over."

Mom looks at me, and I notice the frown lines in her forehead. Were those there before? Or did I just never notice them? "I understand that you feel close to him, but be careful with this boy, Penelope. We don't know much about him. And what we do know…"

"Is not much, I get it. We can talk about him later. Right now, I just need someone I can hang out with. Feel normal with." I kiss her cheek again and then bound out of the kitchen, in a hurry to put some regular pants on. I quickly text Cass to let him know he can come over, along with my street address, and then I go about fixing myself up.

By the time he's knocking on the door, I'm wearing jeans but still in the hoodie, and I tamed my hair so it's now in a normal ponytail versus a sloppy bun. Plus, I put a little makeup on. Face brightener cream stuff and mascara, plus some tinted lip balm. I want to look nice for Cass. I want to pretend just for a little while that this is a normal day, even though I know it's not.

I answer the door and smile at him. "Hi."

"Hey." Cass looks good in jeans and a gray-and-black plaid button-down shirt, the faded black Converse on his feet. He's wearing a black beanie that hides most of his hair, which is a total shame. His hair is one of my favorite things about him. "Can I come in?"

"Let's sit outside." It's not that I don't want my parents to see him. I just want to get some fresh air. I've treated my bed like a refuge, but now that I'm out of it, I realize how cooped up I've been.

He shrugs. "Okay."

I pull the door shut behind me, and we go to sit on the front porch steps. He sits close to me, his thigh pressed against mine, and I lean into him, absorbing his strength, his warmth.

It's funny, how I went from thinking he was totally weird and not knowing him at all to wanting to get as close to him as possible. And that's because I *feel* close to him. What happened Friday night brought us closer together.

Despite everything that happened, I can at least hold on to this. Hold on to Cass.

"You don't look awful," he says after we've been quiet for a few minutes. His gaze meets mine, and I can see the sincerity shining in his eyes. "I think you look pretty great."

I lean my head on his shoulder, then push away from him. "You say the nicest things."

"I mean it." His gaze meets mine once more. "I've been worried about you."

"I've been thinking a lot about you, too," I admit, my

voice soft. "I'm sorry I didn't reach out yesterday. It was…a hard day."

"I understand." And I know he does. I can tell. "It was hard for me, too. What happened Friday brought back a lot of old memories I'd rather forget."

"About your mom and dad?" I probably shouldn't have asked, but I want to be there for him. I want him to know he can say anything to me, and that I get it. I won't judge. I won't gossip. I just want to be his friend.

And maybe something more…

"Yeah." He spreads his legs and rests his arms on his thighs, his clasped hands hanging between his knees. "I found him, you know."

My heart trips over itself at the sound of his voice. "You found who?"

"My dad." He turns to look at me. "I came home from school and I thought no one was there. My mom was *always* there. Sometimes I'd come home and she'd still be in bed, but she was there, you know? I could count on her." His expression is harrowed, like he's back in that moment, reliving it. "I called for my mom, but she didn't answer. I looked in every room, saving their bedroom for last. The door was shut, and that never happened. So when I opened the door, I did it real slow. Like I knew something bad was waiting for me. And I was right. There he was, sprawled across their bed, blood everywhere. I didn't even recognize him at first. I thought it was a stranger. I thought it was fake."

I blink, unable to form words. All I can do is reach out and rest my hand on his forearm.

"She stabbed him." He takes a deep breath and exhales shakily. "Thirty-two times, once for every year he stole from her. She claimed he stole all her years, because she was thirty-two when she did it. Thirty-three when she went to trial. Almost thirty-four by the time she was sentenced to life in prison with no possibility of parole."

"How old were you?"

"When I found him? Ten."

I press my lips together, overcome. The tears are there. I can feel them, desperate to burst out of me, and I give in and let them flow. They streak down my cheeks, drip from my jaw to fall onto my hoodie, and when Cass sees them, his expression turns pained. He reaches out, catching each tear with his thumb.

"Don't cry for me," he whispers, his thumb still stroking my cheek, trying to capture every tear. But they keep falling, faster and faster, and then he pulls me into his arms, crushing me to him.

"I can cry for you if I want," I murmur, making him chuckle. He strokes my hair. Strokes my back. Holds me close and offers me comfort when I'm the one who should be offering him comfort. He just told me the most horrific thing I've ever heard, and he ends up consoling me.

"I'm all right, I promise. I've spent many years in therapy," he says against my hair. "I still do."

"You see a shrink?"

"Yeah." His voice turns hard. "Those asshole detectives were real interested in that, too."

I pull away from him so I can look into his eyes. "Tell me what happened. What did they ask you?"

"The usual. Where was I, what were we doing before we went up the stairs and found Courtney and Dani." Despite what happened, he manages to smile faintly. "Glad you came clean with them, because I did too. Thankfully, our stories matched up."

"You told them about being in Courtney's room, then?" I'm so glad I told the truth.

"Yeah. About her bringing Brogan to her room and us hiding in the closet. How we, uh—kissed in the closet and heard them do a lot more in her bed." His cheeks turn the faintest red.

"I told them that, too. The only thing I left out was about us searching Courtney's room. I didn't think they needed to know about it. I was afraid that would open us up to even more questions." I feel bad keeping something from the cops, but what does it matter? We only found that letter and I'd bet money it was from Brogan.

"Same." He holds up his hand and I give him a gentle high five. "Thought it was best if I didn't mention it, and they never brought it up, either, so I figured we were off the hook."

"They seemed very interested in Brogan."

Cass nods. "I thought so, too. Not that I think he did it."

"I don't think he did, either," I agree. "They didn't tell me anything about Courtney. Nothing."

"Same. I think she's a suspect."

"I think she did it," I say firmly.

"Do you?" The skepticism is in his voice. I can hear it. "Why do you say that?"

"They're all linked to her. Court hated Gretchen. She hated Lex, too. The Larks, how Courtney has said so many awful things about all of them, and she was cheating with Dani's crush. Who's to say Dani didn't confront her and Court got so mad, she killed her? I know we said she was too obvious, but…"

"I don't know, Pen. That sounds so crazy. Do you really think Courtney would *kill* Dani because she's having sex with Dani's possible boyfriend? More like Dani should've been mad at Court," Cass points out.

"So what made you change your mind? You're the one who told me you thought she was capable. Courtney has a temper. Plus, she's been irritated with or hated every single one of us at some point or another. She was really mad at me this week. I'm surprised she didn't come after me."

"You're damn lucky she didn't come after you, if she's the murderer." He shakes his head. "But I don't think it's her."

"Why not?"

"Too cut and dry. I think it's someone else. Someone more devious who's trying to pin it on Court."

"That's saying a lot. Courtney is pretty devious."

"I know. I believe whoever's doing this is smarter than Court, maybe smarter than all of us. He's trying to frame her."

"Who's to say it's a he?"

Cass shrugs. "Maybe it's a she, then."

"So you think it's someone we go to school with?"

"Maybe. I'm not sure. But I'm not going for that random stranger bit the news keeps trying to make us believe," he says. "It's all they can say. No one wants to hear it could be one of our own."

They don't want to tarnish the town's reputation. Cape Bonita has always been known as a safe haven. I don't remember any murders happening here while I've been alive—with the exception of Cass's mom stabbing his dad to death, though that had always been just a rumor floating around.

"I don't believe it, either. I think it's someone we know. It could be anyone from the staff. They have access to all the students." An idea sparks in my brain. "Maybe it's Coach Smith. She's been inconsolable since Gretchen died. What if she killed her by accident and now she's going after all the Larks?"

"Come on. That makes no damn sense and you know it. Sally Smith may have had a strange fascination with Gretchen Nelson, but she didn't *murder* her. She didn't murder the other girls, either." Cass nudges me in the side with his shoulder. "Think, Pen. Could it be someone you're close to?"

"What do you mean?" Who could he be referring to?

"I don't know." He shrugs, but I can tell by the look on his face that he has someone in mind. "It feels like it's someone who could be closer than you think. Maybe someone who's jealous of all of you."

"Like who?" That could be anyone at school. "Are you thinking of someone specific?"

"Maybe it could be one of the junior Larks?" I part my lips, ready to speak, but Cass rushes on. "You never know. I'm just pulling theories out of the sky. But have you ever thought it could be one of them?"

"No freaking way." I make a face. "Have you seen those girls? They're all scared of their own shadows. I can't imagine one of them taking down Gretchen. She would've kicked their ass. Or Lex. Or even Dani. I can't wrap my head around all five of them getting together and taking down one of us, let alone one of them acting on her own. They're that timid."

"They might not be as timid as you think."

There's no way any of those girls could be a killer. "It must be Courtney then," I say firmly. "All roads lead to her."

"I don't think so," he says, leaning in close. "So don't be disappointed if you're wrong."

I press my forehead to his, our gazes locking. "Don't be disappointed if I'm right either, okay?"

He touches my cheek, a faint smile curling his lips. "Okay." He tilts his head to the side and kisses me, and I'm lightheaded the moment his lips touch mine. The kiss is far too brief. "Can I confess something to you?"

I nod, hoping he'll kiss me again.

"Promise you won't make fun?"

"I promise," I whisper.

Cass smiles. "I can't believe I'm with you right now, kissing you. I'm with Penelope Malone, the head cheerleader, one of the most popular girls in our class. It blows my mind."

I smile and kiss him this time around, my lips lingering on his as I slip my hand around the back of his neck, my fingers playing with the ends of his hair. "Can you stay for dinner?" I murmur against his lips. "My mom said it was okay."

"I need to ask Grams, but I'm sure she won't mind." His mouth settles on mine, warm and firm, and I close my eyes. Lose myself to the sensation of his persistent lips, his wandering hands, the beat of his heart, the sound of his breath.

I don't want to forget this moment. Though I can't tell Cass why.

Deep down, I'm afraid it might be one of the last good moments I'll ever have.

CHAPTER TWENTY-NINE

Well, that was quite the weekend, right, folks? I may be down, but I'm definitely not out.

Friday was a total fiasco. The entire night felt off from the very beginning. Nothing went as planned. My original target somehow slipped through my fingers and I had to settle for my second—wait, make that my *third*—choice. As reluctant as I was to take her down, it was too late. I was already in the moment. I had to make it happen.

I didn't want to *completely* deviate from the plan. Bad enough I had to make a few quick changes.

Poor Dani. She was in the wrong place at the wrong time. Drunk off her ass, saying the stupidest crap you've ever heard. Whining on and on about Brogan until I wanted to puke.

Does he like me?

He never tells me he likes me, not like that.

He won't commit.

I think I got friend zoned.

He's so cute.

He kisses me when no one's looking.
Is he just using me?
Fuck it. Maybe I'll let him.

And on and on and on she went, until I wanted to poke pencils in my ears to make her stop. I had zero sympathy for Dani. She's the classic, *want what you can't have* type of girl. She's adorable, she's sweet, and she was fun, but she wanted some jackass who likes his nickname Bro. It fits him, though. He is a *total* bro. That guy was tapping every ass he could at Cape Bonita Prep.

I should know. He tapped mine.

The craziest thing is Dani didn't even know it was coming. One minute she's crying over Brogan and asking me to give her advice—sorry that's your best friend Penelope's job, doll—and then I'm grabbing hold of her by the front of her dress, making her gasp in shock. Those big brown eyes of hers went even bigger, which is quite the feat. I placed the tip of the knife against her throat, pricking her just enough to make blood appear, and she screamed. She screamed and screamed and I slashed and slashed her throat to shut her up. Right there in the middle of the hallway, until I could hear her gurgle, choking on her own blood.

Dani was by far the messiest one of the bunch.

And she was also the least satisfying.

CHAPTER THIRTY

People stare as I walk down the hall Monday morning. I can feel their eyes on me as I move past them, and I keep my posture straight, my head held high as I go to my locker, even though my knees are quaking. No one speaks to me, not even a random hi tossed carelessly in my direction. They all keep a wide berth, as if they're afraid to get too close.

I guess I can't blame them. I'm the girl who found Dani and Courtney—well, Cass and I found them. I'm also the girl who's linked to every single one of the victims. I don't think anyone suspects me, though. I mean, come on, it's *Courtney* who did it.

It has to be.

"Hey." I feel a large hand touch my shoulder just after I get my locker open, and I whirl around, relieved when I discover it's Cass. "You didn't text me this morning."

"I was supposed to text you?" I frown, fighting the guilt. It was so nice, having him spend time with my parents and me last night. They were wary at first, but they warmed up to him quickly. He was polite and respectful, seemed genuinely interested in what they had to say, and I know he was interested in everything I had to say, too. We even laughed a few times.

And that explosive good night kiss he gave me on the porch just before he left made my toes curl.

"I figured you would." He's frowning, his thick, dark brows knitting together. "I don't like the idea of you coming to school alone."

"My dad dropped me off. I still don't have my car back from the police." It's kind of annoying, how the cops are keeping it as evidence, but I guess I understand why. My dad swore he'd get it back by the end of the day, and I hope he's successful. No way do I want to be dependent on my dad for a ride.

Though really, I'd rather lose my car for a while than my life forever, so I need to get over myself.

"Oh, good." The relief on his face is evident. "Wait, not that the police still have your car, but that your dad drove you."

"You approve of my having a chaperone?"

"I can't help it. I worry about you, especially after everything that's happened." He steps closer to me, speaking low so no one else can hear. "I'll take you home, though. And tomorrow, we're riding together, even if you do have your car back by then. I'll come pick you up."

"But that's a total pain in the butt for you." He'd have to drive past campus to get me. We live in opposite directions of the school. "I can drive myself."

Cass shakes his head, his expression firm. "I'll drive you. I don't mind." When I open my mouth to argue, he cuts me off. "Come on, Pen. Let me do this one thing for you."

"Okay." I like how protective he is. He wants to watch over me, and right now, I need that. It's like I have no one on my side. All my friends are gone. There's no one else but my family and Cass. And my family can't follow me to school every day.

So I'm going to need to start counting on Cass—and myself.

I can handle this. I have to.

"Did you see the news report this morning about Courtney?" he asks.

I shake my head, fighting the nerves that have suddenly taken residence in my stomach.

He pulls his phone out of his pocket and taps at the screen, pulling up the video before he hands it to me. I watch in dull horror, my mind cataloging all the images but not really hearing what the reporter is saying. There are clips from the most recent crime scene—Courtney's house—featuring lots of yellow tape and flashing red and blue lights streaking across the dark night sky. Dani's school photo from last year appears, as do Gretchen's and Lex's. Then they show Courtney's senior photo—of course *her* photo is more current. She looks beautiful.

Perfect.

My stomach churns.

"Cape Bonita Prep senior Courtney Jenkins was released from the hospital yesterday afternoon, upon which she returned to her family's residence. The police have been mum in regards to Jenkins's involvement in the three recent murders, but Jenkins hasn't been officially dismissed as a suspect, either. We're keeping close watch on this situation, and will report as soon as we learn new details."

The video ends.

So she's home. I wonder if the detectives spoke to her. I wonder what she said. I wonder why the hell she's not behind bars.

I wonder if she's going to get away with murder.

"That was depressing," I tell Cass when I hand him back his phone. "A known lunatic is now wandering the streets. What's it going to take to lock her up for good, huh? Another murder? Do *I* have to die in order for Courtney to finally pay for what she's done?"

Cass sends me an incredulous look. "Are you serious right now? Come on, Pen."

"Isn't that how the judicial system works in America?" I slam my locker door shut and turn to face him once more, lowering my voice. "I'm freaking out, Cass. Everyone who's died is a Lark. Even if Courtney isn't the murderer, it still means only Court and me are left. I'm a target."

"I agree. You're definitely a target," he says firmly. "Whoever's doing this seems focused on the most popular girls in the senior class. Or they're after the most beautiful girls. Hell, I don't know. None of this makes any sense. But I do know one thing." He hesitates, then goes for it. "Courtney didn't do this."

I glare at him. "You don't know her. You don't know anything about her."

"I know more than you think," he says somberly. "We have a past. She's my friend. We went to rehab together."

My mouth drops open. *Rehab?* And the secrets just keep on coming. "Are you for real right now?"

Cass shrugs, looking irritable. "What's the big deal? You know we had a past. Well, there it is. My secret shame, along with Courtney's. We went to rehab together. We supported each other. We haven't seen each other as much lately, but I want to do the right thing."

"And what's that?" I ask, my voice a tiny whisper.

"Talk to her. Make sure she's okay. Make everything between us right." His mouth goes firm. "She was acting so crazy, and at one point, I truly believed she was the killer. But there's just…no way it could be her. I know Courtney. She can be rotten, and selfish, but she's not a murderer. I feel bad that I suspected her at first, so I need to make amends. She's always stood by me in the past, so I want to stand by her."

Dude. I can't freaking believe it. Why does he care if she's okay or not? Why does he feel the need to make "it" right? What exactly is he talking about?

No one I know.

"You can't talk to her," I tell him.

He frowns. "Why the hell not?"

"She's deranged. Delusional. She'll work her way into your brain and convince you that you shouldn't see me anymore."

Cass literally scoffs. "Give me a break. She wouldn't do that."

"She so would."

"I won't let her."

"Trust me. She can be very convincing."

"Are you calling me weak?"

Oh. He sounds pissed now. "No. I never said you were weak. Don't put words in my mouth."

"I can talk to whoever I want, Pen. Courtney was my friend before I really even knew you."

"So she matters more to you than I do." Okay, now I sound like a jealous, crazed girlfriend. Maybe I'm the one who's deranged. Clearly I'm not thinking straight.

"Now who's putting words in someone's mouth?" Cass says snidely.

Blowing out a breath, I start walking down the hall, Cass right along beside me. "Go away," I tell him, as if he's an annoying bug. "I need to get to class." If we keep this up, I'm going to start crying, and I promised myself I would stay strong today.

"You really want to end it like this?"

I come to a stop, as does he, and people pass us by, in a hurry to get into their seats before the first period bell rings. "End it? What do we have that's even started?"

My words hurt him. I can see it in the way he flinches ever so slightly, and by the quick flicker of emotion in his gaze. "I think we both need to cool off."

"Yeah, maybe you should go cool off with Courtney. Your very dearest, closest friend." I really need to shut up. "Though from what we saw Friday night, I think she's a better expert at heating things up." Oh, that was petty and rude, but it's all I've got, and I'm freaking mad.

I don't give him a chance to speak. Instead, I storm off, ignoring Cass when he calls my name. I don't even bother looking back. I can't believe he's siding with Courtney. So what if he's known her longer than me? I've known her longer than pretty much everyone in my life besides my family, and while I originally believed no way was she capable of hurting someone physically, now I can believe it.

And I believe she did it.

"Penelope." A female voice calls my name when I walk past, and I'm so startled I turn and look for her, slamming my backpack into someone's side as I do.

"Watch it," the guy mutters before he stalks off.

"Penelope! Over here!" I finally find the source and it takes everything I have not to roll my eyes. Even in my anger and fear, I can turn on bitch mode with the flip of a switch.

Something I'm not really proud of, either. A few weeks ago, I would've flipped them total attitude. Now I just want to ignore them. Pretend they don't even exist. Neither option is nice, though, is it?

Alyssa and Maggie, two of my junior Larks, are standing by the lockers, nervous smiles on their faces. They look downright excited to see me and as I approach, I note the way they both stand up straighter, as if they're presenting themselves to me.

This, I can appreciate. This, I understand. Maybe I really *am* the queen bee, not Courtney. This is *my* school.

And I'm not about to let Courtney Jenkins and her evil, psycho ways ruin everything.

"We've been so worried about you," Alyssa breathes, her dark brown eyes wide and her entire demeanor dramatic. "But you look great! Your hair is so shiny this morning."

I hate that they're trying so hard to please me. "You could've called," I remind them. "Or texted. Or Snapchatted. Or sent me a DM on Twitter or Instagram—"

"We get it," Maggie interrupts, her expression immediately contrite when I glare at her. "Our bad for not reaching out to you. But we were scared! Everything that's happened is straight out of a scary movie!"

"We're…afraid for you, Penelope," Alyssa adds, her tone much more sincere. "You're a senior, you're in charge of the Larks, and we admire you so much! We just don't want anything awful to happen to you."

"I appreciate that," I tell them quietly, meaning every word I say. "Really."

I'm scared—and I firmly believe Courtney is a direct threat. Yet Cass wants to hang out with her. Forgive and stand by her, or whatever crazy thing he said. I don't get it.

I don't get *him.*

"Let's call a meeting," I tell the girls, making their eyes go wide. "Today, after school. In our usual spot at the usual time."

"Are you…sure?" Alyssa asks hesitantly.

I nod. "We can discuss what needs to happen next. Maybe we should disband. At the very least, go on a temporary hiatus. I don't know. But we need to talk."

"Sounds good," Maggie says cheerily right as the last bell rings. "See ya later, Penelope!"

I watch them go, not caring that I'm late. Like any teacher is going to give me a tardy notice today.

I'm practically a walking dead girl. Who's going to give me shit after I've lost three of my very best friends?

CHAPTER THIRTY-ONE

"I'm so glad you made it today," I tell the Larks—all five of them, plus me. We're sitting in conference room three at the library and not a one of them was late. "I appreciate your promptness."

They nod and smile, visibly squirming in their seats. They're clearly uncomfortable and I suppose I can't blame them, but I'm not here to coddle them. It's business as usual today, though I have a feeling we're going to shut down business—on a temporary basis. I don't have the heart to close the Larks permanently.

But I might not have a choice.

"How are you feeling, Penelope?" asks Jessica, another one of our quiet junior Larks. I bet you didn't even know she existed, huh?

Well, she does. And while I appreciate her question, I don't want to look weak in front of these girls, either.

I'm running on pure adrenaline, fear, and anger. Cass and I haven't talked about—or made up from—our earlier conversation in the hall before first period. I'm still angry, and he knows it. He's keeping his distance.

Whatever.

He's just like everyone else at this school. They've all kept their distance. Brogan Pearson wasn't here today, and his fellow "bros" stared at me in the caf during lunch like I was going to come after them with a machete and chop them to bits. Courtney wasn't at school, either, and I'm guessing she's the one they really fear. Since she's not here, though...

They're focused on me.

I was called into Mrs. Adney's office yet again after lunch, and she offered me grief counseling.

"We're worried about you," Mrs. Adney said, her expression as soft as her voice, which was unusual. "Especially after what happened to Danielle. I know you two were exceptionally close."

"She was my best friend." I was so proud my voice didn't shake.

"I know she was. You and Dani were very close. Everything that's happened these last few weeks has taken a toll on you, I'm sure." Her gaze met mine. "We'll understand if you might need a break from school."

"I don't want a break," I told her. "What I need is for things to return to normal. If I stay away and hide at home, then nothing's fixed. I need to get back to my routine."

Mrs. Adney nodded, but she didn't look convinced. "Just know my door is open to you, always. If you need to talk, if you need advice, want me to introduce you to the grief counselor, whatever. I'm here for you, Penelope."

Her words meant a lot. I could tell she really was worried about me.

But I need to soldier on, not wallow in my sadness. Courtney isn't here. They'll figure out soon enough she's the one who did it.

"We took it upon ourselves to organize another candlelight vigil," Alyssa says, breaking through my thoughts. "This time to honor all three girls, but especially Dani, since we just lost her."

I'm stunned. "You planned it without me?"

"Well, we figured you were torn up over Dani's death. We wanted to be there for you and help out in any way we could," Alyssa explains.

"We're not trying to take anything away from you, since you're the Larks president," Maggie adds, ever the diplomat. "We just wanted to help."

"I…appreciate it. Thank you." I'm not used to the juniors taking initiative and making decisions. I didn't do it when I was a junior. Yes, I was groomed to become the president, but when I was a junior, I never challenged the seniors. What they said was truth. What they told us to do, we did without question. They were the leaders, grooming us to take over. We went along with their decisions, never once challenging them.

Circumstances have changed. Our seniors are gone, and I need the help. I appreciate that they're taking the lead.

They both look pleased by my approval. Alyssa is practically bouncing in her seat. "The candlelight vigil is tomorrow night at seven here at the school. We have everything arranged, and Mrs. Adney wants to speak. Maybe—if you're feeling up to it—you could talk about Dani and the girls, too."

"Maybe." I'm surprised Mrs. Adney wants to talk, but this is her school and she's been quiet these last few weeks, letting Mr. Rose do all the official talking. "I don't know if I'll be able to talk about Dani without crying."

The sympathetic looks on all the girls' faces make me feel better—and also push me to the verge of tears.

"If you don't want to do it, that's okay," Grace says, and

the other girls nod. "We'll be here for you. We'll all stand around you tomorrow night when you talk, if you want our support."

"That would be great," I say softly. My anger has deflated, and I can't believe it, but I've actually got the warm fuzzies for my fellow Larks. Most of the time we treat one another like the competition—and not the friendly kind. We're all fighting to be the top girl, the leader, the one who gets the most college acceptances, the most votes at homecoming, the most…everything. The only one I got along consistently with was Dani, and only because we've been best friends since the sixth grade.

I wipe away the tears that try to fall, sniffing discreetly. I miss Dani so much it hurts.

"We've got your back, Penelope," Maggie says with a smile.

I'm tempted to hug them all. So I do, quickly and quietly, stepping away from them before we all collapse into a flood of tears.

"Okay." I clear my throat. "Now that we have that handled, we should move on to other business. Is there anything else one of you would like to discuss?" I look around the table, but no one is raising their hand or nodding. They all look at one another, like they're unsure, and so I decide to go for it. "I think we should seriously consider putting a temporary halt to the Larks activities."

"Are you sure?" Grace asks, her voice hushed.

I nod, pressing my lips together so I don't break out in a sob. "All the seniors are gone except me. Courtney probably won't come back to school, and I don't want to find replacements. I don't have the strength to go out and recruit new Larks members. We usually reserve that until spring. So I'm thinking…"

My voice is shaking, and I close my eyes to ward off

another round of tears. I hate that this is happening. My entire high school career I strove toward this moment, and now that I have to close down the Larks, a group that meant everything to me for more than a year, it's heartbreaking.

"Wait until the spring?" Alyssa adds when I don't say anything else.

"But that's months away!" Maggie looks crushed.

"I know, and I'm sorry. I know you girls wanted the full Larks experience. But we aren't full Larks right now. We've been cut down. And I think we need to take some time off to regroup, and recuperate. I believe it's for the best," I tell them. "So let's vote on it. All in favor to temporarily retire the Larks for the next six months?"

They all reluctantly raise their hands, even me.

"Then it's settled." I rest my laced hands on the table. "We'll be back in business in March. Until then, let's stay in touch, take care of one another when someone is in need, and please, think about who you'd like to recruit to become a Lark for next year."

Alyssa's gaze meets mine. I can see it in her more and more every time we're together. She's going to make a perfect Larks president. "Thank you for everything, Penelope. You've been a great leader."

"So sorry this has all happened on your watch," Maggie adds.

"We'll be there for you tomorrow, too. Don't forget," Alyssa continues, a reassuring smile on her face.

We wrap up plans for tomorrow's candlelight vigil and then one by one, each girl files out of the conference room, until I'm the last one left. I gather my things, grab my backpack, and leave the room, walking through the mostly empty library and waving at the librarian before I exit the building.

Outside, it's cloudy, the air cold and bringing with it the possibility of rain. I head toward the senior lot on the other side of campus and tug my sweater closer, walking briskly through the school grounds.

No one is around, not even for after school practice, which is odd. But things have been canceled or postponed, just like the Larks, so it's not too surprising. Everyone's in mourning, they're all afraid to have a good time or admit that they weren't affected by the girls' deaths. But eventually life goes on.

Even if we don't want it to.

I hear a noise, like a snapped twig or a kicked rock, and I glance over my shoulder, seeing no one. I walk faster, looking around, hyperaware of my surroundings.

And then it hits me.

I didn't drive my car to school.

My dad brought me.

My shoulders sag and I blow out a harsh breath. Cass said he'd take me home, but he's nowhere to be found, considering we got into that stupid fight. He totally brushed me off.

That hurts.

I stop in front of the main office and pull out my phone, trying to call my dad. He never responds to texts, and he rarely answers his cell if he's working.

No surprise, the call goes straight to voicemail.

I try my mom next, which is an even bigger shot in the dark. She's the worst with her phone. Dad says she only uses it for outgoing calls, and he's not too far off the mark. She doesn't really text. She rarely carries her phone with her—like she legitimately forgets it at home most of the time. She claims she'd rather live "a real life," versus being glued to her phone twenty-four-seven.

Like a miracle, though, she answers on the fourth ring. "Penny, are you all right?" Mom sounds breathless.

"Can you come pick me up at school? I forgot I didn't have a ride home."

"I'll be there in ten." She ends the call before I can even say anything and I glance around, hating how quiet campus is. How desolate it feels.

I'm stuck here for the next ten minutes. All alone.

And I don't like it. At all.

"Hey."

I turn at the sound of the familiar voice to find Maggie standing about ten feet away, a weird look on her face. "Oh hey, Maggie."

She's frowning. "What are you doing here?"

"My dad brought me to school this morning, and I don't have my car." I smile weakly, but her expression doesn't change. "My mom is coming to get me, though."

"Oh." She takes a few steps toward me, tilting her head to the side. "Do you want me to wait with you?"

Relief floods me and I nod, curling my fingers around my backpack strap. "That would be great."

A car engine suddenly sounds, and I whirl around to see a silver Lexus SUV suddenly pull up to the curb. The passenger-side window rolls down, revealing Cass behind the wheel with a grim look on his face. "You thought I'd ditched you, huh?" His voice is flat. "You didn't even text me."

I shrug, hating that he's right.

"I saw you head toward the library right after school, so I figured you had a Larks meeting." I nod my answer as I start to approach the SUV. "I've been waiting around for the past thirty minutes for you to appear. Just noticed you, so I thought I'd come over here and get you. If you still want a ride, that is."

"You don't mind?"

The look Cass sends me is part annoyance, part affectionate. "Of course I don't mind, Penelope. Get in the car."

Remembering Maggie, I turn to tell her I don't need a ride after all, but she's gone.

Huh. Maybe she got the hint and decided to take off.

I open the door and climb in, dropping my backpack on the floorboard. He puts the SUV in drive and off we go, tearing out of the parking lot so fast, his tires squeal when he turns onto the street.

I'm hunched over my phone texting my mom that she doesn't need to come get me after all because I'm with Cass, when he asks me a question.

"Who was that you were talking to?"

"Maggie. She's one of the junior Larks." I don't want to talk about the Larks anymore. It hurts my heart, what I just did. So I change the subject. "Driving your grandma's car again?"

"Yeah." He doesn't even look my way.

"What about the old Mercedes you were driving yesterday?"

"That's my car. Well, it was my grandma's, but she gave it to me when I was thirteen."

I gape at him. "Thirteen?"

"I've been driving since I was thirteen, yeah." He glances over at me, looking amused at my surprise. "My grandma doesn't like to drive. I helped her out when I could."

"By driving without a license."

"Only to the store and stuff. It was no big deal."

"You could've gotten in trouble."

"I could've gotten in trouble for a lot of things. But I didn't."

"Does that make it right?"

We come to a stoplight, and he really looks at me. "I don't think we're just referring to me driving without a license here."

"You're right. We're not." I cross my arms, hating how confused I am. I don't know how to feel about any of this, about him. My emotions are a confused jumble. I'm upset over shutting down the Larks. I'm still mad at Cass, but he's all I have right now. I don't really know or trust the Larks girls.

But I don't really know or trust Cass, either. Not anymore.

When the light turns green, he turns right versus driving straight, and within minutes he pulls into the parking lot of a small city park. "We should talk," he says the moment he turns the car's engine off.

"So talk."

"Pen." I look up and our gazes lock. "Don't act this way," he says softly. "I'm sorry about what happened earlier. I don't want us to fight."

"I don't want to fight, either, but I can't trust Courtney right now. I don't know how you can."

"Court and I, we've been through a lot. Like I said, we were in rehab together. We got close in there. We were all each other had." He sounds distant, like he's remembering what it was like, being with Courtney in rehab.

It couldn't have been that great.

"So you were close friends."

He makes a face, one I can't decipher. "I guess. We didn't define what we had."

My heart is racing. I don't want to ask this question, but I must know. "Did you have sex with her?"

Now he looks away, remains quiet before he finally says, "No. I already told you that. But we did…kiss once. That's it, though."

My reaction is automatic. I climb out of the car. It's like I have no control of myself. I'm out of the SUV, slamming the door behind me and running toward the kiddie playground, which is currently—thankfully—empty. I hear Cass call my name but I ignore him. I run until I'm standing next to the swing set and I clutch the pole with grasping hands, the cold metal seeping into my palms and making me shake.

Or maybe I'm shaking because I'm angry. Upset. Sad. Annoyed. It's like Courtney touches what I want and leaves it a toxic, ugly mess. The Larks, the school, my friends, Cass.

I'm sick of it. I'm sick of *her*.

"Pen." Cass is standing right behind me. He places his hands on my shoulders and I shrug them away, immediately full of regret. I wish he would try and touch me again.

But he doesn't.

"Don't be mad. What happened between Court and me was a long time ago."

"How long?"

"Sophomore year. We were fifteen." He takes a deep breath. Exhales slowly. "I was a total mess, she was a mess, too. We recognized each other from school. Well, she claims she didn't know who I was, but I knew her. They put us together in counseling because we were the same age, and we got close pretty fast. We felt like we had no one else in there, only each other."

I can relate. That's exactly how I feel about Cass right now. I have no one else.

Just him.

"Once we got out of rehab, she pretended like she didn't even know I existed when we were at school, and that fucking hurt. I can't lie. It was such a slap in the face. I'm good enough to hang out with in rehab, but not where her friends could see her?" He smiles, but it looks more like a baring of teeth. My stomach sinks, because I've done that, too. Ignored him. Acted like he doesn't exist.

But not anymore.

"So I got pissed," he continues. "And she knew it, but she didn't care. When I went to the addiction meetings, she'd be there sometimes. And then one day...Gretchen appeared. We were surprised and she was embarrassed, but she got over it pretty quickly. She was a mess, too, and her parents made her go whenever they caught her smoking weed or whatever. Her mom was very controlling of every aspect in her life. It made Gretchen lash out. The woman had no idea that if she would've eased up on Gretchen, she probably wouldn't have done half the shit she did."

"I remember that about her mom," I murmur. "She fell completely apart at Gretchen's funeral."

"Yeah, it was sad."

"Did you spend a lot of time with her, too? With Gretchen?"

"Sort of. At first, yeah. She was a lost soul like me, and we started to get closer. Though trust me, there was nothing between us, I was just trying to help her out, and once Courtney saw us together, she got jealous. She and Gretchen were very competitive. They always wanted to one up each other."

He's right. I remember that, too. I feel that way now with Courtney. Like she's trying to outdo me all the time.

"But is Courtney a violent person? Would she *kill* her competition to end up on top?" He shakes his head. "I don't think so."

"Maybe she could." We don't really know what pushes a person to do terrible things. "I wouldn't put it past her."

"It makes no sense." He shakes his head.

"You'd rather see the good in people, am I right?" He says nothing. "You were close to Courtney. You hung out with her during a vulnerable time in her life, and a vulnerable time in your life, too. Of course you're going to get close to her. And you only want to believe she's a good person."

"You don't think she is?"

"Not really."

"Well, she doesn't think you're a good person, either."

CHAPTER THIRTY-TWO

My mouth drops open. "What did you just say?"

His mouth twists into a frown. "Courtney has never believed you were a good person."

"And when exactly did she tell you this?" My voice is sharp, but I don't care. I can't believe he just told me that.

"A few days ago, before Friday night. But don't worry," he reassures me. "I didn't believe her."

That is not reassuring. And I am rendered speechless. He's talking about me to Courtney? And she's ready to throw me under the bus as soon as she gets the opportunity? God, I hate her.

Seriously.

I do.

"She saw us talking at school and she warned me about you." He looks away. "I told her it wasn't necessary. I knew what I was dealing with."

The only time Courtney could have seen us together was Friday afternoon, when no one else was really around. Which means she was somehow...spying on us.

A shiver moves down my spine. That's super weird. When I don't say anything, Cass keeps on talking.

"Since everything that's happened, I think you've turned into a better person. You're nicer. Gentler. Not strutting around the school all the time looking like you want to tear someone's head off."

"You really thought I acted like that? Looked like that?" My voice squeaks. I think it's because I'm in total shock. He made me sound awful.

Not that I was the nicest person, I realize this. I had a reputation as a snob, yet it never bothered me. I was just following in my sister's footsteps, who also ruled the school back in the day. Most of the time, I secretly liked it when people would scurry away when they saw me coming. That crowds would part to allow me to walk through and people called my name because they were desperate to be my friend. It made me feel powerful.

That was still happening a few weeks ago. Heck, it still happened today. But it's not right for me to act that way—to glory in my so-called power and throw it around. It's not even real.

It's freaking *high school*, people.

Time and people are fleeting. I've lost three friends, one of them my very best friend, and I finally see it.

Life is short.

I need to make the most of it.

And being a total bitch is not the way to go.

"I'll be honest. My early assumption of you wasn't flattering," he finally admits. "But I only looked on the surface, and that's all you wanted us to see anyway. I didn't know you. And you never acted like you wanted to know me."

"You're right. I'm sorry." I didn't want to know anyone

but my close circle of friends and the occasional boy. And even then, the boys drove me crazy and I knew my friends were jerks. "I thought you were weird," I admit softly.

He laughs. "I *am* weird. Your early opinion of me is pretty accurate."

"But I've come to realize you're really nice." I smile when he grimaces. "You're smart. You've led an…interesting life."

"Don't forget you also think I'm devastatingly handsome, right?" He wags his brows.

I laugh and slowly shake my head. "Who fed you that line?"

"My grandma. She calls me that at least once a day, usually in the morning before I leave for school. She's good for my ego."

"I bet," I say drily. "But you are devastatingly handsome — if you're fishing for compliments."

"Hey, thanks. You're not so bad yourself." His smile falters and his expression grows serious. "I really am sorry about what happened earlier. I don't want to fight with you. I really do like you, Pen. I like you a lot. I've always felt drawn to you, I just didn't know how to approach you."

"I like you, too," I whisper. I've never actually admitted that to a boy out loud before. I usually just…fell into relationships. It's always like next thing I knew, I'm with a guy and he's my boyfriend. That's what happened with Robby. One minute he was talking to me, the next minute I agreed to go out on a date with him, and the next minute after that, we were a couple.

Everything's different with Cass. And I like that. I feel like what we have is special and unique, too.

"So let's just see where this goes, okay? After everything that happened last weekend, I feel extra close to you. I don't want to lose that connection." He reaches out and touches my face, his fingers drifting across my cheek, making my skin tingle. I like it when he touches me. I feel light, like a balloon that could float high into the sky, never to be seen again.

"I don't want to lose it, either," I agree in a whisper, my lids growing heavy when he keeps lightly stroking my cheek.

"I have a suggestion."

"What?" I sound breathless, but I don't care. This is what he does to me. He may as well know about it.

"Let's go over to Courtney's house and see if she'll talk to us."

That balloon feeling deflates, just like that. "Are you kidding? No way." I jerk away from his touch and he drops his hand. "I don't want to talk to her. She'll probably try to kill me."

Irritation flashes across his features. "Come on, Pen. You're being ridiculous. She's not going to try and kill you with me there."

"What, she treats you special?" I ask snottily. Ugh, I need to shut up.

"No, if she really is the killer, it seems she's only interested in murdering girls. Right? So I'm a dude. She won't touch me."

I stare at him, the wind suddenly kicking up, whipping my hair across my face. I can't even believe I'm considering this. But maybe we should go talk to her. Confront her even. What's she going to do, lunge at me with a knife? We'll be in her house and her parents are home. They had to cut their European vacation short once they found out what happened Friday night.

"Your idea is crazy," I mutter, looking away from him.

"It's crazy, but you can't deny it's a good one, right?" He nudges me with his elbow. "Come on, let's go over there."

"What if they won't let us see her?"

"Then at least we tried." He shrugs.

"What if she starts yelling at us? What if she accuses one of us of being the killer?"

Cass's eyes go wide. "You think she'd do that?"

"I wouldn't put it past her."

"Then that's the risk we'll have to take." He grabs hold of my arm and gives it a gentle tug, pulling me into his embrace. He's tall and warm and safe, and I relax against him when he holds me close, even though I'm scared.

"You in, Pen?" he asks.

"I'm in," I murmur reluctantly against his chest.

Hope I don't regret this decision.

"Penelope, we're so glad you stopped by." Courtney's mom sweeps me into a hug, squeezing me extra tight. She pulls away and holds me at arm's length, her gaze raking over me as if she's searching for obvious flaws. "How are you holding up?"

"As best I can," I tell her somberly.

Mrs. Jenkins nods. "Understandable. Poor Courtney has been an emotional wreck. This entire thing has shaken her to her core. We keep encouraging her to talk, to get it all out, but she won't. She claims she's fine."

"Maybe she's not ready to talk about it yet," Cass suggests.

Mrs. Jenkins's gaze flickers to him. "Who are you?"

I find it weird that a boy who claims he was so close to Courtney has never met her parents, ever. They were in rehab together, and Mrs. Jenkins acts like she's never seen him before.

Though I guess I shouldn't find it *too* weird. This sort of thing happens a lot, especially when two people aren't that serious about each other. Meaning I don't think Courtney was that serious about Cass.

No surprise. She's not serious about anyone.

"This is Cass Vincenti," I tell her, and Cass reaches out to quickly shake her hand.

"Your grandmother is Sue Vincenti, no?" Mrs. Jenkins asks politely.

"Yes, ma'am. We live just down the street."

"Of course. In the ivy-covered house." Her lips curl the slightest bit with seeming distaste. "I'll go see if Courtney's feeling well enough to come down and chat with you. Please, have a seat."

The moment she's gone, Cass starts pacing around the sitting room she brought us into. "This room is smaller than the one they kept us in Friday night."

"Yes. This room is for intimate gatherings."

He smirks and rolls his eyes. "I don't know how they keep track of all their many rooms."

"They have hired staff to do that," I joke, though I'm also serious. His nervous pacing reminds me of a giant cat and within seconds, he's making *me* nervous. I grab my phone, scrolling through it so I don't have to watch him. There's nothing going on. Even social media is quiet lately. I think people go to school and go home, keeping their heads down the entire time. We're all afraid. And we'll continue to be afraid until the killer is caught.

"Do you think she'll talk to us?" I ask Cass.

He stops his pacing. "Yes. I think she will."

I slowly shake my head when he resumes his pacing. "I think she'll blow us off."

"Does she normally do that?"

"You tell me. Has she ever blown you off?"

"Yeah. A couple of times." He scowls, as if he's remembering those few times.

"Same. So I wouldn't put it past her."

"I think she's itching to talk. To someone who was there, who saw it all," he explains. "Like us."

That isn't a bad theory. Maybe she's eager to show off what she knows. She always did love a juicy story. We all did.

"*Penny.* I can't believe you came to see me."

I stand and turn to find Courtney in the doorway, and she is absolutely…beautiful. Her blond hair is perfectly curled in luxurious waves that spill down her back, and her makeup is expertly applied. She's wearing a long sleeved, fitted black sweater dress and black tights with black knee high boots. She looks like she just walked off a fashion runway as she glides toward me, her rosebud lips parted, her eyes sparkling and bright.

"Courtney…" My voice drifts. What do I say? The last time I saw her, she'd been covered in blood and screaming uncontrollably, denying her involvement. Now she looks like a freaking regal princess, cool and calm. "Are you all right?"

"I'm…well." She draws me into a hug, holding me close for a beat before she lets go, her gaze then heading to Cass. "Oh, Cass. You're here, too? It's so nice to see you." She hugs him, then backs away, her hands clasped in front of her.

"You look great, Court," Cass says, and I fight the jealousy bubbling within me. I have no reason to be jealous. Cass came here with me. He's not interested in Courtney.

"I went to the spa for most of the day," she tells me in that hushed, intimate tone she likes to use when she drops an interesting bit of information. "It was so refreshing. Just what I needed after everything that happened." She waves a hand, like she can dismiss all the bad stuff with a few wiggling fingers.

I chance a glance at Cass, who's frowning at me. He looks just as disturbed as I feel. Courtney's not acting right.

Not at all.

"Please, sit down." She indicates the couch with her hand and I sit, Cass joining me. We're close, our arms brushing, and Courtney notices. I see the way her gaze lingers as she sits in a high-backed chair across from us. She crosses her legs, her skirt riding up to mid thigh, and I wonder if she did that on purpose.

"Are you coming back to school soon?" I ask her.

"Oh, I'm not sure." She shrugs. "Mother thinks I should stay home and recuperate first."

"Are you hurt?" Cass asks.

"Yes, I am. Right here." She rests a hand on her chest, over her heart, her expression solemn.

Okay. That was creepy.

"Finding Dani like that was—horrible. One of the worst things I've ever experienced, and I will never forget it," she continues, her voice even, her expression blank. "I don't know if I can ever un-see that moment. It's embedded in my brain forever."

Maybe she's on drugs?

"What exactly happened when you found Dani? Was she already there in the hallway?" Cass asks.

"Yes." Courtney nods continuously, like she's a robot stuck on repeat. "I went upstairs because Brogan sent me a text, asking me to meet him there."

"Wait a minute…Brogan?" Well, that's new information.

"Uh-huh. We were flirting the entire night." It takes everything within me not to say something. Cass looks like he wants to burst, too. That was some *serious* flirting going on with Brogan in her room. "I mean, I know he and Dani were kind of a thing, but it wasn't real, you know? Not like what Brogan and *I* have. I adore him. And he adores me."

She was so rude to him that night. Or is she forgetting?

"Brogan sent you a text to come meet him in the east wing upstairs hall?" Cass asks, his voice full of disbelief.

"He did. And so I did. I went up there, ready to sneak a kiss with him or whatever." She giggles, then sobers quickly. "I shouldn't laugh. It was a terrible night. One I won't ever forget."

She's repeating herself. I feel like some of the stuff she's saying to us is rehearsed. Like someone had her practice saying it before she came downstairs to talk to us.

"Have you seen Brogan since that night?" Cass asks her.

She shakes her hair back from her shoulders and plasters a phony smile on her face. "No. I haven't. But I've missed him. I don't know what's going on." Her eyes light up and she leans forward on the edge of her chair. "Have you seen him? Did he go to school today?"

"I didn't see him," I say.

"I didn't, either." This is from Cass.

Courtney's face crumples. "I hope he's okay."

"I'm just glad you're okay," I tell her.

Her face brightens once more. "I'm fantastic. Well. As fantastic as I can be, considering what's happened."

"We're having a candlelight vigil for the girls tomorrow night," I say. "You should come. If you're up for it." Yikes, why did I tell her? We don't need a repeat performance from the last candlelight vigil.

"Oh, I don't know. Last time I went to one, I sort of made a fool of myself." Well, at least she's honest. Her smile is sweet and she shakes her head, like she's so saddened by her actions. The Courtney I know doesn't give a crap. "But thank you so much for the invite."

"The Larks want you there, Court. I hope you can go."

It's weird, how my anger toward her has evaporated. I think it's because of her odd demeanor. How spacey she's acting, like she's hopped up on a load of prescription pills.

"Oh!" She claps her hands once, startling us both. "The Larks! I miss them. How are they?"

"We are…" How do I tell her that we're temporarily disbanding? "We're doing the best we can considering the circumstances."

"I'm sure. Well, now that we've lost three girls and I won't be around much, it sounds like we don't have much of a group anymore."

"We don't," I assure her. "In fact, we took a vote and decided to stop meeting until the spring."

"*What?*" Courtney leaps to her feet, her face red with anger. "Are you serious? You're *shutting down* the Larks?"

"We're not shutting down," I say as I rise to my feet and go to her. I want to touch her, hoping it will calm her down, but she seems too agitated. "It's just a temporary thing. I'm the only senior left, and then the juniors, and we don't think it's proper to continue on, what with everything that's happened. It doesn't feel right."

"Maybe it doesn't feel right to you. But for the rest of us, it's everything. The Larks are *everything*! How dare you close them down? What gave you the right?"

She rears back her hand and slaps me soundly across the face. So hard, the impact jars my teeth and my head bounces. Yeah. Bounces.

"Court, what the hell!" Cass rushes to my defense, wrapping his arms around my waist and pulling me away from her. "Why did you hit her?"

"She doesn't care about anything or anyone but herself! Can't you see? She's destroying everything! The Larks are the only thing keeping us together, keeping us alive, and she's tearing it down!" Courtney is screaming at the top of her lungs, her face tomato red, tears streaming down her cheeks. "I hate you, Penelope! I hate you!"

Mrs. Jenkins bustles into the room, her face full of horror and shame. "Courtney! What in the world? Are you all right?"

"Get her out of here." She points a shaky finger right at me. "I never want to see you again, Penelope!"

A man in a black suit strides into the room. I've never seen him before, but he sends me a glare as he places his arm awkwardly around Courtney's shoulders and steers her out of the sitting room.

"I'm so sorry," Mrs. Jenkins says the moment they're gone, her eyes full of sympathy as she watches me. "She's been having…outbursts ever since Friday night. I don't know what brings them on."

"She's mad at me, I guess." I gingerly touch my cheek. It's warm. I bet she left a mark.

"I'm afraid I'm going to have to ask you to leave." The pleasant smile on Mrs. Jenkins's face feels as false as the emotion Courtney displayed those first few minutes she spoke to us.

Once she became angry, though, it felt like the real Courtney came out.

"No problem," Cass says with a curt nod. Anger radiates from him, making his movements stiff. He curls his arm around my shoulders and guides me out of the sitting room. "We'll see ourselves out."

"Thank you for coming," Mrs. Jenkins calls after our retreating backs.

So. Weird.

The moment we exit the front door, Cass comes to a stop, making me stop too. "What the hell was that?" He examines my cheek, his fingers gently pressing into my skin. "Are you all right? Does it hurt?"

"Not anymore." I lift my gaze to his. "I can't believe she hit me."

"I can't believe she did, either," he says grimly. "I wanted to hit her, too."

That shouldn't make me feel good, but it does. "She acted so strange. Not like her normal self. I think she's pumped full of prescription drugs. Maybe anti-anxiety stuff."

"Probably," he mutters, shaking his head. "You ready to go?"

"Definitely."

We're almost to his car when he speaks again.

"I have another idea."

"What is it?" I ask warily.

"Do you know where Brogan Pearson lives?"

"Kind of. Not exactly, but I could find out."

"Let's try. I want to talk to him." His expression is serious. "I have a few questions I'd like to ask him."

CHAPTER THIRTY-THREE

W e find Brogan's house after I do a little internet sleuthing. He doesn't live too far from Cass and Courtney, though he's in a smaller gated community up off Hot Springs Road. The small neighborhood isn't as exclusive, not as ritzy, though the view is amazing, just like everyone else's is up here. When we pull into the driveway, Brogan is outside, shooting hoops by himself in the driveway. Cass parks the SUV on the street in front of Brogan's house.

I get out of the car and start walking toward him. "Hey, Brogan."

"What are you doing here, Penny?" He throws the basketball and it hits the closed garage door, the metal clanging loudly.

"We wanted to talk to you," I say as I approach him.

His gaze flickers to Cass, who's coming up behind me. "Why are you with this freak?"

Why's Brogan being so awful? "Don't be mean," I tell Brogan, automatically irritated.

"Aren't you the guy whose mom killed your dad?" Brogan

asks, a giant smirk on his face.

"Aren't you the guy whose recent hookup most likely killed the girl who's crushed on you for years?" Cass throws back at him.

Brogan's anger is immediate. He tosses the basketball to the side, so it lands in the front yard, and starts for Cass, his expression thunderous. Like he wants to throw down on him. "What the hell did you just say?" he says between clenched teeth.

Oh God. Here we go with the macho showdown. I am totally over this and we've been here less than a minute.

"You heard me." Cass's voice is eerily calm despite Brogan thrusting his face in his. They're standing so close to each other I'm afraid Brogan's going to chest bump him. Or Cass might chest bump Brogan. And then the fight will be on.

I so do not want to deal.

"Stop it, you guys," I tell them, but they're not listening to me.

They don't even look in my direction.

"We just came from Courtney's house," I tell Brogan, hoping that will ease the tension simmering between them.

Thankfully, it works. Brogan turns away from Cass, stepping closer to me. "You did? Is she okay? Does she look all right?"

"She looks good, but she's…very upset." Understatement. My cheek still tingles where she slapped me.

The misery on Brogan's face is immediate. "Did she ask about me?"

"She talked about you," Cass says. "Mentioned something about you texting her to meet upstairs that night."

Brogan frowns, looking at Cass then back to me. "What night are you talking about?"

I send him a *duh* look. "Friday night, when Dani...died."
I struggle with the word. It's still hard for me to believe she's
really and truly gone. "Courtney said she received a text
from you. Said you asked her to meet you upstairs."

"We did meet upstairs, but that was before the—thing—
with Dani." Brogan at least has the decency to look sheepish,
even though he doesn't know *we* know all about that meeting
in Courtney's room. "Yeah, it was definitely before she found
Dani. We, uh, went up to her room."

"You and Courtney?" Cass asks. Our gazes meet for a
quick moment before we look away.

I can't believe he's being honest.

Brogan nods, his cheeks turning red.

"What did you two do up there?"

"Messed around a little. We were drunk." Brogan shrugs.
"Then we came back downstairs. I never talked to her again.
I still haven't."

Wait a minute. "So you didn't text her to meet you in
the east wing?"

"I don't even know where the east wing is. Her house is
so freaking big, I get lost in there. That's why most of the
time I just stay outside. It's easier," Brogan explains.

Cass and I share another look before he continues. "You
sure you didn't text her?"

"What are you, the police?" Brogan makes an irritated
face. "Those assholes kept coming around over the weekend
asking me a bunch of questions, but I haven't seen them at
all today."

"Why weren't you at school?" I ask.

"Didn't want to. My mom's worried about my mental
state or whatever, so she kept me home. I'll be back
tomorrow," he says just before he goes to the front yard and
grabs his basketball. He starts dribbling it on the driveway,

the rhythmic *thwap* of the ball bouncing again and again setting me on edge.

"We're having a candlelight vigil for Dani tomorrow," I tell Brogan, wishing he would stop dribbling that basketball. "Actually, it's for all three girls. I hope you can make it."

"I'll be there. For sure. Will Courtney come?" He looks so hopeful. I almost feel sorry for him.

"I don't know," I tell him. "I mentioned it to her, but I'm not sure when she's returning to school."

"You should try to reach out to her," Cass suggests. "She might like to talk to you, or even see you."

Brogan's entire face brightens, and he stops dribbling the ball. Thank God. "That's a good idea. I'm gonna go Snapchat her right now. Talk to you later, bro. Maybe she'll let me come over." And with that, he dashes inside, the front door slamming behind him.

Cass and I turn to look at each other, the both of us still standing in the middle of the driveway. "That was weird," I say.

"Sometimes I wonder if that guy had a lobotomy." Cass shakes his head. "He acts like he's brain dead most of the time."

"I know. I don't get what Courtney sees in him." Or Dani.

We walk back to the SUV and climb inside before we resume our conversation.

"Do you believe him when he says he didn't text Courtney to meet in the east wing?" Cass asks.

"Yeah, I do. I think he would've admitted it if he did. He doesn't think about what he says. Like, ever," I say. "Plus, someone texted Gretchen about that emergency Larks meeting the night she was killed. That's too similar if you ask me."

"You're right." Cass shakes his head as he starts the SUV.

"That was a lead that went nowhere."

"There's still something to consider, though," I say. Cass glances in my direction. "Either Courtney is lying and no one sent her a text to meet up, or someone pretended to be Brogan to lure Courtney upstairs."

"But who? Could it have been Dani? Maybe she was angry. She could've found out that Courtney and Brogan were hooking up, and she got pissed off. So maybe she got a hold of Brogan's phone and sent a text to Courtney?" Cass slowly pulls out into the street, frowning. "Do you think Dani would do that?"

His theory has merit. I can almost envision Dani doing exactly that. "Maybe. She's been after Brogan for so long. Everyone knew she had a major crush on him. I wouldn't blame her for getting mad at Courtney for moving in on him." I stare unseeingly out the passenger-side window, my mind going over everything that happened Friday night. Most of it I would rather forget, but I need to remember.

I need to figure this out. For Dani.

"She was so drunk," I finally say. "I don't know if she was capable of grabbing Brogan's phone and sending Courtney a text to trick her to come upstairs. He said he left her on the lounger passed out. Besides, Court scared Dani. Everyone is pretty much scared of Court, except for me."

"She doesn't scare you?"

"Court's all bark and no bite." Most of the time.

"Did you just compare the beautiful Courtney Jenkins to a dog?" Cass shoots me a grin.

I don't particularly like that he just called Courtney beautiful, even though she is. I'm still a little jealous over what went on between them. Is he downplaying it? Were they more involved than he's letting on?

A realization hits me and I turn to look at him. *Really*

look at him. "You said to me last night that you couldn't believe you were with me. That you were actually kissing me."

His grin fades and his gaze meets mine for the briefest moment before he returns his attention to the road. "Yeah, so? It's true."

"But you've been with Courtney."

He starts to look uneasy.

"And you had a…what? 'Special friendship' with Gretchen, too?" He says nothing, so I continue. "You try to act like you're some quiet weird guy or whatever, but you've been with a few popular girls. More than a few." I almost say, *I don't get it,* but I stop myself in time.

Seriously, though. I really don't get it. I mean, Cass is nice. He's good looking. But he has this way of blending into the background. At least, that's how I viewed him for the longest time. But maybe I'm a recovering narcissistic bitch who never paid him much attention before. Maybe he's been on everyone else's radar and I missed it. Missed him.

Why didn't I see him until a few weeks ago? He sort of forced himself on me, if I'm being truthful. Did he do that on purpose? Was there some sort of plan put into place? Did he want to get to know me for ulterior reasons?

I watch him, fighting the unease that seeps into my skin, sinks into my bones. It's already getting dark outside, and the looming storm clouds put me in a dark mood. I remember what Cass told me about his past. I think of all the things I've seen these last few weeks. The things I've heard, I've been told, and my three friends who died…

What-if. What-if—*Cass* is the one who did it? What if he's the killer? It's not too farfetched. He has a connection to Gretchen. He also has one to Courtney—but she's not dead. He didn't really know Dani. What about…

"Were you friends with Lex?"

He's quiet for a moment.

Too quiet.

"Were you?" I ask again, my voice sharp.

"Sort of." He exhales loudly. "We kind of hooked up. Once."

"What?" I might've screamed the word. Actually, I'm pretty sure I did. He's looking at me like I lost my mind, and he pulls over near the front gates of Brogan's neighborhood so he can turn to look at me.

"It was the very end of our freshman year at some stupid party. She was drunk. I was drunk. We kissed. That's it. It was nothing. She barely remembered it," he explains.

"But you remembered." Oh. My. God. It all makes sense. It all makes total freaking sense. He has reason. He has motive—all the popular girls who get with him and then dissed him over the years. He's exacting his revenge. "You hooked up with all of them."

"What do you mean, all of them?"

"All the girls who are dead! Did you hook up with Dani?"

He slowly shakes his head. "No. I didn't. I hardly knew Dani."

I blink at him, my mind a twisted mess involving too many things. Courtney and Lex and Gretchen. He's been with them. Maybe Dani wasn't the intended victim. Maybe it was supposed to be Courtney who should be dead.

If Cass is the killer, that makes sense.

"I hooked up with those girls because I was their freaking drug dealer, okay? They wanted meds and I got them meds. Prescription pills. Sometimes I had the weed connection, too, but mostly it was pills. I provided them with whatever they wanted and in turn, I got invited to the best parties. Got to hang out with the most popular girls, but it was all kept hidden. They kept *me* hidden," he says, sounding bitter. "So there, Pen. That's my dirty little secret. Do with it what you want. Go ahead and tell the world I'm the reformed drug dealer hell-bent on killing every girl who's ever wronged me."

My eyes go wide and I part my lips, but no words come out. Was I that obvious?

"I know exactly what you're thinking," Cass confirms. "It's written all over your face. You'd be a terrible poker player, Pen. At least, you would be with me. I know what you're thinking pretty much all the time." He leans over the console, his gaze zeroed in on mine. His voice is low, and deathly serious. "I didn't do it. I didn't murder those girls. I considered them friends. I didn't know Dani, but I have no reason to kill her. I had no reason to kill any of them. Hell, I was with *you* when Dani was murdered. I can't be in two places at once, right?"

I close my eyes and press my lips together, trying to focus. He's right. I know he's right. But still. Why is he connected so closely to them? He looks suspicious and I wish he didn't. I don't want the connection.

I don't want the doubt.

"Do you believe me?"

Opening my eyes, I find him watching me carefully, his gaze unwavering. I study his face, wishing I'd known him longer, so we could've had more time to build our friendship or whatever.

Oh my God, that sounded so corny in my head. What the hell is wrong with me?

I'm torn. That's my problem. I want to believe him. I do. But it's difficult. I barely know him. Worse, I don't know what or who to believe anymore.

"Penelope." He whispers my full name, something he rarely says. He always just calls me Pen. "Tell me. Do you believe me?"

"I want to." I swallow hard, my throat raw. "It's just…we haven't known each other for very long."

"Do you ever feel afraid when you're with me? Have I given you any reason to make you think I might hurt you? Or I might hurt someone else? I can't help my past, it's just there. It's my burden to carry for the rest of my life. I had nothing to do with what my mom did to my dad."

"I know you didn't. You're right." I want to touch him, but I'm scared. Nervous.

There are too many what-ifs running through my mind.

"You're just as connected to them as I am. Even more so," he reminds me, his voice soft. "I could think you did it."

My heart drops. *Seriously?* "Do you?"

"No, of course not," he says emphatically. "I trust *you.* We haven't known each other long, but I can tell what kind of person you are. And you're definitely not a murderer."

We're quiet for a moment, and all I can hear is our soft breathing, the sound of the occasional car passing by. I don't know what to do or what to say. I decide to go with my gut instinct.

"I don't think you're a murderer," I whisper shakily. "I don't."

The faintest smile curves his full lips. He almost looks triumphant. "Good to know, because I'm not. Come here." He tugs on my hand and pulls me closer so he can kiss me. And it's a searing kiss, his lips hot and almost hungry as they linger on mine. "We'll figure this out together, okay?" he murmurs against my lips once the kiss is over. "I think we're getting closer to the killer."

"You do? Who is it?" His lips are a distraction and I want him to kiss me again. Make me forget everything but the touch of his mouth on mine. But maybe I don't. When he kisses me, I can't think straight.

"I have some theories." He puts the SUV back into drive and turns onto the main road. "Want to grab some dinner and we can talk about it?"

He moves at lightning speed, I swear. One minute we're fighting, the next we're kissing. Now he's easygoing, like we have zero problems, yet only a few minutes ago, I thought he could be the killer. Now he's asking me if I want to go out to dinner.

I'm so confused. My head freaking hurts.

"Um, sure. Okay. Let me text my mom." I pull my phone out of my pocket and send her a quick text, telling her I'm going to dinner with Cass. Usually I just say I'm going with friends. For some reason, I want to be specific tonight. "Where did you want to go?"

"That pizza place on Main?" he suggests.

"Sounds good." I tell Mom that's exactly where we're going.

After all, I can't be too safe, right?

CHAPTER THIRTY-FOUR

We remain quiet for much of the drive, and after a while, I start to feel like something's wrong. Cass is eerily quiet and I glance over at him. His body is stiff, and his hands are gripping the steering wheel so hard, his knuckles are white. The tension radiates off him in palpable waves, making me nervous. He's usually so calm.

The way he's acting right now, he's…scaring me.

"What's wrong?" I finally ask when the growing silence becomes almost unbearable.

"There's a car just behind mine, tailing me close."

"So?" There are jerk drivers everywhere.

"Pretty sure it's following us." His voice is low, filled with grim truth, and I glance in the side mirror, my breath catching in my throat. I watch the car, noticing that it keeps a decent enough distance that it might go undetected if you weren't inclined to notice.

But I notice. And so did Cass.

"Maybe you should turn off on one of the side streets," I suggest, my gaze locked on those two bright headlights in the mirror. They seem to inch forward and then retreat, as if the car is playing some sort of chicken game with us. Or maybe it's just my overwrought imagination. Today has been nonstop drama. I'm tempted to tell Cass to just take me home.

"What? So it'll follow us when we're on an unfamiliar street and we end up trapped?" Cass shakes his head. "No way. I'm staying on the main road."

"Speed up and make a sudden right or whatever. Pull into someone's driveway and shut off the lights. You can throw him off our trail." I've seen them do it on TV and in the movies, but does that sort of thing really work?

Probably not. But I don't know what else to do.

Cass's foot presses down on the accelerator, and the engine roars as the Lexus SUV picks up speed, making me reach out and grip the handle on the inside of the door. I hate that he's going so much faster, but we need to get away from this car.

"Who do you think it is?" I ask quietly.

"I don't know. Brogan? Maybe Courtney?"

I can't imagine Courtney chasing after us. Or Brogan. But I can't imagine them killing someone, either, so…I don't know what to think.

"Maybe we're being paranoid." I want to think that. It's so much easier to believe, especially after the day we've had.

"I don't think so," Cass says, his voice firm.

"Then what are we going to do?" I'm whispering. Panicking. My gaze never leaves the side mirror and that car is right there, on our ass, and I'm quietly freaking the hell out.

"I've got an idea," Cass says, readjusting his hands on the steering wheel and flexing his fingers. He maintains a steady speed, his eyes never leaving the road, and I realize

as we round a tight corner that we're getting closer to the
narrow canyon road. The one that twists and turns as it leads
us back down into town. "But you're not going to like it."

"How do you know?" My voice is sharp, and I immediately
regret my tone.

"I could get rid of him, but it'll be risky," he continues. I
hear the engine rev, the car shoots forward, and my stomach
twists with nerves.

"Aren't you driving a little too fast?" I ask, my voice high
pitched, revealing my fear.

He slides me a look, dark eyebrows raised, lips curled
into a little smirk. Oh, he's cute when he does that.

Fine, he's *hot* when he does that. Even in our time of
crisis I'm cataloging all the ways Cass Vincenti is attractive.
The dark hair and eyes, how he doesn't say much, but it's like
he never really needs to. He's infuriating and frustrating and
sexy and I like his voice, how deep and measured it is. He is
the rare boy who thinks before he speaks. There is nothing
spontaneous about Cass, though he can be surprising.

How he's looking at me at this very moment is both
infuriating and tantalizing, all at once. There's this arrogant
tilt to the corners of his full lips, and it screams that he's
totally got this handled. And maybe he really does, but I'm
not sure.

I still can't help but wonder if he's a consummate liar
who's got everyone snowed—including me.

"Don't worry. I know every crook and turn in these roads,"
he drawls as he relaxes his grip on the steering wheel. "I've
been driving them for years."

"For *years*?" Doubt fills me. He's totally pushing it. "Give
me a break."

"I'm serious—remember how I told you I've been driving
since I was thirteen?" He sends me a look. "I've driven up

and down this road hundreds of times."

"Hundreds?" I ask weakly. I do remember him telling me about the driving thing, but I thought he was joking. Exaggerating.

"Oh yeah. My grandma's eyesight isn't so good anymore, and she'd become anxious every time she got behind the wheel."

"That's so sad." I like his grandma. She was nice, though a bit odd. And I like the fact that Cass is so good to her. It seems he really wants to take care of her.

"She's fine. She likes bossing me around, so me driving and her telling me where to go works for her." He glances in the rearview mirror, and the flash of a passing car's lights casts a bright white stripe slashing across his face. "That car is still trailing us."

Glancing in the side mirror, I see that the car is behind us. Cass chooses that moment to take a curve extra fast, making the tires squeal, and I gasp. "You're scaring me," I murmur. It feels like my heart just flew into my throat.

"Just wait. What I really want to do is going to scare you even more," he says cryptically.

"What do you want to do?"

"You'll have to trust me on this."

"Okay." I clamp my lips shut. I shouldn't automatically agree, right? I'm still having trust issues, even though I'd never say that out loud. This entire day has been confusing. I don't know who to believe anymore.

"No demanding we back out once we commit," he says, his gaze never wavering from the road. "That's a surefire way to get ourselves hurt."

His words are ominous. Like a warning. "Fine. I'm all in."

He eases up on the gas pedal, just the slightest bit. The car slows, the vehicle behind us drawing closer. So close I swear it looks like it's going to eat the back bumper. "I don't want you to freak out."

"Oh my God, Cass." Why is he slowing down? "Just tell me."

"You have to promise me one thing first." His gaze meets mine, lingering a moment too long. He should be watching the road, not staring at me. "Say you'll promise."

"I promise," I readily agree, frowning. "But what am I promising?"

He's staring straight ahead once more, his fingers sliding over the steering wheel, almost like a caress. "You can't scream."

What?

"I mean it. No screaming. No yelling. You must remain quiet. I need you to trust me, Pen." He hesitates, his voice dropping lower. "Do you trust me?"

Do I? He's already asked me once and I said yes, but the doubt still creeps in. He scares me a little. He also—God, I am so ridiculous thinking this, but—he turns me on. He does. There's something about him. He has this edge that other boys don't have. And when he touches me, kisses me…

I'd probably do just about anything he asks me to.

So how can I doubt him when we've already gone this far together?

"I won't scream," I tell him quietly. "And I won't yell. I promise."

"Okay." He nods once, then hisses out a breath between his teeth. I chance a glance at him, the way his dark hair falls over his forehead, how he's squinting his eyes. What he's about to do, what's about to happen, feels…dangerous. "Here it goes."

With a flick of his wrist he turns the car's headlights off. Like, completely off. The road goes dark. I suck in a breath, hold it until I feel like it's choking me. He hits the gas pedal hard, the SUV roaring to life as he flies down the road. A dangerous, winding road where multiple car crashes occur every year. The windows are down, the wind blows through my hair, blasts against my face, and I close my eyes.

I'm scared, and I can't make a sound. Not a peep. I hold on to the handle right above the window, gripping it with both hands as Cass takes the twisty road with ease. My gaze is trained on the side mirror and I watch for the car lights behind us.

They're still there.

I want to yell at Cass, *go faster! He's still following us!* But I clamp my lips shut. I can't talk, I can't yell. I can't even freaking cry, and I sort of want to.

Cass hits the accelerator even harder and he jerks the wheel to the side, cruising down the road like it's no big deal. The car lights behind us start to get farther away, and the quietest whimper leaves me.

If he keeps up this pace, we'll get rid of them soon.

He takes another turn, and the vehicle sways. The SUV is top heavy and tall, and it could probably topple over if Cass turns too hard. I close my eyes and hang on to the handle above my head, my body flopping back and forth as I struggle to keep myself still. I'm clenching my teeth so tight my jaw hurts.

"Hold on," Cass suddenly yells. "Hold on, hold on, hold on."

I do as he says, my eyes popping open and automatically going to the side mirror. There's even more distance between us and the other car now. I'm trembling from a mixture of fear and excitement. I can hear the matching excitement in Cass's voice. He's not scared. I'm starting to believe he's enjoying this.

Without warning, he hits the brakes, the car squealing to a stop as he jerks the steering wheel left, sending the SUV careening down a narrow side street. We shoot straight down a steep hill, the car flying at high speed. We hit potholes and bumps, the car rocks and the tires squeal. Until finally, *finally* Cass makes a sharp right and we're headed down a long gravel driveway, toward a house in the middle of a clearing. There are no lights on within the house, and I almost hope someone comes out through the front door to help us.

As we draw closer, though, I can tell, even in the dark, that the house is abandoned. The front yard is run-down and there are no cars parked anywhere. There's no sign of human life to be found at all.

Cass drives past the house, whips around directly behind it, and immediately shuts off the engine.

It's over. I hear nothing but the sounds of our accelerated breaths, the tick of the engine as it cools, the wind blowing through the trees outside. The other car never appears, even after we sit there for a few minutes.

We lost them.

Cass leans back against the seat, staring up at the roof of the car. He pushes both of his hands through his hair, shoving it off his face, and all I can do is stare at him, aghast. At a complete loss for words.

"Fuck, that was crazy, wasn't it?"

And then he laughs. Actually *laughs*.

CHAPTER THIRTY-FIVE

I'm trembling. My entire body is shaking so hard, my teeth are chattering. "You drive like an absolute maniac."

"I know." He laughs even harder. Now he actually *sounds* like a maniac. "I didn't know I had it in me."

I want to hit him. Just beat the shit out of him for scaring me so damn bad. "You're crazy."

"You know it." He's grinning like a lunatic and that's it. I give in to my urges and punch his arm. Hard. So hard, my knuckles hurt because he is solid muscle. I hit him again, then one more time for good measure. "You scared the shit out of me!"

"Ow." He rubs his arm, glaring at me. "I told you it was going to be scary."

"You could've killed us!"

"But I didn't." Oh, he has some nerve to sound smug.

"You are such an asshole." I just let loose and start pummeling him, hitting him where I can, smacking and punching his arms, his chest, his shoulders. Cass finally grabs hold of my wrists, wrapping his fingers around them so tight

I can't hit him anymore.

"Chill out. We're okay," he murmurs, his gaze locked with mine. We're both breathing heavily, our frantic inhales and exhales loud in the otherwise quiet of the car's interior. The windows are still down, and I can hear the chirp of the bugs outside, the howling wind, the occasional dog barking.

"Duck," Cass whispers, jerking me down so we're both practically flat across our seats, facing each other over the center console. It's so freaking uncomfortable, and I'm about to tell him he's overreacting when car lights sweep over us, illuminating the SUV's interior for the briefest moment.

I'm still trembling. Even harder this time, but I realize fast the car was coming down the hill and has already driven by. Cass sits back up, running a hand through his unruly hair, messing it up even worse. "The car's gone. It wasn't them." He glances down to where I'm still curled up, half hanging over the seat, my lower body curled onto the floorboard. "Pen. You okay?"

I look up, my gaze meeting his. He must see something in my eyes because the next thing I know he's pulling me up, up, into his arms. He's somehow pushed back his seat to give us more room and he's cradling me in his lap, rubbing his hands over my arms. Holding me close, murmuring nonsensical words into my hair as I continue to shiver.

"Hey." He nudges me and I pull away from him so our gazes meet. It's dark, but my eyes have adjusted, so I can just make out his features. The air between us is crackling. Electric. I can feel him. His body is vibrating with this sort of restless energy and it's pulsating from within him and straight into me. "You're coming down from the adrenaline rush," he says as he reaches out and tentatively touches my hair.

I say nothing. What can I say? I've never felt anything

like this before. It's almost…sexual, I swear.

"Pen," he whispers, and I feel his breath. Feel it waft across my face, warm and soft and reminding me that he is very much a boy and I am very much a girl and we are sitting together intimately. I'm on his lap and his arms are around me and I have my hands on his chest and somehow, they move of their own accord. Until they wrap around his neck and my fingers are in his hair and his mouth is just a hair's breadth away from mine.

And then his lips are on mine and I feel sparks spread all over my skin. My lips are hot. Tingling.

"Did you feel that?" he asks, just before he kisses me again, deeper this time. "Pen. Did you?"

His hands grip me tighter and his legs shift beneath me. Yes, I feel him. I feel him all over me. "Feel what?" I whisper.

"This." He kisses me again, his tongue sweeping inside my mouth, circling around mine, and I moan. It's like I've lost all control with this boy, and I never do that.

Except with Cass.

"Tell me," he urges, and I whisper *yes* against his lips, because I *do* feel it. I feel the energy between us surge under my skin, and it sings in my blood. I wiggle against him and he groans low and deep, his chest vibrating with the sound.

It is the sexiest sound I've ever heard. Hands down.

"That was a wild ride," he whispers against my mouth, and I nip at his lower lip with my teeth, making him smile. "Did you like it? Tell me you liked it."

"No, I didn't." I try to bite his lip again but he gently pushes me away.

"Don't lie, Pen. You fucking loved it." His mouth lands on my neck and he's whispering close to my ear. "You felt the rush. You wanted more of it. I saw it written all over your face."

"It was too dangerous. You could've killed us." So dangerous, yet somehow also sexy.

"But I didn't. You're fine. I'm fine. It's okay to like dangerous things." His mouth lingers on mine, the kiss gentle until he sinks his teeth into my lower lip and tugs.

"What are we doing?" I ask him, running my hands across his shoulders.

"We're just coming down from all the adrenaline." More kissing. It's hot and deep and wet and our hands wander. I readjust my position, straddling his hips, and he groans.

"We should leave. I don't want to get caught."

He kisses my neck, his damp lips blazing a trail of fire across my skin. "Don't worry. No one will find us."

"I don't want to get in trouble." I tilt my head back, loving the sensation of his mouth on my neck, his hands on my waist. Being with him is addictive. Like eating a sinful dessert when I should be on a diet.

"Not everything's black and white, you know," Cass mutters against my throat. "You're allowed to be bad every once in a while."

I frown and try to pull away from him, but he won't let me go. Was he trying to prove a point with that crazy stunt? Trying to bring a little danger into my life because… what? I'm too boring? Haven't I been through enough? I lost my best friend, my two other friends, and my life has been turned completely upside down. Now he's trying to scare the hell out of me and possibly even kill me?

"What do you mean about the black and white thing?" I look at him, our gazes meeting.

"You're too rigid," he whispers, gently touching my face. "You need to relax and trust me."

I try to shove him away. He thinks I'm boring. He believes I see things one way or another and there's no in-between. Maybe old Penelope thought that way, but I don't think like that anymore. Not with Cass.

Not with anyone.

"Don't," he murmurs, grabbing hold of my arms again and keeping me still. "Why are you fighting me?"

"Why are you being so mean?" My voice cracks and I hate it. I need to be stronger. Yet he makes me feel weak.

"I'm not," he whispers. "I'd never be mean to you, Pen. I like you too damn much."

His words are just what I wanted to hear. I still want him. Desperately.

And then we're kissing again. Wildly. No finesse, no precise skill or teasing tongues and lips. It's raw and it's carnal and his hands are everywhere and my hands are everywhere and then I hear the quick *chirp, chirp* of a police siren. I open my eyes to see the flash of blue and red lights illuminate the SUV's interior.

That's when I realize there are two police cars parked on either side of the SUV, their lights going but not the sirens.

"Shit," Cass mutters, and I lean into him, my face pressed against that warm, solid spot between his neck and shoulder. He is strong and comforting yet also terrifying, all at once.

He scares me. And I don't know what to do about it.

There's a knock on the window, and I jerk my head up to find Detective Spalding standing next to the driver's-side door. He peers in closer, and Cass rolls down the window.

"That was some crazy ass driving, son," Spalding drawls, slowly shaking his head.

My heart falls into my toes. "Wait a minute. *You* were following us?"

Spalding ignores my question. "Why were you two running?"

"We thought someone else was following us," Cass admits.

Spalding frowns. "Like who?"

I'm about to open my mouth, but Cass shoots me a look. One that says, *keep quiet.* So I do.

Hughes suddenly appears, shoving Spalding out of his way. He looks ready to reach through the open window and grab Cass by the throat. "What the fuck was that little stunt?"

"Calm down—" Spalding starts, but Hughes cuts him off.

"That was some bullshit driving, Vincenti. You could've gotten yourself killed." He points a finger at me. "And her!"

"I didn't, okay?" Cass sounds just as irritated as Hughes. "I had no idea you guys were cops. Why didn't you flip your lights on?"

"We were following you in our car," Spalding tells us. It's like Detective Hughes can't even speak, he's so angry. He stalks away from us, pacing in front of the Lexus and glaring in our direction every few seconds.

"You should've given me a signal," Cass mutters.

"Like what, a bat signal?" Detective Spalding starts to laugh, shaking his head. "You've got some explaining to do, son. Afraid we're going to have to ask you to come down to the station with us."

"There's nothing for me to explain," Cass says, running a hand through his hair, trying to fix it.

I slide off his lap, straightening my skirt, my hair, utterly embarrassed. They just caught us making out after Cass drove like a crazy man to get away from them. I bet we look guilty.

It doesn't help that I actually *feel* guilty.

That moment was so intense. I can't believe I actually became—aroused by that car ride. And the way Cass talked to me, touched me, kissed me…he was aroused, too. It was crazy. If the detectives hadn't interrupted us, I bet we would've taken that moment further.

Like get naked and have sex in the back seat of the Lexus further.

"Can't we just talk here?" Cass asks. "It's been a long day. The last place I want to go is the police station."

"Then tell us exactly what you two were doing this afternoon." He sends us both a stern look. "And no bullshit, either. We've been tailing you two since you left the school. We know where you've been—first Courtney Jenkins's house, then Brogan Pearson's. What are you up to?"

I look over at Cass, who then turns to Spalding, possibly ready to spill, but Spalding puts a halt to it.

"Step out of the car, Cass. You, too, Penelope. Come outside and let's hear what you have to say."

I can't look at Cass. I can't look at the detectives, either. My entire body is vibrating, and I inhale shakily, trying to calm my racing heart. The adrenaline is wearing off quickly, and now the only emotion I'm experiencing is...

Fear.

We told them everything we could, only leaving out our suspicions and theories. They don't need to know what we're thinking. Let them figure that stuff out on their own.

After an hour-long interrogation behind an abandoned house on a moonlit night, they finally let us go.

"I'm too tired to go to dinner," I tell Cass as we start to drive. "Can you take me home?"

"Sure. You're not hungry?"

I shake my head. I just want to take a shower and go to bed. Today has drained everything out of me.

"I'm glad you didn't tell them what we talked about," Cass says, his voice soft.

I glance over at him. "They don't need to know."

"Exactly. I'm sure they have a bunch of theories and suspicions and they're not telling us dick," he says irritably.

"As well they shouldn't. They are the cops."

Cass sends me a look. "Spalding mentioned the FBI is coming back to Cape Bonita to investigate further. They think there's a serial killer on the loose."

"*Duh.* Glad they finally realized it." There's too much cover-up in this town, all for the sake of image. They won't reveal too many details about the crimes for fear it'll taint the reputation of our bucolic seaside town. It's complete crap. "I don't understand why they won't reveal any details to the media."

"Because they're looking for the killer. If you withhold information, the guilty party could slip. Give up details that no one else knows *but* the killer," Cass explains, like he has lots of experience with this type of stuff.

"Is that what your mom did? About your dad?" I ask quietly.

He slowly shakes his head. "She fessed up right at the start, claiming she killed him. Then she turned around and said she didn't do it when she had to plead in front of the judge. That's why they went to trial. It was a mess."

"Sounds like it."

We're quiet as we drive back into town. I'm still a little shaky, I realize as I hold my hands out in front of me. They're quaking, and I link my fingers together, trying to calm myself down.

But it's hard. I still feel shot full of adrenaline. I wonder if Cass feels it, too.

We don't really talk again until he pulls up in front of my

house fifteen minutes later. The windows shine with golden light, and I can imagine my mom still in the kitchen while my dad watches TV in his recliner. I wonder if they missed me. I know I've missed them.

What I miss the most is normalcy. The mundane things in life. There's nothing mundane about what I've experienced these last few weeks. I wish I could get my friends back. I wish I could get my old life back.

"I hate this," I tell Cass, turning to look at him.

He's already watching me. "You hate what?"

"Everything that's happened. Gretchen and Lex and Dani dying. Courtney's turned into a mental case. We're running for our lives from the freaking *police* like we've lost our minds. My life has turned into a made-for-TV movie!"

"I'm sorry, Pen," he says, his voice soft. "I probably shouldn't have driven like that."

"You definitely shouldn't have done that," I agree. "You could've killed us."

"You think I'm the killer, don't you." His voice is flat. It's not a question, more like a statement. I must hesitate too long, because now he's glaring at me. "You do."

"I don't know what to think anymore," I admit, my voice quiet. Shaky. I can't even believe he said that. It's like he's peering into my brain and can see all my worries and fears.

"You know me, Pen—" he starts but I shake my head, cutting him off.

"No, I really don't know you at all. I wish I did." I take a deep breath and let it all out before I speak again. "It's like we were on the run from the police, Cass. Like you didn't want to get caught. Is that what you were doing? Did you know the detectives were following us?"

"I didn't realize it was the cops, Pen. Swear to God. They were chasing us in an unmarked car. I thought it was

Courtney or Brogan or whoever the hell is doing this!" He punches the steering wheel, making me jump. "I don't know how to fix this. I don't know how to make it stop."

"I don't either," I whisper. I grab my backpack and reach for the passenger door handle. "I think we might need...a break. Just for a little while. Until we both get our heads on straight."

I don't even know what I'm saying anymore. Or what I want.

He looks away from me and shrugs. "Whatever."

What do I say to that? Tears threaten, and I close my eyes for a quick moment, fighting them off. "Good night, Cass."

He says nothing. Doesn't bother looking in my direction when I climb out of the SUV, slam the door, and start toward my front door.

"I wish you could trust me," he calls out.

I turn to find him watching me, the driver's-side window rolled down. "I wish I could trust you, too."

He says nothing. Just stares at me with that intense gaze of his before the window slides closed, he starts the engine, and pulls away.

CHAPTER THIRTY-SIX

I t's time for me to make a move.

I've waited long enough.

I tried to let the drama and the speculation die down. But it won't.

It keeps getting bigger. And bigger.

And bigger.

Until it feels like it's going to explode in my face.

What's worse is that my intended victim didn't even go down that night. I didn't want Dani to die. What I really wanted to do was tear open Courtney's throat and watch the life bleed right out of her.

The bitch deserved it.

But no. Dani showed up first. I don't even know exactly how that happened. She was staggering around in the hall like a drunken idiot, crying for Brogan. No Courtney in sight, when she should've been up there. I tried my best to draw her out with that bogus text.

I had to kill Dani to shut her up. I couldn't risk her revealing me. That was a major glitch in my plans, when everything else had been going so smoothly.

Now everything's a mess. The cops are sniffing around. So are Cass and Penelope. Who knew those two would end up a pair? Not me. I didn't think he was her type, though he seems drawn to the popular girls. And for some reason, they're drawn to him, too.

Me, I prefer jocks. Like Brogan.

Stupid, idiotic Brogan, who pretends I don't even exist. *Asshole.*

But yeah. Penelope. She's messing everything up. Her and that stupid man whore Cass. Maybe I shouldn't worry about Courtney. She's acting so crazy, people might start thinking she's the one doing this. Not that I want her to take all the credit but...

I don't need Penelope sniffing around me. She could figure me out. Or Cass might. But if Penelope's done for, maybe Cass would fall apart. And then...it would be over.

Tonight is the candlelight vigil. Where I must pretend to be sad and pretend to cry and pretend to give a shit. I don't. I don't care about any of them. They were awful to me. They all deserved to die, even Dani. If everything had happened according to my plans, I would've gotten around to Dani eventually.

Sometimes you have to readjust. It's a part of life. We can't all get what we want. But if we're patient, we can get pretty close.

I smile, thinking of tonight. Forget Courtney. Penelope is who I want. Courtney probably won't even show up. So I'll focus on Penny. I'll have to make nice with everyone and act like I care about her, and by doing so, maybe I can get her alone.

And if that happens...

She's done.

CHAPTER
THIRTY-SEVEN

"There are so many daisies," Alyssa murmurs as she glances around. "They're everywhere."

"Daisies were Dani's favorite flower," I say softly as I go to a giant arrangement and pluck one of the flowers out. I stroke the smooth petals, mentally counting each one. "She said they made her happy."

And now she can never be happy again.

We're in the school quad, setting up the final touches for the candlelight vigil, which is in less than an hour. A small stage has been set up, each of the girls' senior portraits blown up to poster size and set on easels. Alyssa was right— there *are* daisies everywhere, filling up every empty spot, and they look glorious. There are a few rows of white plastic folding chairs for the parents and family members, plus the faculty. Everyone else will have to stand.

"Where are the rest of the girls?" I ask Alyssa as she straightens out the rows of chairs. "This is our last Larks duty for a while. I want to take a photo of us together."

"Oh, what a good idea." Alyssa smiles. "I'll go get them."

I watch as she gathers them up, then I pull out my phone to double check the list I made. I've pretty much covered everything that needs to be taken care of for tonight. The media is here and set up, the local TV news stations with their vans parked out in front of the school. I see a few reporters lingering on the far edge of the quad, talking among themselves. I wonder if they're comparing notes.

The police are here, too—of course. I spotted Detectives Spalding and Hughes earlier, along with uniformed officers as well as a few guys in suits. Men that are unfamiliar, making me think they might be FBI investigators.

My life is so surreal right now. I almost can't take it.

Mrs. Adney and Mr. Rose show up, hanging out by the stage. Mrs. Adney is going to give a speech tonight, and so is Gretchen's father. He plans on pleading with the killer, asking him to turn himself in.

That's what Mr. Nelson kept telling us earlier, when he first arrived. He kept talking about *him*. How *he* should be stopped. How *he* is a monster.

But what if the killer is a she? I still can't shake my suspicion of Courtney. She didn't come to school today. No surprise. Brogan did, but he moved through the halls like a zombie, looking lost and sad. Cass wasn't in our physics class and I became worried. But I saw him at lunch in the caf, though he wouldn't even look in my direction.

"I found everyone!" Alyssa says cheerily, knocking me from my thoughts. I glance up to find her standing with Maggie, Kayla, Grace, and Jessica. My five junior Larks and me, all that's left.

"You girls look fabulous," I say, and they do. They're all dressed in somber yet fashionable black, and they worked so hard today to put this together. "It looks great out here. Thank you so much for all your help."

"We wanted to do it," Maggie says, taking a step forward. "For Dani, and for Lex, and for Gretchen. For all of us, really."

I hug her, because I'm overcome with emotion. I've been holding it together pretty well since the weekend, and after everything that happened yesterday, I'm surprised I didn't cry. But now the tears threaten, and I want to let go. Just let it all out.

After, I tell myself. *Once this is all done, then you can cry all you want.*

"Let's take a photo," I say, sniffing and wiping discreetly beneath my eyes. I whip out my phone and wave the girls over to gather around me. "One last selfie, for old time's sake."

Holding the phone up, I correct the angle so I can get everyone in the frame. All of us are smiling widely while I snap a few photos. I see Alyssa shift as I'm still snapping away, her eyes widening and then she calls out, "Courtney! Hey! Come here!"

I look over to see Courtney standing nearby, dressed in elegant black, her hair pulled back into a simple ponytail. She smiles when our eyes connect. "Hi Penelope."

Wariness fills me as I watch her approach. The last time we saw each other, she slapped me across the face. And that was only a little more than twenty-four hours ago. "Hi, Court. How are you?" I ask coolly.

She reaches out, making me flinch, but she only takes my hand. "Don't be mad," she whispers. "I'm sorry for what happened yesterday."

I don't know if I should accept her apology. I'm still worried she might hit me again. But it's easier to play friendly with Courtney, so I do. "I'm glad you could make it."

"Do you guys need any help?" she asks brightly as she lets go of my hand.

"I think we have everything under control, but thank you for offering." I take a deep breath, telling myself to get over my anger. It's been an emotionally fraught time. She's suffering, just like I am. "Would you like to take a photo with us?"

"I would love to." She steps into place, right next to me, and we bend our heads together, our cheeks almost touching.

"One more photo, ladies!" I tell them as I raise my phone up once more. I snap a few extra pictures and then we disband, though Courtney remains with me. "Are you really all right?"

She takes a deep breath and lets it out slowly. "As all right as I can be considering what's going on, I guess. I really do feel bad for what happened yesterday. I had way too many pills coursing through my system and I-I overreacted."

"I figured," I murmured. "Are you better today?" She seems better. Isn't acting so out of it, like she did yesterday.

"I am. I feel much better." Her smile blooms and she nods. "How about you? How are you holding up?"

"I'm all right," I say with a shrug. "It's been good, having the candlelight vigil to focus on."

"I'm sure. Gives you something to do." Her smile fades and she steps closer. "How's Cass?"

"He's...good," I tell her. "He should be here any minute, if you want to talk to him."

"Hmm." The noncommittal sound she makes tells me she doesn't really care about talking to Cass. And this makes me feel better, jealous shrew that I am. "Oh, look. There's Brogan."

And she's gone.

More and more people are showing up, and I mingle through the crowds, greeting those I know and helping to hand out the cups and candles. The other Larks are doing the same, some of them at the quad entrance, handing out a short program Maggie made up today in her journalism class. Family members of the victims come in, and I guide them to the chairs.

The turnout is huge, much bigger than we had for Gretchen's candlelight vigil, but now we're also attracting those who are simply curious. I can't help but wonder if the killer is here with us tonight.

And who it might be.

I spot Cass among the growing crowd, and our gazes meet. Linger. He offers me a sad smile and I look away, my heart thumping hard. I want to go to him. I want to tell him I'm sorry.

But I can't.

Turning, I find Courtney watching me watch Cass, her eyes dark, her smile long gone when our eyes lock.

I look away.

"The turnout is huge." Courtney appears by my side, her bright smile back in place.

"I know. It's almost overwhelming. Mrs. Adney is going to speak first, then Gretchen's father. I hear even the chief of police has something to say."

"Really? Wow." Courtney slowly shakes her head as she surveys the crowd of people.

"They're anxious to catch the killer," I tell her, thinking how just last night I thought she was the killer. I still sort of do, which means I'm crazy to talk to her like this. But she wouldn't dare touch me. Not right now. "The residents of Cape Bonita are outraged. They want this all to stop."

"I'm sure," Court murmurs.

When Mrs. Adney starts to speak, I can't help it—I zone out. I didn't go to bed last night until late, and I've been helping the other Larks set up the vigil, so I'm exhausted.

Plus, I can't stop thinking about Cass. I hate that we're not talking. But last night shook me so hard, I still don't know what to think about him.

Or how to act around him.

I open up my phone and start to scroll through the photos I just took, smiling a little. We look pretty good, even in the photo when Alyssa yelled at Courtney and some of us aren't looking straight at the camera.

Frowning, I stare at Maggie. She looks…pissed. I zoom in on her face, see the scowl, her narrowed eyes as she looks right at Courtney, who's off camera. I scroll through the remaining photos, the ones with Courtney in them. We're smiling, all of us staring straight at the camera.

Except for Maggie. She's glaring at Court and me. Like she wishes she could rip our heads off.

I glance up, searching for Maggie in the crowd. She's standing on the opposite end of the quad with Alyssa, who is focused on Mrs. Adney's speech. Maggie is searching the crowd, a sullen expression on her face. Her gaze snags with mine and we stare at each other for a moment. I smile at her.

She looks away.

Huh.

I don't even try to hide it—I keep a close watch on Maggie throughout Mrs. Adney's speech, never taking my eyes off her. She looks around irritably, crossing her arms in front of her chest.

My gaze snags on Courtney, who's standing with Brogan. He's behind her, his arms around her waist, his hands clasped in front of her stomach. They look awfully cozy. I guess grief and tragedy have allowed them to become closer?

Ugh, whatever.

Cass is nowhere to be found, which, of course, makes me suspicious. I lock gazes with Maggie again and she sends me a cold smile before leaning over to whisper something in Alyssa's ear.

After a few minutes, I see Courtney tear herself away from Brogan and leave the quad, headed in the direction of the bathroom.

Maggie soon leaves, too.

I'm tempted to follow her. Follow them both.

But that would be stupid. So incredibly stupid. Right? Not that anything could happen. There are people everywhere. I'll be fine.

Yeah.

Just fine.

CHAPTER
THIRTY-EIGHT

I hang back on the dimly lit trail, not wanting Maggie to see me, since there's no one else around. I don't even see Courtney, and can only assume she's in the bathroom already. Everyone else is in the quad, the crowd quiet as Mrs. Adney's voice booms through the speakers set up around the perimeter. Hundreds of people have shown up tonight, yet I've never felt so alone as I do at this moment.

Chills race over my skin when I realize it's Maggie. Oh my God, it's freaking *Maggie* who's the killer. Sweet little gung-ho Maggie — but why?

Why?

Taking a deep breath, I tell myself to stay focused. Maggie is oblivious to my following her as she heads down the path, her steps determined. The bathrooms loom ahead and the women's door swings open, a shard of golden light shining bright before the door slams shut again.

It's Courtney.

"Oh," she says when she spots Maggie. Her voice is flat, devoid of any emotion. "It's you."

"It's me." Maggie's voice rings clear. She almost sounds cheerful. "I was hoping we could talk."

"What about?"

"I haven't seen you in a while."

"That's because I haven't been at school."

I jump behind a tree so they don't see me. I hope I'm close enough that I can listen to their conversation.

"I know that," Maggie says slowly, as if she's talking to an imbecile. "I wanted to make sure you're okay."

"Since when do you care?" Courtney asks snottily. Her tone shocks me, only because it's the first time I've heard her sound like her old self in days.

"I told you before, I wanted us to be friends," Maggie says, almost pleadingly.

"Well, like I told *you* before, I'm not interested." Courtney starts to walk away, but Maggie grabs hold of her arm. "Hey! Let me go!"

"Tell me something." Maggie's voice changes, goes deeper. "Are you with Brogan?"

"What? Why do you care?" Courtney struggles. "I said let me go!"

"Answer me. Are you and Brogan a thing?"

"Not that it's any of your business, but yeah. We're together." Courtney finally jerks out of her hold. "You satisfied?"

"No. I'm not." Maggie's voice is eerily calm.

Courtney turns to leave, but not before Maggie grabs hold of her arm once more, pulling so hard Courtney stumbles, trips, and falls to the ground, landing flat on her back. Maggie stands over her, reaching into the voluminous folds of her black dress and pulling something out of her pocket.

It's a knife.

"What the hell are you doing?" Courtney yells just as I move away from the tree and run toward them.

"Stop!" I scream at Maggie, causing her to whirl around. She clutches the knife in her hand, the long blade gleaming in the dim moonlight, and I stop only a few feet away from her, trying to catch my breath.

Holy. Freaking. *Crap.* It's not Courtney who's the killer. It's Maggie?

Her shoulders sag and she rolls her eyes, laughing. "What are you doing here? Jesus. Why can't everything go my way for once?"

"Put the knife down." My gaze drops to meet Courtney's. She's sprawled on the ground, her knees scraped from the fall, but otherwise, she looks okay.

"Are you kidding me? No way. This actually works out better. I'll take care of Courtney first, considering she stole my man."

She stole that line from Courtney, who said the same exact thing about Gretchen.

"I never stole Brogan from you!" Courtney yells indignantly. "What the hell are you talking about?"

Maggie sends her a withering glance before she looks back at me. "Then I'll take care of you. And finally, it will be over."

"What will be over?" I need to keep her talking, and hopefully someone will find us. There are so many people here, surely someone will need to use the restroom.

And if that's all I'm banking on, we are so screwed.

"My plan. Once you're gone, I'll reopen the Larks and *I'll* become president, not Alyssa." She smiles, her eyes sparkling. "Everyone will be so relieved I'm there to take care of them. It'll be easy."

Don't tell me she planned this only because she wants to be the president of the Larks? That's crazy. The seniors choose who becomes the next president...

Though it's hard for us to make a choice when we're all dead.

"Why are you doing this? Why did you kill them?"

Maggie shrugs and starts waving the knife around. "I tried my hardest to become everyone's friend, and you all made fun of me. You would laugh and push me to the ground so my skirt got muddy and my shoes were ruined. All the boys would point and call me names, because you guys encouraged them. You don't remember?" she asks when she catches my confused expression.

I slowly shake my head. "What are you talking about?"

"I couldn't go back to school, couldn't face all you stupid bitches again. I told my mom she couldn't make me. I mean, I threw the *biggest* fit. I didn't know I had it in me." She shakes her head, a faint smile on her face, like she's thinking of a fond memory. "I missed so much school they had to hold me back a year. My mom homeschooled me until I came back halfway through the tenth grade, though I should've been a junior, like you. Like all of you."

I rack my brain, trying to remember her. She's talking about the past, when we were little kids. But I don't remember anyone who looked like her, and I definitely don't remember a girl named Maggie.

"I was plain. And poor. A scholarship kid, and you all knew it. I wore glasses and had braces and was just so... awkward. None of you pretty, rich girls want to be seen with a girl carrying a few extra pounds. I ruined your image." She kicks hard at Courtney's leg, making her yell out in pain. "Come on, Penelope! *Think*. You have to remember me. I'll be totally insulted if you don't."

It comes to me slowly. There was a short, round-faced girl, back in sixth grade and the beginning of seventh. The middle school years were bad, and there was a miserable little thing who was an easy target for a bunch of mean girls like Gretchen. And Lex. And Courtney.

Sometimes even Dani and me.

Her name was Margaret.

"Ah, you do remember me. I can see it on your face. Do you remember what you used to say? How you all used to taunt me and call me names? God, Gretchen was the worst. That's why I killed her first. She was *such* a bitch." Maggie shakes her head, her expression disgusted. "And Lex wasn't much better. They finally recognized me when I came back, did you know that? That's why they had to go first. I couldn't risk them telling you about me."

"Maggie, come on," I say, trying a different tactic. "We were just kids back then. We didn't know any better."

"Bullshit! You knew better, but you didn't care. So I worked my hardest to be the perfect little do-gooder like you wanted me to be. I was determined to become a Lark so damn bad, and now when I finally am, when I'm finally close to getting what I want, you take it away from me! You shut down the Larks! Who *does* that?" Maggie smiles and glances down at her knife, stroking it gently with her fingers. "A selfish bitch like you, that's who."

A chill races down my spine at the sound of her flat voice, goose bumps rising on my skin. She's mad at me. She's just as mad at me as she is at Courtney, maybe even more.

"It'll give me great pleasure to end you both tonight, though it's bound to get messy. Dani sure was messy, but her death wasn't according to plan, so when you deviate from the plan, shit goes bad, right?"

She's looking at me like she expects an answer, so I nod, feeling helpless. I look over at Courtney to see she's now sitting up. She rests her finger over her lips and I look away, my gaze locking with Maggie's once again. "Right."

"Be a good girl, then, and let me take care of Courtney first. Not like you two get along. And she's the real man stealer of the group, not Gretchen. She hooks up with *everyone*." Maggie still hasn't noticed that Courtney is slowly rising to her feet. "Courtney doesn't care if she hurts anyone's feelings. The only person she cares about is herself."

Courtney chooses that exact moment to charge into Maggie from behind, knocking her to the ground. They claw and scratch at each other, the knife falling from Maggie's hand, clattering onto the sidewalk. Courtney kicks it away, sending the knife skidding across the path.

I run toward them, screaming at the top of my lungs for help as I head for the knife. I try to snatch it up, but Maggie beats me to it, grabbing the knife and thrusting it in my face. "Back off," she fumes, her face red. There's a scrape across her cheek and her mascara is running. "I will cut a bitch if you get too close. I swear to God."

"Maggie," I start but Courtney grabs hold of her leg from behind, sending her toppling.

Toppling into me.

We fall onto each other, and I scream when Maggie lunges for me. I'm grabbing at her arms, her wrists, trying to keep that knife away from me. Courtney is screaming, and then I hear another voice.

A male voice.

Cass.

"Pen!" He's yelling my name, his voice drawing closer, and I thrust my leg up, trying to knee Maggie in the stomach. But then I feel a prick, a sharp pinch in my skin, and I cry out before I roll over and away from her.

"Get away from me!" Maggie yells, and then Cass is there, struggling with her, trying to grab the knife. I stare up at the starry night sky, pressing my hand against my side.

When I pull my hand away, I see it's covered in blood.

"Stop! Don't move!"

I recognize that voice, too. Swiveling my head to the side, I see Detective Hughes, and he's got a gun trained on Cass and Maggie. Courtney's struggling to her feet, and he yells at her, too. "Freeze, Courtney!"

She goes completely still, her eyes wide. "Don't shoot me! I'm not the killer!"

"She is," Cass says, pointing at Maggie.

"I need you two to separate from each other right now!" Hughes commands Cass and Maggie, waving the gun at them. "Get on your knees with your hands up!"

More police show up, every one of them with their guns drawn as they surround us. I can feel the blood flowing, spurting out of my side, and I press my hand hard against my hip, trying to stop it. I turn my head to see Maggie leap to her feet, her hands high up in the air.

"I didn't do it, Officer! I swear! It's Courtney! She's the killer! I tried to stop her before she murdered Penelope!"

"No," I gasp, shaking my head. But it's like I can't speak. And the more I shake my head, the dizzier I get. I close my eyes and swallow hard, trying to find my voice, but it's not there. No one can hear me over all the yelling and screaming.

"Get on your knees!" Hughes tells Maggie again, and she just stands there, her eyes wide, hands still up in the air.

"Why won't you listen to me? I didn't do it! I swear to God!" she screams at the top of her lungs.

Cass is on his knees, his arms raised above his head, and Courtney does the same. They're both staring at the cops, not saying a word.

Sometimes silence speaks louder than words could ever say. I hope the cops realize this.

And that's the last thing I remember thinking before the world goes black.

CHAPTER THIRTY-NINE

I wake up slowly, and it feels like my head has been stuffed with cotton. My brain is fuzzy, and my eyelids are so heavy. I struggle to open them, and when I finally do, I find I'm not in my bed at home. I'm in an unfamiliar place.

I realize quickly I'm in a hospital bed, not in my own room.

"Oh, Penny. There you are." It's Mom. She's standing by my bedside, tears shining in her eyes. "How are you feeling? Are you uncomfortable? I can call the nurse—"

"No," I interrupt her with a croak. I clear my throat and wince. "Can you get me some water?"

She pours me a glass and hands it to me, helping me sit up so I can take a sip. The water is cool relief considering my mouth and throat both feel like the Sahara desert. "Why am I here?" I ask. "What happened?"

"You were injured." Mom's face becomes serious. "Stabbed, but luckily enough, no major arteries or organs were hit. They called it a shallow wound, though it certainly didn't look shallow to me."

"Maggie." I close my eyes, sink my head into the flat pillow. It all comes rushing back now. The candlelight vigil. Me suspecting it was Maggie and following her as she followed Courtney. "Maggie did it to me."

"I know. We all know. She's been taken into custody." Mom pats my arm gently.

"What about Courtney?" I struggle to open my eyes again, but it's so hard. "Is she okay?"

"She's fine. Everyone's fine, including you." Mom's voice starts to drift. She sounds like she's so far away. "It's okay. We can talk about it later. Get more rest. You need it, darling. You've been through so much."

I want to say something more. Ask about the cops. Where's Courtney? Where's Cass? Why isn't he here? Is he okay?

My head is too heavy to fight it, though. I give in.

And sleep.

They release me from the hospital the next afternoon with little fanfare, thank goodness. I couldn't stand being in there. Thankfully, the wound wasn't that bad, but they wanted to keep me overnight for observation. What made me so groggy was the pain medication they pumped into me. The doctor prescribed pain meds for me to take home, but I don't like being so foggy headed.

I felt completely out of control. And after what just happened to me, I don't ever want to experience that again.

Once I change into a pair of yoga pants and a T-shirt Mom brought me from home, I'm ready to go. The nurse pushes my wheelchair outside into the blinding midafternoon sun, and I see my dad's car is parked right in front of the main entrance. Mom is walking beside me, and she helps me get out of the wheelchair, then into the backseat of the car. She's treating me like a total invalid.

But that's okay. I sort of feel like a total invalid.

Once we're in the car, Mom doesn't stop chattering. I think she's trying to keep me focused, so I won't feel sorry for myself or think too much about what happened last night.

"Your sister and brother wanted to come see you right away, especially Peyton. But I told them to wait until this weekend, after you've had a few days to recuperate. I didn't think you'd be up to visitors just yet, don't you think? You need as much rest as possible after everything you've gone through."

"Yeah. Sure," I say distractedly.

"Courtney's mother called me this morning, checking on you. That was nice, wasn't it?" she asks.

"Have you talked to Cass?" He didn't come to the hospital to see me, and I don't know why. I need more details. I want to know where Maggie is, what did the cops say, how Courtney is and what happened to Cass. I'm worried about him.

He saved me.

"He called this morning, but I told him you couldn't talk yet."

"What?" I say it so loudly Mom turns to look at me. "Why did you do that?"

"You were sleeping."

"But I want to talk to him." He's my freaking hero.

"You can do that later." She waves a hand, as if dismissing the subject.

"I want to talk to him now, Mom." I'm so tired of her controlling my life all the time. "Do you have my phone?"

She reluctantly hands it over and I power it on, watching all the notifications rack up, one after the other. I scroll through everything, relieved when I see the Snapchat selfie from Cass that came early this morning, captioned I MISS YOU, accompanied by a sad emoji.

I send him a Snapchat message back. A selfie with the caption I MISS YOU TOO.

My phone rings. It's Cass. I bring the phone up to my ear, smiling. "You saved my life."

"I told you I wasn't the killer."

I'm smiling. I can't believe he's joking about this right now. "Guess you couldn't wait to talk to me?"

"Yeah. I couldn't. Where are you?"

"I'm on my way home. They released me from the hospital."

"So you're okay."

"Yeah. I'm fine."

"Thank God." I can hear the relief in his deep voice, and it makes my skin go warm.

I lower my voice. I can feel my parents spying on me and I wish I were by myself. "My mom told me you called. I'm sorry I didn't call you back."

"It's okay, she said you were sleeping and I didn't want to disturb you. I can't lie, though, I've been worried sick." He hesitates, and I can't help but think he's being so sweet. "It's been crazy, Pen. I had to stay at the school last night, since I was an eyewitness. The cops questioned me. Then I went home and my grandma was completely freaked out. I had to reassure her that everything was okay. She wanted me to tell her everything. So I did, staying up half the night spilling it all. Spalding called around midnight to let me know that you were all right. He knew I was worried."

Aw. Spalding was actually nice to Cass. I can't believe it.

"I just called the hospital about a half hour ago, trying to get them to put me through to your room, but they said you were taking no personal calls."

"Come over to my house," I whisper. "I want to see you."

"I'll leave in a half hour. Is that okay?"

I smile. "That's perfect."

The moment I end the call, Mom starts in.

"Are you sure you should have visitors? You need to rest."

"I want to see him, Mom."

"I don't know if it's a good idea—"

I interrupt her. "I know you don't approve of him one hundred percent, but he saved my life, Mom. He means a lot to me, and we've been through so much together. No one else understands, except for Cass. And I understand him, too."

"It's just that…" Her voice trails off and she shakes her head before looking over her shoulder at me. "I just want to protect you, Penny. You're our baby. And we could've lost you."

"But you didn't, thanks to Cass," I say firmly. "And I want to see him. I care about him, Mom. A lot."

She relents. I witness her sag in seeming defeat. "Fine. He can come over. But I don't want him to stay too long. You need your—"

"Rest," I finish for her. "Yeah, I get it."

The minute we arrive home, Mom's helping me walk to my bedroom. I'm not as strong as I thought. The stab wound is throbbing and I practically collapse into bed, sighing when Mom pulls my comforter up and over my body.

"My bed is the best bed in the whole wide world," I tell her, making her laugh.

"There's nothing like sleeping in your own bed when you've been missing it," Mom agrees, sitting on the edge of my mattress. She tucks the comforter around me, acting like a typical mother. "That call from the police last night was one of the most terrifying I've ever experienced in my life."

I meet her gaze, see the sadness and worry written all over her face, and I feel awful. "I'm sorry, Mom. I should've never followed after Maggie like that. But I just knew she was going to attack Courtney. And I was right."

"Why don't you start at the beginning of this story," Mom says with a gentle smile.

So I do. I launch into all the details from the last few days, trying to ignore the dawning horror on her face. I did some stupid stuff. I realize it now. But every move I made last night was impulsive—and potentially life threatening. Following after Maggie is where I made my biggest mistake.

Luckily enough, I paid for it with only a minor stab wound, versus my life.

"I'm just glad you're safe. These last few weeks have been an absolute nightmare," Mom says.

I roll my eyes. "Tell me about it."

We both smile wanly, and then Mom dives in for a hug, making me wince with pain. "Oh, I'm so sorry!" She moves away, shaking her head. "I didn't mean to hurt you."

"It's okay, Mom." I grin at her. "I've realized I'm pretty tough."

"Of course, sweetheart." She pats my cheek. "That you are."

CHAPTER FORTy

A knock sounds on my partially closed door and then Mom pushes it open, Cass standing behind her. "Your friend is here," she says cheerily, sending me a pointed smile.

She shifts out of the way and Cass moves past her, nodding in her direction. "Thanks, Mrs. Malone."

"Keep the door open," she warns us before she leaves my room.

Leaving us alone.

Cass stands by the foot of my bed, watching me with a faint smile curling his lips. "You look good."

I haven't taken a real shower, my hair is greasy, I'm wearing raggedy old sweats and a beat-up T-shirt. Oh, and I was just stabbed. I know for a fact I look like hell. "You look good, too."

He does. He's wearing a blue plaid button-down shirt and jeans, his dark hair a little wild about his head. His gaze is soft as he studies me, his full mouth curved in that smug smile I used to despise but now adore. "Can I sit with you?" he asks tentatively. "On your bed?"

I scoot over as best I can, wincing with the movement. Cass rushes to my side, trying to help me, and I let him. Then he kicks off his shoes—the beat-up Converse—and climbs into bed with me, him on top of the covers while I'm beneath them. He's solid and warm and when he curves his arm around me so I can rest my head on his shoulder, for the first time since this wild situation started, I actually feel safe.

"I thought I was going to lose you," he murmurs against my hair, his voice shaky.

"I'm too tough." I poke him in the ribs with my index finger, making him laugh.

"Seriously, I should be mad at you for not telling me what you were doing last night." He hesitates, then gives me a squeeze. "I would've helped you."

"I know. But I didn't want to jump to conclusions, I guess. I kept thinking I was wrong, though my gut told me it was her."

"Why Maggie, though? Why was she targeting the Larks? I thought she *was* a Lark," he says.

I explain what she told me. How she went to middle school with us, how Gretchen and Lex made fun of her, and how Maggie could never let it go. That she was seeking her revenge and she almost got away with it. She was never a real suspect. At least, not in my eyes.

I don't know what all of this is going to do to the Larks. Or to my relationship with Courtney. I know Maggie is in jail. The media is losing its mind over the story. An eighteen-year-old girl is a criminal mastermind on the verge of becoming a serial killer. It's straight out of a teen slasher movie.

"I wondered at one point if it was a Lark. Remember?" Cass muses as he twirls a thick strand of my hair around his finger. "I know you believed it was Courtney, but I never really thought so."

I'm so relieved it wasn't Courtney after all. "I don't remember you telling me that you suspected a Lark, so your suspicion is void," I tease, though the more I think about it, the more I kind of do remember him mentioning his suspicions.

"The cops were shocked, too. Spalding told me straight up Hughes thought it was Courtney."

I glance at him. "Are you serious? Hughes and I were thinking the same thing? I hate that guy!"

Cass chuckles. "He's not that bad. Neither of them are. They were just doing their job."

"Says the former suspect and reformed drug dealer."

"Hey, don't be mean." Now he pokes me in the side, but gently. Not anywhere close to my wound.

"I'm sorry. I was just teasing." I tilt my head back to meet his gaze, and he bends down, dropping a soft kiss on my lips. "I'm sorry I ever doubted you."

His answer is a kiss. A long, sweet, warm, tongue-filled kiss that leaves me wanting more when he finally breaks away. I don't even care if Mom or Dad finds us making out on my bed. I missed Cass that much.

"I can't blame you," he murmurs against my lips. "I'm sorry we fought."

"Thank you for saving me."

"No problem," he says jokingly, making us both laugh softly.

"Seriously, Cass. I don't know what would've happened if you hadn't shown up," I tell him.

"We've been through a lot together," Cass says as he runs his fingers over my hair.

I close my eyes. That feels so good. I could fall asleep if he keeps this up. "We have."

"I'm really sorry you had to experience that. And that

you lost your friends."

"I'm sorry, too," I murmur.

"But at least you're safe."

I snuggle closer to him. "At least you are, too."

"I think we make a good pair."

"I do, too."

"Are you willing to give this a shot? Even though there isn't a murder mystery to solve anymore? Now you might find me kind of boring." I hear the amusement in his voice, and it makes me smile.

I open my eyes to find him watching me with a faint smirk. "Trust me, I could never consider you boring, Cass Vincenti."

"Right back at ya, Pen," he whispers.

Just before he kisses me.

ACKNOWLEDGMENTS

I love reading young adult books. I also love reading thrillers. So when I was watching the first season of *Scream Queens* (#RIP), I became inspired by those snarky mean girls who said and did the worst things ever. A few months before that, I saw a nonfiction book that explored our society's fascination with, and I quote, "pretty dead girls." I thought, *that would make a great book title,* and I wrote it down in a notebook I always keep with me.

That's how this book was born.

Inspiration is a funny thing. You never know where it's going to strike, what little thing you see or read or hear will make you think, *hmmm.* I'm asked all the time, where do you get your inspiration (fellow writers, can I get an amen), and I always say, "It comes from everywhere. It's all around me." And that's the truth.

So a big shout-out to that nonfiction book about pretty dead girls and to the first season of *Scream Queens*—thanks for inspiring me.

Also, I should say thanks to my family for putting up with me stealing bits and pieces from their lives and inserting them into my books.

And to the readers. Without you, I'm nothing. I appreciate your support.

GRAB THE ENTANGLED TEEN RELEASES READERS ARE TALKING ABOUT!

BY A CHARM AND A CURSE
BY JAIME QUESTELL

A kiss is never just a kiss.

Le Grand's Carnival Fantastic isn't like other traveling circuses. It's bound by a charm, held together by a centuries-old curse, that protects its members from ever growing older or getting hurt. Emmaline King is drawn to the circus like a moth to a flame... and unwittingly recruited into its folds by a mysterious teen boy whose kiss is as cold as ice.

Forced to travel through Texas as the new Girl in the Box, passing out fortunes and searching for the poor soul she can transfer the curse to with one frosty kiss, Emmaline begins to fall for the quiet carnival carpenter Benjamin Singer. Ben is just as desperate to start a life outside the carnival as Emmaline is to escape her destiny—but giving in to their undeniable attraction means Ben's fate would be sealed.

Breaking the curse seems like their only chance at happiness—but no curse means no charm, either, endangering everyone who calls Le Grand home. Ben and Emma will have to decide if the cost of their freedom is worth the destruction of the Carnival Fantastic...and everyone they've grown to care about in the process.

BREAKING THE ICE
BY JULIE CROSS

Haley Stevenson seems like she's got it all together: cheer captain, "Princess" of Juniper Falls, and voted Most Likely to Get Things Done. But below the surface, she's struggling with a less-than-stellar GPA and still reeling from the loss of her first love. Repeating her Civics class during summer school is her chance to Get Things Done, not angst over boys. In fact, she's sworn them off completely until college.

Fletcher Scott is happy to keep a low profile around Juniper Falls. He's always been the invisible guy, warming the bench on the hockey team and moonlighting at a job that would make his grandma blush. Suddenly, though, he's finding he wants more: more time on the ice, and more time with his infuriatingly perfect summer-school study partner.

But leave it to a girl who requires perfection to shake up a boy who's ready to break all the rules.

WICKED CHARM
BY AMBER HART

Nothing good comes from living in the Devil's swamp.

Willow Bell doesn't think moving to the Okefenokee is half bad, but nothing prepares her for what awaits in the shadows of the bog—or for the boy next door, who might just be the trouble people speak of.

Beneath his wicked, depthless eyes and the allure that draws girls to him, Beau Cadwell is mystery to his core. Where Beau goes, chaos follows. *His lips are full of twisted grins and lies*, the girls say. *He's evil in disguise*, warns Gran.

It isn't until girls wind up dead in the swamp that Willow wonders if maybe Beau is more intense than she can handle. His riddles tell her that he's someone to be wary of, but his touch tells her that she can trust him. Problem is, which is true? It's hard to tell with a boy like him...

NEVER APART
BY ROMILY BERNARD

What if you had to relive the same five days over and over?
And what if at the end of it, your boyfriend is killed…
And you have to watch. Every time.
You don't know why you're stuck in this nightmare.
But you do know that these are the rules you now live by:
Wake Up.
Run.
Die.
Repeat.

Now, the only way to escape this loop is to attempt something crazy. Something dangerous. Something completely unexpected. This time…you're not going to run.

Combining heart-pounding romance and a thrilling mystery *Never Apart* is a stunning story you won't soon forget.

THE NOVEMBER GIRL
BY LYDIA KANG

I'm Anda, and the lake is my mother. I am the November storms that terrify sailors, and with their deaths, I keep the island alive.

Hector has come to Isle Royale to hide. My little island on Lake Superior is shut down for the winter, and there's no one here but me. And now him.

Hector is running from the violence in his life, but violence runs through my veins. I should send him away. But I'm half-human, too, and Hector makes me want to listen to my foolish, half-human heart. And if do, I can't protect him from the storms coming for us.

entangled teen

an imprint of Entangled Publishing LLC